Postcards
from Cedar Key

Also by Terri DuLong

Spinning Forward

"A Cedar Key Christmas" in *Holiday Magic*

Casting About

Sunrise on Cedar Key

Published by Kensington Publishing Corporation

Postcards from Cedar Key

TERRI DuLONG

KENSINGTON BOOKS
www.kensingtonbooks.com

KENSINGTON BOOKS are published by

Kensington Publishing Corp.
119 West 40th Street
New York, NY 10018

All Kensington titles, imprints, and distributed lines are available at special quantity discounts for bulk purchases for sales promotion, premi-
ums, fund-raising, and educational or institutional use.

Special book excerpts or customized printings can also be created to fit
specific needs. For details, write or phone the office of the Kensington
Special Sales Manager: Kensington Publishing Corp., 119 West 40th
Street, New York, NY 10018. Attn. Special Sales Department. Phone:
1-800-221-2647.

Kensington and the K logo Reg. U.S. Pat. & TM Off.

ISBN-13: 978-0-7582-6866-2
ISBN-10: 0-7582-6866-1

First Kensington Trade Paperback Printing: November 2012
10 9 8 7 6 5 4 3 2 1

Printed in the United States of America

In memory of my son, Shawn Timothy DuLong
With love

ACKNOWLEDGMENTS

Thank you so much to Chuck and Freddie Smith, owners of Angell & Phelps Chocolate Factory in Daytona Beach. Your wonderful tour of the factory and all of the information you shared with me about the making of chocolate helped a lot in creating my fictional shop for Berkley.

For this novel I have some canines that deserve a thank you:

I'm always captivated by the dogs that accompany their owners to the yarn shops where I've done book signings. In this story I've included the real Yorkie, Addi, who belongs to Pat Capistrant, owner of Lovin' Knit in Marietta, Georgia. And also Lola, the little terrier, who belongs to yarn shop owner Debbie Davis at Yarns To Dye For in Charlotte, North Carolina. It was fun incorporating both dogs into my story, so thank you for sharing their charm with me.

Thank you to Mary Bates, from Quincy, Washington, for introducing me to your beloved Oliver, who really does participate in a very worthy reading program at the local school.

The gorgeous Otis is the namesake of the Black Dog Bar & Tables on Cedar Key. Thank you to this very friendly Labradoodle for always making me feel welcome when I stop by.

And thank you to my own cockapoodle, Brie, for the inspiration to create Annie, and to my Scottie, Duncan, who never fails to make me smile.

Berkley's friend, Jill, was fictional for my story, but I owe a large thank you to Roberta Webber Pearson, owner of the real Rumination Farm in North Yarmouth, Maine. Thank you so much for sharing all the information about your alpacas, the process of turning the fiber into yarn, and the correct terms used.

I very much appreciate all the time given to me from Molly Brown and Dottie Halderman for answering my numerous questions about the soft-shell crab industry.

Another thank you goes out to Corallee Morgan, of Quincy,

Washington, for giving me the inspiration to create the character of Corabeth. She was fun to develop, and I enjoyed weaving her into my story.

I receive quite a bit of e-mail from fans asking if the Lighthouse is a real place or fictional. It is indeed a real structure and the private residence of my Cedar Key friend Skip Drake. So thanks, Skip, for allowing me to include your unusual and beautiful home in my novels.

A huge thank you goes out to the Cedar Key Chamber of Commerce for endorsing my Cedar Key series and being the only place on the island for my fans to obtain autographed copies. To the President of the Chamber and my friend Andrea Dennison, thank you so much for your support and encouragement. To Tina Ryan, Secretary, another thank you, and to Mary Farrell, thank you so much for the promoting you do for the Cedar Key series with tourists visiting the Welcome Center.

As always . . . thank you to my personal assistant, Alice Jordan; my husband, Ray; my daughter, Susan; and all of my wonderful fans who have come to love the Cedar Key series as much as I do.

1

"So you were looking for a small, quiet town where you could relocate?" I heard the woman ask as I carefully placed her truffles in the box.

I nodded and smiled while focusing to make sure that I had each chocolate perfectly lined up.

"Yes," I told her, although it wasn't the entire truth. "Unfortunately, Salem became too busy for my liking."

"That's right. Chloe said you were from the Witch City. Oh, and I'm real sorry about the loss of your mother."

"Thank you," I said, and wondered what she'd think if she knew Mom was upstairs in my apartment.

I closed the box and attached the island-shaped gold seal that displayed my shop name, Berkley's Chocolate & Gems, before ringing up the sale.

"Well, I'm Polly," the woman said. "I own the Curl Up and Dye Hair Salon over on Third Street. If you're lookin' for a new style, drop on by."

I noticed that her glance strayed to the deep purple streak that ran along the side of my dark brunette hair.

"Thanks," I told her even though I couldn't remember the last time I'd crossed the threshold of a hair salon. A few months before,

I'd decided it was time to get rid of the long hair that had hung to my shoulders for years. Using a good pair of cutting shears I'd proceeded to snip away until I was left with a one-inch pixie style that complemented my oval-shaped face, only requiring a shampoo and a bit of mousse and I was good to go. I'd never been one to fuss with fancy styles, nor was I one to follow current trends. Hence, the purple streak fit me.

Polly reached across the counter to take her chocolates. "I'm very anxious to try these. I've been counting the days to your opening since last November."

"I know, and Chloe understood about my delay. I was lucky that she was willing to hold the apartment and this shop for me. My mother took ill shortly after I returned to Salem from my visit here. She passed away in November, and then I had a lot of things to tend to."

"Oh, I can only imagine. Losing a family member brings so many tasks that need to be done. I remember when I lost my mother and had to clean out her house. My sister and I spent a couple months trying to decide what to keep and what to get rid of."

"Right," was all I said, and thought of the postcards tucked away in my desk drawer.

"Well, I won't keep you any longer, but it was nice to finally meet you."

"Same here, and I hope you'll enjoy the chocolates."

She turned toward the door and then paused in front of the circular table where I had arranged my display of crystals and other gems.

"Oh," she said, reaching out a finger to touch a rose quartz crystal. "How beautiful. You also sell these?"

"Yes." A customer had been in earlier, and I now saw that my display wasn't in the symmetrical arrangement that I'd created. I repositioned the amethyst above the pyramid-shaped crystal. "Do you like gems?"

"I don't honestly know. What are they used for? I mean, what do you *do* with them?"

I smiled, both at her question and the fact that my display was again in balance.

"Well, all gems have energy," I explained. "Crystals are used for healing and to bring positive changes in the mind. Many people use them for meditation. Our bodies have a complex electromagnetic system, and nature has created crystals to be perfect electromagnetic conductors. Each one has a unique vibrational resonance, and they've been known to have a positive effect on our body systems. Pick one up and hold it in your hand."

Polly reached out, allowing her hand to pause briefly before choosing a six-sided prism. She folded her fingers across the gem. "Oh, it feels quite warm," she said, after a few moments.

I nodded. "Right. That's the energy of the crystal interacting with your energy."

"Well, I'll be darn," she said, replacing the gem on the table. "I always say you learn something new every day. Thanks for explaining that to me. Now I'm going home to savor these chocolates."

"My pleasure," I told her as I moved the crystal a smidgeon to the left of where Polly had placed it.

I heard my stomach growl and glanced at my watch. Twelve-thirty. No wonder I was hungry—it had been over seven hours since I'd had breakfast. I flipped the cardboard clock on my door to one-thirty, got my keys, locked the door, and stepped outside onto Second Street.

I stood there for a few moments breathing in the clean March air. Spring had arrived on the island of Cedar Key with warm temperatures and the scent of tropical blooms. March in the Boston area could be very iffy, and it wasn't unusual for a St. Patrick's Day blizzard to descend on winter-weary residents, so I was relishing my first spring in the Sunshine State.

I walked around the corner, through the courtyard, and up the stairs to my apartment. Stepping into the living room, I heard a meow and saw Sigmund come running from the bedroom.

I picked him up to cuddle in my arms and rubbed my chin back and forth across the top of his large, dome-shaped head. "Have a tough morning sleeping, did you?" I received another meow in reply as we headed to the kitchen.

"Time for us to eat, fellow," I told him as I opened a can of

Fancy Feast. After placing his bowl on the floor, I heated up some of the squash soup that I'd prepared the night before, and then settled myself at the table that overlooked SR 24.

Chloe had been right. I noticed more traffic entering town for the start of the weekend. She'd told me that my busiest days in the shop would probably be Friday, Saturday, and Sunday.

I had been fortunate to hook up with Chloe the previous year during my first visit to Cedar Key. I recalled wandering into the coffee café across the street and being greeted by Grace, her sister Chloe, and their friend Suellen. All three had been friendly and made me feel welcome. Although I'd only come at that time to see the town—the town where my mother had chosen to disappear when I was five—I knew now that deep down inside I'd planned all along to eventually spend a significant amount of time here. Enough time to discover the answers that I'd wanted for the past forty years. So when Chloe told me that she'd recently purchased the Hale Building across the street and had both an apartment for rent and retail space for a shop, I knew my stars were aligned in a way that wouldn't allow me to postpone my decision.

But that decision was delayed due to the sudden death of my mother. When I'd called Chloe to explain that I wouldn't be able to come in November as planned, and that I'd understand if she had to cancel our rental agreement, she wouldn't hear of it. She insisted that she wasn't desperate for the rental money and a few more months would be fine. I offered to at least pay the rent during the time I wasn't there, but she wouldn't hear of that either. During the two weeks since I'd arrived on the island Chloe had been helpful with whatever I needed, and since she had the other apartment down the hall, I felt certain that over time we'd become good friends.

I rinsed out my bowl, placed it in the rack, and decided to make myself a cup of tea to go with the oatmeal cookies I'd baked that morning.

I took the tea and cookies into the living room and saw that Sigmund had resumed his position on the wide windowsill in the bedroom. From the day we'd moved in, he'd claimed that patch of sun as his own. I heard his loud purring and smiled. Sigmund was an extralarge black cat and my best buddy. We'd been together for ten years, since the morning he'd shown up at the back door of my chocolate shop in Salem.

I nibbled on a cookie and looked around the living room. Perfect for a woman alone. Just three rooms and a bath, but spacious, bright, and airy. I was especially happy with the oversized kitchen, which gave me plenty of room to make my chocolates. Although now that I was going to be purchasing most of them wholesale from Angell and Phelps in Daytona, I wouldn't have to make quite as many chocolates as I'd had to in Salem. Hopefully, this would enable me to have more time for spinning the fiber from my alpacas.

I thought of Bosco and Belle, the source of my fiber, and felt a momentary stab of homesickness, but I wasn't sure which *home* I longed for—coastal Maine, where I'd lived only till age five, or Salem, Massachusetts, where I'd resided until a couple weeks ago?

I recalled my phone conversation from the day before with Jill. Jill had been my first girlfriend when we lived in Maine, and when I moved to Salem with my mother and grandmother, Jill continued to keep in touch with printed letters enabling us to then become pen pals the summer before we began first grade. Our friendship had grown over the years since I'd left Topsham, and during those years, Jill had moved a few towns away, gotten married, divorced, and became the owner of Rumination Farm in North Yarmouth. Her alpaca farm was where I boarded Bosco and Belle, knowing they were well cared for, which Jill had assured me of the previous morning. But I still missed the fact that I wouldn't be able to jump into my car and make the two-hour drive to visit both her and my alpacas.

My eyes strayed to the oak rolltop desk, and I let out a deep sigh. The postcards that I'd found after my mother died were safely stored in the top drawer—waiting for me to unravel their meaning. Waiting for me to understand things that my mother and grandmother would never discuss. And the postcards were the reason why I'd come to Cedar Key in the first place.

I pushed aside thoughts of Bosco and Belle and went into the kitchen to place my cup and plate in the sink before going to pat Sigmund.

"Be a good boy, Siggy. I'm closing at five . . . unless I get an on-slaught of business, of course."

2

When I came downstairs and walked to the corner of Second Street and SR 24, my plan was to run across the street to get myself some coffee at the coffee café, but I was surprised to see a gentleman sitting on the pavement in front of my shop reading a book. Obviously waiting for me to reopen. I glanced at my watch and saw that it was only one-twenty. I still had ten minutes—but business was business.

As I walked toward my shop I could see the man was probably mid- to late fifties, had curly gray hair, and seemed to be deeply engrossed in whatever he was reading.

Even when I stood just a few inches away from him, he didn't acknowledge me or look up until I cleared my throat. The expression on his face was one of embarrassment as he pulled himself to a standing position while brushing off his jeans.

"I'm so terribly sorry," he said, and I immediately recognized a very proper British accent. I believe people referred to it as the King's English. "I have no doubt you're the proprietor of the chocolate shop and I'm blocking your way to reopen."

In addition to the British accent, I also noticed my loitering customer had a very pleasant face. One of those faces that isn't just nice to look at but is wholesome and open and tempts one to want to know him better. Deep brown eyes stared back at me with a hint of interest.

I smiled and for the first time in ages, I felt the urge to flirt coming over me. Reaching out to put my key in the lock, I said, "Yes, that would be me, and I'd have to say this is a first. Finding a gentleman sitting on the pavement waiting for me to open. Any chance you're a chocoholic?"

He followed me inside and his laughter filled the shop.

When I turned around, I noticed that he was about five inches taller than my five feet seven and that he was wearing a store-bought cable pullover sweater. Knitters noticed things like that.

"Now, that's a first for me," he said, a huge smile on his face. "Although I do admit to having quite a passion for chocolate, I've never been referred to as that."

I hoped I hadn't offended him. "Well, having that passion can be a good thing. Chocolate is actually quite good for people, as long as it's not overdone."

"Oh, yes, I've read all the studies on chocolate and they're quite convincing. And I do limit myself to just two pieces per day. I must admit I've been waiting patiently for you to open since I heard about your shop last fall. Now I'll be able to eliminate my monthly forays into Gainesville for my chocolate supply."

"I didn't realize there was a shop in Gainesville." In addition to his height and sweater, I now noticed that this man had a most charming dimple in his chin when he smiled.

"Well, if there is one, I'm not aware of it. I go to Publix and purchase bags of Lindt Truffles. They're quite good, but nothing compares with fresh, handmade chocolates. By the way, I'm Saxton," he said, extending his hand across the counter. "Saxton Tate the third."

I reached for his hand and let out a chuckle. "Seriously? That's quite a name you have. Are you descended from royalty with that British accent along with the name?"

Without releasing my hand, he let out another burst of laughter. "I tend to doubt that, but you never know what skeletons families hide in their closets, do you?"

If you only knew, I thought.

He gave my hand a squeeze before letting go.

"No, I was just named for my father and my grandfather. Hence, the third. Grew up in a small village in the Cotswolds, but no royalty, I'm afraid. Oh, I also wanted to offer my condolences on the loss of your mother. I heard that was what detained your arrival in Cedar Key."

I nodded. "Thank you. Yes, she passed away in November and I had to tend to various tasks before I could move down here. Do you live on the island?"

"I do. I've been here a few years now and I can't see myself ever living anywhere else. I'm an author, and I receive much of my inspiration being surrounded by Mother Nature."

I smiled. "You *look* like an author, and you certainly have a great name for book jackets. What type of books do you write?"

Saxton threw his head back laughing. "What exactly does an author look like?"

"Oh, well," I mumbled, and felt myself getting flustered. "What I meant was . . . you know . . . a bit bohemian with, ah . . ." I gave him a full body scan. "Curly hair, the pullover sweater, jeans . . ."

"Well, then you should see me on a chilly day when I'm sporting my tweed cap and scarf."

I wasn't sure whether to believe him or not because I was already getting the impression that this man possessed a good amount of wit and humor.

Another smile crossed his face. "I write mysteries," he told me. "Most of my novels were released in the UK, but I'm now with a publisher in New York and my second book with them will be out this fall."

"I'm an avid reader, so I'll have to be sure to pick one up."

"I highly recommend the one released last year, *A Deadly Secret,* and I hope you'll enjoy it. Lucas carries it at his bookshop across the street."

What the heck was it all of a sudden about family skeletons and secrets? "Well, I'll be sure to pick up a copy, and maybe you'll autograph it for me."

"It would be my pleasure, but you haven't yet told me your name."

I felt a smile cross my face and extended my right hand again. "Berkley," I told him. "Berkley Whitmore, and it's nice to meet you."

A chuckle escaped him as once again his hand encircled mine. "Berkley? And you're questioning the oddity of *my* name?"

Now it was my turn to laugh. "Right. Yeah, it is a bit unusual. My parents were students at Berkeley during the sixties when my mother got pregnant with me."

"Ah, I see, and yes, that makes perfect sense."

It did? Although I didn't dislike my name, I always thought it was a bit silly of my mother to name me after her alma mater.

"Well, I'm definitely due for my chocolate, so it's time for me to make my decisions," he said, walking over to the glass case. "They look wonderful, and you make them yourself?"

I walked around the counter and pointed to the dark chocolate pieces shaped like clams. "I make those," I told him. "Cedar Key is the number one place in the country for farm-grown clams. So I designed a mold to depict these. But those on that side," I said, gesturing to my left, "are purchased wholesale from the wonderful chocolate shop in Daytona Beach, Angell and Phelps. I order my truffles and all the other chocolates in the case from them. I agree with their policy on selling only fresh chocolate, and they have no preservatives, so if I happen to be out of what you might like, I can order them and have them for you in just a couple of days."

"I've been to that chocolate shop," Saxton said. "I've done book signings on the east coast of Florida and found my way to their shop. You're right, they're quite wonderful chocolates."

"So what can I get for you?" I asked, putting on a plastic glove.

"I'll take four of your truffles, please. That'll do me for today and tomorrow . . . and then I'll just have to come back on Sunday to restock."

I placed the chocolate into one of my extra small boxes, applied the seal, and rang up the sale. "Here you go," I said, passing them across the counter.

"Thank you, and I'll see you in a couple of days."

I watched him leave the shop, and three things struck me: He was one of the few people meeting me for the first time who had avoided any comment on the purple streak in my hair. I had very much enjoyed conversing with him. I wasn't displeased at all that Saxton Tate III would be returning to my shop on Sunday.

Before the afternoon was over I had made quite a few sales. All of the customers had been tourists visiting the island for the weekend, most of them purchasing chocolate, but a few had bought some of my smaller gems.

Just before five I stepped outside to see how busy Second Street was and saw Eudora Foster walking at a brisk pace toward my shop.

"Hello," she hollered, and waved. When she got closer she said, "Have you already closed? I was hoping to get some chocolate."

"You're in luck. The shop is still open."

Chloe had introduced me to Eudora, known to the locals as Miss Dora, the week before. She had taken over the yarn shop down the street, Yarning Together, and Chloe was her business partner.

"Come on in," I told her.

Before walking to the glass case, Dora paused at the table that held my gems.

"Oh, goodness. Aren't these gorgeous. I'll have to tell my daughter, Marin, that you also sell crystals. She just loves those. Where do you get them?" she asked, picking one up and allowing it to lie in the palm of her hand.

"From Sedona in Arizona. I visited there a few years ago and I was quite impressed with the quality of their gems. So I order them wholesale from a shop there."

"They're just lovely." She replaced the crystal on the table as her attention was drawn to the glass case of chocolate.

"Oh, what a nice selection." Dora leaned forward to get a better look. "I see you have my favorite—raspberry truffles. Those are from Angell and Phelps, right?"

I nodded as I slipped the glove onto my right hand.

"Well, I'll have one pound of those, please. Were you busy today?"

I began placing each chocolate into the box. "Yes, fairly steady with tourists, so I think I had a good first day."

"You'll find that the weekends will be your busiest times. That's how it is at the yarn shop too. Oh, I wanted to ask you . . . Chloe said that you own your own alpacas?"

"I do. Bosco and Belle stay with my friend at her alpaca farm in Maine, Rumination Farm. I'd always knitted, but Jill got me into spinning a few years ago and that led to me purchasing a couple of my own alpacas. I had no place to keep them in Salem, so I'm fortunate that she boards them for me. Plus she does the shearing along with the process of turning the raw fleece into fiber and then she hand dyes it, so that really saves me time. By the time she ships it to me, I'm able to just sit down and spin it."

"I see. And Chloe said that you have a small Internet business?"

"Yeah, I set up a website and I take orders and ship the yarn. A lot of my customers have particular requests for colors, and since Jill does the hand dyeing, I can accommodate them."

"Well, Chloe and I were talking, and we wondered if you might be interested in selling some of your yarn to us for the shop. We get quite a few tourists looking for hand-spun alpaca yarn in the hand-dyed colors."

I was certainly not one to turn away business. "Oh, that's a great idea. Sure, I'd be very interested in doing that." I rang up the sale and passed her the box.

"Okay, then," Dora said. "I'll get with Chloe and we'll have you come over to the yarn shop so that we can discuss details. Thank you for the chocolate."

"I hope you'll enjoy it."

She turned at the door to give me a wide smile. "Oh, I have no doubt that I will."

After she left I walked to the table and rearranged the position of the crystal that Dora had picked up.

Then I emptied the cash register, placing the money into the zippered bag that I'd drop at the bank in the morning, shut off the lights, locked the door, and headed back upstairs to my apartment.

Not a bad first day, I thought, as I stepped into my living room and was immediately overcome with a sense of my mother's presence. I heard Sigmund meow as my eyes flew to the mahogany credenza where I'd placed the marble urn containing the ashes of Jeanette Whitmore. Walking over, I reached out a finger to touch the smooth stone and traced an invisible circle along the side.

"Sorry, Mom," I said out loud. "You're staying put for a while. I'm not about to release you back into the universe until I get some answers."

3

I can't say that I was overwhelmed with business the following day, but it was a steady flow of customers. Mostly tourists, but some of the locals also dropped by to meet me and sample my chocolate.

Two of those locals were Sydney Webster and her daughter, Monica Brooks, along with Monica's triplets and stepdaughter, Clarissa. I'd briefly met both women at the coffee café the previous year.

"It's nice to see you're open," Sydney said, pushing the oversized stroller into the shop. "Welcome to Cedar Key. You remember my daughter, Monica? And this is my granddaughter, Clarissa, and Saren, Sidney, and Candace, my triplet grandchildren."

I smiled as a wave of melancholy came over me. Seeing the women together brought back childhood memories of walking Essex Street with my own mother, stopping in various shops. Although I had good memories of time spent with my mother when I was a child, we had been far from close. Her overprotectiveness accounted for part of the reason, with me always wanting to rebel. But unlike my grandmother, who showered me with affection, I always felt my mother withheld a part of herself from me. And that was only enforced the summer that she chose to go away and leave me behind.

"Yes," I said. "I remember Grace introduced us last year. Gosh, these babies are growing way too fast." I bent down to stroke their little hands.

"They certainly are." Monica laughed. "They had their first birthday last month."

I stood up and noticed Clarissa beaming proudly at her siblings. "I bet you're a great big sister. How old are you now?"

"I'm eleven, and yeah, Monica says I'm a big help to her."

Monica ruffled the top of Clarissa's head and smiled. "I don't know what I'd do without you. Now let's get some chocolate. I think we earned it."

They made their choices as I filled the box.

"Oh, what are those?" Clarissa asked, pointing to the case.

"Those are my Cedar Key clams—rich, dark chocolate. Here," I said, reaching for one. "Try a sample."

Before I reached in for two more to give Sydney and Monica, Clarissa exclaimed, "Oh, I want these. They're really good."

Both women nodded after taking a bite. "Delicious," Sydney said. "Add some of those to the box also."

I rang up the sale and passed the box to Sydney, who slid her charge card across the counter.

"This is a great shop," Monica said. "I think you'll be very successful here. And why did you choose Cedar Key? I can't remember what Grace told me."

"Oh, I had seen an article about it someplace. It seemed like the perfect small town I was looking for. I love Salem, but it's become pretty crowded there, and besides, who can resist this great Florida weather in March?"

Sydney laughed. "Right. We'll check back with you on that come July and August."

In the afternoon Suellen stopped by to bring me a latte.

"This is so nice of you," I told her, taking a sip of the delicious coffee.

"Well, Grace is covering the coffee café, and we thought you might enjoy an afternoon pick-me-up. Have you been busy?"

"Yeah, pretty steady. How about you?"

Suellen nodded. "The coffee café has been pretty much nonstop all day, and I think Lucas is selling a fair amount of books too, so looks like it'll be a good weekend for the merchants. Well, I have to get back. Enjoy the coffee."

"Thanks," I hollered as she swept out the door.

I smiled and watched her run across the street. I liked Suellen. She had an energy about her that gave off positive vibes.

I was taking an inventory of how much chocolate I'd need to make on my days off to replenish for the coming week when I looked up and saw an older woman enter the shop, a huge smile on her face.

"Hi," she said, extending her hand. "I'm Maude Stone, Chloe and Grace's aunt."

"Oh, hello," I told her, returning her smile. "I've heard a lot about you from Chloe. It's nice to finally meet you."

"I was delighted to hear we'd have a chocolate shop opening in town." She glanced at the glass counter and nodded. "And everything looks so good. Do you happen to have ... well, I always called them Turtles."

I smiled and pointed to the case. "Right there. I order those from Angell and Phelps in Daytona and their candy maker calls them Honeybees. We have them in milk or dark chocolate, and you have a choice of cashews, Georgia pecans, or macadamia nuts."

"Oh, my," Maude said, and I swear she was an instant away from drooling when she spied them.

I let out a chuckle. "Yeah, they're really good."

"Well, then, I'll take one pound with the dark chocolate and cashews, please."

I began arranging them in the box. "You do knitting retreats, don't you?"

"Yes, once a month. Women come from across the country and it's quite a fun time."

"Chloe had mentioned it to me. All of you gather at the carriage house in your garden and it's an entire weekend of knitting. That does sound like fun."

"Yes, and then we always have our Blue Moon ceremony on the final evening, which I sometimes think is the highlight of the weekend."

"Oh, she didn't mention that. What's that about?"

A smile crossed Maude's face, and I could tell she was in her element discussing something that meant a lot to her.

"We gather on the beach over at the City Park. No two are ever the same, but we play music, dance around, read quotes that are meaningful to us—basically, we just bond as women and friends."

"It sounds wonderful. How did you ever come up with such a clever idea?"

Maude laughed. "Oh, I'm afraid I can't take credit for that. The original one was held back in the forties. Have you met Eudora Foster yet?"

"Yes, she was in here yesterday."

"Well, it was Dora and her sister, Sybile, who came up with the idea many years ago, and then shortly before Sybile passed away, her daughter and granddaughter, Sydney and Monica, decided to resurrect the old tradition. So I'm afraid I copied their idea."

"And I'm sure Sydney and Monica didn't mind in the least."

"I think you're right. Actually, Dora told me she thought it was a wonderful way to keep her sister's memory alive. You'll have to come sometime, Berkley. Chloe and Grace still attend now and then."

"Thank you so much," I said, passing the box of chocolate across the counter. "I'm sure I'd really enjoy that. And I hope you'll enjoy these chocolates."

Maude laughed again. "Oh, there's no doubt that I will."

I rang up the sale and took her cash. "So you're not from the island originally?"

"No, I came here last year from Brunswick, Georgia. I bought the old Coachman House on F Street and then decided to turn the carriage house, which is in my garden, into a venue for my knitting retreats."

"But Dora is from Cedar Key?"

"Oh, my, yes. Born and raised here. Never even left when she married. Some people call her the town historian."

So, I thought, *maybe it's Dora Foster that I need to talk to about the past.*

"Well, welcome to the island. I hope your business will be very successful," Maude said before leaving.

I got some last-minute customers, and after standing on my feet for most of the day, I decided to order a pizza for supper rather than do any cooking.

I had just finished cleaning up the kitchen after eating when there was a knock at the door.

"Hey," I said when I saw Chloe standing in the hallway, holding a bottle of wine and two wineglasses. "I was beginning to think you really didn't live in that apartment down the hall. Come on in."

Chloe laughed. "I know. I've been so darn busy at the yarn shop recently I haven't even had a chance to welcome you properly. So I thought maybe you'd like to join me on my porch and we can indulge in this great chardonnay and have a gabfest."

"That sounds great," I said, and followed her down the hall and through her apartment, which overlooked Second Street from a good-size second-floor porch. "You sure have a bird's-eye view of the town from here, don't you?"

"Yeah," she said, filling the wineglasses. "Except I haven't had much time to just sit out here and see what's going on."

"It's good that the yarn shop has been busy. I've had a pretty good first weekend also."

"And we have to enjoy it now, because come September it'll be pretty slow."

I took a sip of wine. "Hmm, good. I met your Aunt Maude today. She was telling me about the Blue Moon ceremonies that she does with her knitting retreats. Did you know Dora's sister, Sybile? I guess they did the first one."

"Yeah, they did, but no, I never met Sybile. She passed away before I came here last year. From what I hear, she was quite a character."

"So Dora must know a lot about the island, huh?"

"Oh, yeah. She was born and raised here." Chloe cut a wedge of cheese from the platter on the table. "Why? Is there something in particular you want to know about?"

"Nah, it just must be nice to know your roots."

I saw the look of surprise that crossed Chloe's face. "But you grew up in Salem, right?"

"Yeah, but we were originally from Maine. My grandmother and mother moved to Salem when I was five."

"And there's no other family left in Maine?"

"No. My only other relative is my mom's sister, but they were never really close. I saw her at my grandmother's funeral, and that was only the second time I'd met her. She lives outside of Atlanta now. Her husband was in the military and they had no children. They traveled around a lot."

"Families can be complex, can't they? My parents traveled a lot before they died. They owned an antique shop in Brunswick, and that took them to Europe frequently."

"So it's nice that you have your aunt and Grace," I said.

"Well, Grace and I weren't really close until I moved to Cedar Key, but yes, I'm glad we reconnected. How about your father? Has he also passed away?"

I took another sip of wine while trying to decide how much to reveal. "My parents were never married. They met at college and then he went off to Vietnam, where he was killed shortly after I was born."

"Oh, so you never knew him? How about his family?"

I shook my head. "No, I never met him, and my mother was never in touch with his family. They lived in Houston."

"Well, I can understand how you feel about having roots. Have you thought about getting in touch with your aunt?"

"Yeah, especially after my mother died. Maybe eventually I will."

When I returned to my apartment a couple of hours later, I glanced at the desk drawer that held the postcards, but I didn't remove them. I already knew what they said.

So after giving Sigmund some attention I began my bedtime ritual of preparing the coffeemaker for the following morning, arranging the clothes I would wear across the chair, brushing my teeth, and placing a glass of ice water on my bedside table. My routine never varied, and yes, I knew that the last thing I did was probably the opposite of most people—I switched on the lamp beside my bed, casting light inside the room. As I drifted off to sleep two thoughts crossed my mind: Saxton Tate III would be coming to the chocolate shop the following day, and perhaps the time had arrived to contact my aunt, Stella Baldwin.

4

True to his word, Saxton did stop by the shop to replenish his chocolate. I was waiting on two women when he sauntered through the door. The word *saunter* seemed to fit him perfectly because nothing about Saxton Tate III seemed rushed or swift. The man definitely had a laid-back demeanor. He also had a dashing quality about him that the plaid tam on his head emphasized. I watched out of the corner of my eye as he stood near the table where the gems were arranged.

"Thanks," I told the women after ringing up their sale.

Saxton nodded at them as they left the shop and then turned toward me with a smile.

"It looks like you're being kept busy," he said.

"Yeah, it's been steady all weekend, which is good. What can I get for you today?"

His eyes focused on the glass case as he tilted his head for a better look. After a few moments' deliberation he said, "I think I'll try two of your Cedar Key clam chocolates and two of the truffles, please."

I reached for a small box and began filling it with his request. "Are there a lot of people out and about on Second Street?" I asked.

"Oh, I'd say a fair amount. Poor Lucas just had a run-in with one of them across the street."

"An unhappy tourist?" I rang up the sale and slipped the box into a bag.

"No, no. Not a tourist at all—a local. Not sure if you've met Raylene Samuels yet. Very set in her ways, and she was in the bookshop complaining about Lucas carrying the newest release by Lacey Weston."

Although I'd never read her books, I knew she was a top seller in the genre of erotica. "Really? What was her problem?"

Saxton let out a chuckle. "Seems she was on her soapbox telling him that as a good Christian woman she didn't appreciate his shop stocking those kinds of books. Told him she considered it *smut*."

"I wonder why it bothers her so much. There are plenty of other books in there for her to read."

Saxton reached for the bag I passed him. "That's pretty much what Lucas told her. He explained that as a bookshop owner, censorship isn't part of his job. Lacey Weston's books sell, which means the author has readers."

I nodded. "Yeah, I've never read them myself, but . . . live and let live, I always say. It's too bad she gave Lucas a hard time about it."

"From what I hear, Raylene does this on a regular basis. Even though she knows she has no chance of getting those books banned. Like it's her moral duty to try."

We both looked toward the door as the wind chimes tinkled.

A woman walked into the shop. She was medium height, short salt and pepper hair, appeared to be early seventies, with a distinct frown on her face and somebody I'd never seen before.

Saxton surprised me when he said, "Miss Raylene. How're you today?"

She briefly glanced in his direction before bringing her eyes back to the case filled with chocolate. "Since you just saw me across the street at the bookshop, you should know I'm upset."

Oh, no . . . was this woman here in an attempt to ban my chocolate along with erotica? Chocolate sometimes caused the word *decadent* to come to mind.

"What's that?" she asked, pointing an arthritic finger toward my clams.

"My signature chocolates. Dark chocolate in the shape of clams. Here," I said, putting on a plastic glove and reaching into the case. "Would you like a sample?" With the sour look on this woman's face she looked like she could use a bit of sweetening.

Saxton and I watched as she plopped it into her mouth. "It's good," she said, but her tone indicated surprise. "I'll take a half pound of those. I'm Raylene Samuels, and you are . . . ?"

"Berkley Whitmore. It's nice to meet you," I told her as I filled a box. "You live here on the island?"

"I do. Born and raised here. Like my daddy always said, when ya live in paradise, why on earth would ya wanna leave?"

I smiled. "Why indeed?"

I rang up the sale and passed the box to her. "I hope you'll enjoy them."

"Me too," was all she said before turning around and leaving.

Saxton's deep laughter filled the shop as he shook his head. "She's a piece of work, isn't she?"

I joined his laughter. "I have to agree with you on that. Gosh, she seems like an angry person. I wonder if the poor woman knows how to smile."

"Like the old farmer used to say, people are like crops. You have to weed them out. Well, I better get going. It was nice seeing you again, Berkley. I'll be back on Tuesday for my refill."

A wave of disappointment swept through me. "Oh, I'm closed on Mondays and Tuesdays."

"Well, then, in that case you'd better give me two more of the truffles to tide me over."

After paying me, he said, "You know . . . I enjoy talking to you. Any chance you'd be interested in joining me sometime for coffee or a drink? I know you haven't met many people in town yet, and it might do you good to get away from your shop for a while."

That would be nice. Very nice, actually. "You could be right," was all I said, waiting for him to take the lead.

"Great. Why don't you meet me Tuesday evening over at the

Black Dog on Dock Street? They have good wine and beer and a nice deck where I like to sit with Lola. She's my best friend—a little white terrier mix—and she adores Otis, the namesake for the Black Dog. Why don't we say around seven o'clock?"

"That sounds like fun, and I look forward to meeting Lola."

I watched him walk out the door but instead of thinking about *fun,* I found myself wondering if I really wanted to get involved in another aimless relationship. While I'd always enjoyed having a male companion, before long I would feel smothered or not able to tolerate various quirks he'd have. Either that or my *own* quirks would drive him away, which always led to a parting. Too late to think about this now, since I'd already accepted Saxton's invitation.

After I'd had dinner and cleaned up I sat on the sofa with Sigmund curled beside me, trying to figure out exactly what I'd say to Aunt Stella when I called her.

I needed information to piece together the answers I was looking for. I wasn't at all sure that my mother's sister could assist me, but she was the only family member left that might be able to. People are strange about relinquishing family information, even when the members involved are no longer here, so I didn't want her to think the main reason for my call was precisely that.

I got up, poured myself a glass of iced tea, and wiped up the droplets on the counter as I continued to formulate my thoughts. Twenty minutes later I was dialing my aunt's phone number in Atlanta.

"Berkley," I heard her say with more friendliness than I'd expected. "How nice to hear from you. How are things in Salem?"

I explained about my relocation to Cedar Key and listened intently to see if the name of the town would cause recognition in her voice. It did not.

"Where exactly in Florida is that?" she questioned, leading me to believe that she probably wasn't aware that my mother had come here forty years before.

"Off the west coast. North central Florida, about an hour from Gainesville."

"And it's an island? I'm sure it's delightful. It's really nice that

you're continuing to carry on the family tradition with the chocolate shop. I'm afraid other than eating chocolates I had no desire to
be involved in the business. But your mother and grandmother always loved it." She paused for a moment. "You know, Berkley, I've
always felt bad that you and I never got to know each other better.
Maybe you'd like to come and visit me sometime. . . ."

She left the sentence hanging, but I heard an almost wistful
tone. Stella Baldwin was the last link. The one who could probably
explain so many things about her sister to me, and I had an idea.

"This is my first weekend being open and I really can't take any
time off for a while, but if you're free I'd love to have you come and
visit me here. It's a beautiful island surrounded by Mother Nature."

"Really?" I heard the surprise in my aunt's voice.

"Yeah, you're alone now and maybe you'd enjoy a getaway. The
only problem is that my place is pretty small. I only have a one-
bedroom apartment."

"Hmm, that might be fun. I wonder how long a drive it is from
Atlanta. Don't worry about putting me up. I'm sure I could find a
place to stay . . . but I have a little Yorkie and I couldn't bear to put
Addi in a kennel, so that might be a problem."

"I think it's about six or seven hours from Atlanta to Cedar Key.
I know the Faraway Inn is pet friendly, and it's a great location in
the historic district, right across the street from a small beach and a
great view."

"Well, let me think about it, Berkley, and see when I could
come. I have quite a few social commitments between now and
June, but I'll get on the Internet and check out that place for lodg-
ing. I'll get back to you as soon as I figure out some dates."

"That would be great," I told her.

After hanging up the phone, I walked into the living room and
glanced toward my desk. The urn stared back at me. I wondered
what my mother would think about her sister paying me a visit. But
more important, I wondered if that sister would be able to put together some pieces of my puzzle.

5

It was a nice feeling to wake up Monday morning and know I didn't have to be downstairs in the chocolate shop. After I had breakfast and got Sigmund fed, I sat at the table and looked over my list for the day. Yes, I'm a list maker. According to some people, I'm rather compulsive about this—but these lists, along with Post-its, help me to stay on track throughout the day and accomplish everything that I hope to.

I glanced at the notebook paper: Visit yarn shop and see about supplying yarn to Dora. Stop by coffee café looking for locals to engage in conversation. Finish spinning yarn for customers. Check on supply of chocolate clams. Call Angell and Phelps to order more Honeybees.

I let out a sigh before gulping the last of my coffee and glanced at the clock on the wall. Eight-thirty. Probably too early to do a few of these things, since most shops in town didn't open till ten. But I could get some spinning finished.

Walking into the living room I flipped on the CD player and settled into the chair behind my spinning wheel. I loved spinning not only because I enjoyed the feel of the fiber coming to life in my hands, but also because it afforded me time to just let my mind wander.

Although I had originally only come to Cedar Key to gain information, I had to admit I liked the town and the people that I'd met so far. But I guess I was one of those people that could easily relocate and feel comfortable in my new surroundings. I attributed this to the fact that at age five I had to leave behind my nursery school, my friends, and the only house I'd ever known and make the move from Maine to Massachusetts. Looking back now, it seemed that all of it happened almost overnight. One minute we were living in a small town in Maine and the next thing I knew, my mother was gone and my grandmother was telling me the two of us were moving.

Leaning over to adjust the fiber on the bobbin, I tried to recall exactly what I had been told before my mother left. But much of it was such a blur. What bothered me the most that summer was that my mother hadn't even said *good-bye*. That I still remembered. I recalled getting up one morning, looking for her in the kitchen, where she normally was before I left for school, and she wasn't there. My grandmother was making my breakfast and told me that my mother had to go away for a little while, but we had an adventure ahead because we were moving. I'm not sure any of it made sense to my five-year-old mind. Hell, it still didn't make sense. And beyond that, the only other thing that I could recall was that I didn't go to school that day or the rest of the week, because by the following week my grandmother and I were on our way to a new life in Salem, Massachusetts.

I finished spinning the skein of yarn and realized it was now ten-fifteen. One more skein to go and I'd be able to ship the order to my customer in Chicago. But now it was time to get out and about and see what information I might be able to gather.

I walked into the coffee café to find it pretty crowded. Suellen spied me from behind the counter and gave a wave.

"Hey," I said, walking toward her. "Looks like business is booming here."

She swiped a strand of hair from her forehead and nodded. "Yeah, this time of morning it's always busy. The locals come in to visit and exchange gossip. What can I get you?"

A pound of gossip from somebody recalling a Jeanette Whitmore who stayed here for a summer forty years ago would be great, I thought, but said, "A regular coffee, twenty ounce, and one of those delicious blueberry muffins."

I chose a table next to four women who were having an animated discussion about books.

"So you *have* read her books?" I heard one woman ask with astonishment.

"Yes, I have, and why shouldn't I? I'm over twenty-one by a few years," she said, which brought a chuckle from the other women.

I glanced over to see that the woman speaking appeared to be in her early eighties, and I smiled. From what I could gather, I had a feeling that the erotica author Lacey Weston was once again the subject of conversation on the island.

"Well, yes, Flora, I agree," another woman said. "I guess I was just surprised since you normally read nonfiction books."

"Variety is the spice of life," the older woman replied, and looked over at me. "Do you like to read?"

"I do," I said. "Very much so."

"Visiting here?" she asked.

"No, I recently moved here. I'm Berkley Whitmore and the owner of the chocolate shop across the street."

The older woman's face lit up. "Right. I'd been meaning to get over there, and I see you're closed today. Well, I'm Flora Mathews, and this here is Corabeth, Liz, and Betty. We've been friends for years."

Four potential sources of information. "So you grew up together? Right here on the island?"

Flora nodded. "We sure did, and you know that building where your shop is? I used to own that a long time ago."

A definite source of information.

"Pull up a chair," she said. "Come and join us. We're having a discussion about erotica."

Corabeth laughed and shook her head as I moved my chair to their table.

"Not exactly about erotica," she said. "We're discussing books."

"Did you ever read that author, Lacey Weston?" Flora questioned.

"No, I haven't, but it has nothing to do with the fact that it's erotica. I generally lean more toward women's fiction or mysteries."

The women nodded. "Same here," said Betty. "Not sure if you've met her yet, but Raylene Samuels has her knickers in a twist about the bookshop selling this author's work. She's a member of our book club but very particular about our choices. If Raylene doesn't like the book chosen, she doesn't attend the meeting, and that's fine with us. But she's badgering poor Lucas at the bookshop not to carry Weston's books, which is flat-out ridiculous."

"Exactly," Liz said. "We respect her right not to read certain books, and there's no penalty for missing a meeting, so she should give the rest of the reading public that same respect. But not Raylene—oh, no. Even though none of Weston's books have ever been one of our book club selections, she's taken it upon herself to try and enforce censorship."

I nodded. "I did hear something about this the other day, but I was told that she didn't get through to Lucas about not carrying the books."

"That's right," Corabeth said. "The man is in business to sell books, and obviously Weston's books sell. He has no desire to censor readers' choices."

"I hear you're living in one of the apartments upstairs," Flora said, changing the subject. "That makes it convenient with your shop."

"Yes, it really does. I love the apartment and I love having Chloe right down the hall. Did you have a shop there when you owned the building?"

Flora shook her head. "Oh, my, no. My family has been in the soft-shell crab business since before I was born. My grandson runs the business now. You like soft-shell crab?"

"I love it," I told her.

"Well, then, you'll have to come out to our house and learn all about what you're eating."

Opportunity for information was being dropped right in my lap. "That would be great."

"I live out on Twenty-four, and we'll make plans for you to come over."

"I'd really enjoy that," I told her, and took the last bite of my muffin. "Well, I need to get going. I'll be supplying yarn to Dora for her shop, so I have to stop by there and discuss the arrangements with her."

"That's right," Corabeth said. "Somebody told me you own your own alpacas and spin the yarn. I'm looking forward to purchasing some. Oh, and you have to join our knitting group. I'm sure Dora will tell you all about it, but we meet on Thursday evenings. To just sit around and talk and knit."

"And gossip," Liz interjected, causing the women to laugh.

"Thank you for including me," I said, standing up. "I really enjoyed meeting you ladies and I'll probably see you Thursday evening."

Walking down Second Street toward the yarn shop I hoped that some of the gossip that would be revealed over time might eventually lead me to my answers.

Walking into the yarn shop I was greeted by a large, black standard poodle.

"Well, hello, handsome," I said, reaching out my hand for him to sniff. "And who are you?"

"Berkley, how nice to see you," Dora said, coming from behind the counter. "This is Oliver—my new best friend. I got Oliver a few months ago from the rescue league. He's four years old and I'm afraid he didn't always have the best life with his previous owners."

I bent down to pat him and was immediately struck by the fact that the dog wouldn't make eye contact with me. Instead he hung his head and looked at the floor.

"It's okay, Oliver," Dora said softly. "Berkley is a nice person and she won't hurt you." As she explained to the dog, she gently lifted his head, encouraging him to look at me.

My heart broke to think of the abuse he had probably suffered causing him to have such a lack of self-esteem.

I looked into his soulful brown eyes. "You're such a handsome boy," I told him, and rubbed the top of his head.

"We go to obedience classes in Gainesville once a week. Oliver has done outstanding, and even the trainer is impressed," she relayed with pride in her voice. "I bring him with me every day to the yarn shop because having people fawn over him is a good thing. It gives him the confidence he needs."

"How sweet, and how fortunate Oliver is to have you as his caregiver."

"Oh, I'm the fortunate one," Dora said as a huge smile crossed her face. "I'm glad you dropped by. Did you want to discuss selling me your yarn?"

"If you're not busy, that would be great."

"I just heated some water for tea. Would you like to join me for a cup?"

"Sure," I said, as I settled myself on the sofa. "What a pretty shop you have. I love the fireplace and how you arranged the two sofas to face it."

"I'm afraid I can't take credit for that or the decorating. My niece, Sydney, was the original owner. The shop was called Spinning Forward when Sydney opened it, and then a few years later her daughter, Monica, bought the shop and changed the name to Yarning Together."

"Thanks," I said, accepting the mug of tea. "That's an unusual name for a knit shop, isn't it?"

Dora laughed. "I suppose it is, but when Monica's stepdaughter saw knitting being done, she questioned why the craft wasn't called *yarning* rather than knitting. Clarissa continued to refer to the craft as yarning, and when Monica bought the shop, she decided to change the name based on Clarissa's terminology."

I smiled. "That's really sweet, and I'm sure it made Clarissa happy."

"It did, even though she now refers to it as knitting. So you think you'd be interested in supplying our shop with some of your yarn?"

I took a sip of tea and then nodded. "Yes, I know that hand-dyed, hand-spun yarn is popular with knitters. The average yield from one alpaca is approximately five pounds of raw fleece, and as you know, I own two alpacas. I do have some customers on the Internet, but I'd have enough to do a supply for your shop as well. And if you happened to have a big demand for it, I know my friend Jill would be happy to also sell you some."

"That sounds great. Do you have any samples with you?"

"I do," I said, reaching into my tote bag and pulling out three skeins of yarn.

"Oh, these are gorgeous." Dora reached out to touch the soft fibers of blues, greens, and lavenders. "Okay, well, Chloe was all for the idea, so when you have some skeins ready to sell us, bring them over and we'll add them to our inventory."

"That sounds great." I reached out to pat Oliver, who had edged his way over to my leg. "Oh, Corabeth mentioned that you have a knitting group here on Thursday evenings. . . ."

"Yes, we do, and it would be nice if you could join us. Seven o'clock till around nine. We just sit around and knit, get caught up on what's going on in town, and enjoy each other's company. We also take turns bringing some kind of pastry to go with coffee or tea."

"I'll definitely join you, and it'll give me a chance to meet some of the women from the island. I'm sure they have some great stories to share."

Dora laughed. "Oh, yeah. I think each one is a born storyteller."

"Do you get a lot of people here who only come for the summer?"

"Hmm, not really. We do have a fair amount of snowbirds though. People who own homes here but only stay during the winter months. Or tourists escaping the cold of the north for a few months. But you'll see that during the summer it's mighty quiet here."

All the more reason that old-timer locals might recall a particular woman who came to stay during the summer of 1972, I thought.

6

By the time that Tuesday evening arrived, all of the items on my list had been crossed off. I had finished spinning the yarn for my customer, called Angell and Phelps for an order, and made another supply of my chocolate clams, but I hadn't gathered any information about anybody knowing a Jeanette Whitmore.

I was hesitant to just come out and ask people if they recalled that name. Perhaps I wanted to avoid any disappointment so early in my search. I also felt that it would be more likely for somebody to share information after they got to know me better. So I was in no hurry. Heck, I'd already waited forty years, so a little longer wouldn't matter.

After I applied my kohl eyeliner and a bit of mascara, I slipped into a pair of white cropped pants, black tank top, and sandals. I'm far from a fashion plate, and my normal attire usually consists of shorts or jeans with a tee shirt, but the anticipation of meeting Saxton for a drink notched up my dress code a bit.

I stood back from the full-length mirror to access my image and was surprised that for a split second I saw my mother looking back at me. I never felt that I resembled her, nor had anybody ever mentioned this fact, but within the blink of an eye and for the first time, I did catch a glimpse of Jeanette Whitmore.

Walking slowly over to Dock Street, I knew that my mother had walked these same streets. Although the postcards indicated that the main reason for that communication was to give my mother updates on my well-being, even now, forty years later, I wondered how she could have just up and left her daughter for an entire summer. I had my own theories on this—but no proof whatsoever.

Saxton was already seated at one of the tables on the outside deck when I arrived.

"Hey," he said, standing up as a huge smile covered his face. "I'm glad you could make it."

I felt a smile cross my own face and noticed again that Saxton Tate III was definitely one very distinguished-looking man. Wearing khakis, a pale blue polo shirt, and loafers, he looked every bit the cosmopolitan author.

"Me too," I replied, and glanced down to see a cute white dog on a leash staring up at me. "And you must be Lola." I reached out my hand to allow her a sniff.

"Yes, this is my buddy. Lola, meet Berkley," he said, not taking his eyes from my face.

"She's really sweet. How old is she?" I asked as I settled myself on the opposite stool.

"Lola's five. I've had her since she was a pup. Do you have any pets?"

The waitress approached our table, preventing me from answering. I noticed Saxton had a glass of red wine in front of him.

"I'll have what he's drinking," I told her before turning my attention back to him. "Yes, I have a huge black cat named Sigmund. He's ten now."

Saxton nodded. "Pets are wonderful companions, especially for people who live alone. So how do you like Cedar Key so far?"

"I like it a lot. People are friendly, and of course it's a beautiful place to live, so I'm hoping that my chocolate shop will do well. Thanks," I told the waitress as she placed the wineglass in front of me.

Saxton held up his glass. "Cheers, and let me officially welcome you to the island."

"Cheers," I repeated before taking a sip. "Oh, this is good. What is it?"

"It's called Cycles Gladiator, and one of my favorite red wines here. I heard you had only visited the island once last year before making the decision to relocate. You must be quite an adventuresome woman."

I laughed while shaking my head. "No, I don't think I am. But after visiting here last fall, I knew I could be happy living here."

"Do you still have any family up north?"

"No, my grandmother passed away the year before my mother, so it was just me. I do have an aunt in Atlanta, my mother's sister, and she might be coming to visit in the next few months. But we're not close at all. We hardly know each other. How about you? Do you still have family in England?"

Saxton shook his head. "No, nobody. Oh, some distant cousins, but that's about it. I have a thirty-eight-year-old daughter who lives in Seattle."

A thirty-eight-year-old daughter? She was only seven years younger than me, and he didn't look old enough to have a daughter that age.

As if reading my mind, he said, "I was only twenty when Resa was born. I'm afraid I became a statistic of a young marriage that failed. You mentioned your parents met at Berkeley. Has your father also passed away?"

"Yes, they were never married and he was killed in Vietnam, so I never knew him."

Saxton took a sip of wine and was quiet for a few moments before asking, "Do you feel that affected your life in any way? Not knowing your father?"

I thought it was an odd question and one that I had never given much thought to. "Not really," I said with a shrug. "I guess what you don't know, you don't miss. Do you see your daughter very often?"

Without hesitating, he replied, "I haven't seen her in thirty years. Her mother is American and we met at university in London. Resa was born there, and when we divorced eight years later Muriel took her and came back to the States."

"Oh," I said, hoping my expression didn't reveal too much of my surprise. "But didn't you have visitation rights?"

"I did, but I'm ashamed to admit that I didn't enforce them. I thought perhaps it was best that they both make a new life. I paid support for Resa until she was thirteen, when Muriel remarried and her husband adopted my daughter, so we had no further contact. Muriel had a top position with a corporation in Manhattan and married a doctor, so I'm sure Resa had a good lifestyle and didn't go without anything—except her real father."

He didn't disguise the regret in his tone. "But you know she's in Seattle?" I questioned.

Saxton nodded. "I happened to see the obituary of Muriel's husband in the *New York Times* last year and it said he left a daughter Resa Campbell from Seattle. Campbell wasn't her adopted name, so I assume she's now married, probably with her own family."

"Families can be pretty difficult, can't they?" I said, thinking of my own situation, and before I knew it or understood why, I found myself sharing with Saxton the truth about how I ended up on Cedar Key.

"Wow," he said, and nodded to the waitress for two more glasses of wine. "That's quite a story. So you really came here on a search to find some answers. Have you had any luck yet?"

I shook my head. "No, but I haven't begun to actively search for information. My mother was here forty years ago and although a lot of the locals are still here, I'm not sure anybody will remember a twenty-seven-year-old woman from the northeast."

"Well, if she was here for the entire summer she had to have lived and worked somewhere. Besides, this is a very small town, so I'd say your chances are pretty good about at least finding somebody that knew her. It might be a bit more difficult, though, to actually find out *why* she was here."

"Yeah, I thought of that. My mother was an extremely private person, so to be honest, I'm not sure she would have opened up and told the truth to anybody. Now that she's gone, though, I just felt compelled to come here and try and find some answers."

"What kind of woman was she? Was she outgoing and friendly? Or do you think she would have kept more to herself?"

I let out a deep sigh. "My mother was extremely complex. When she worked in the chocolate shop, she was very friendly to the customers, but I always got the feeling that she had to make an effort to be that way. Like it didn't come naturally to her. She had an isolated life—really no girlfriends to speak of. She never dated, and if she wasn't working she was at home."

"So there's no reason to think that her lifestyle would have been any different here," Saxton said, and reached down to give Lola a pat.

"Right, and why here? It's not like she left Salem for a larger city for work or education. Why come to such a small town, a place that she'd never been before?"

"And you say that the postcards are really only updates on how she's doing? No other information about what she's doing here?"

"None. In her postcards to my grandmother she only mentions the weather or that she's feeling okay."

"Do you think she was ill? That maybe she came here to recuperate from an injury or illness?"

"Even if that were the reason, why keep it from me? Why not tell me that was why she left? I mean, gosh, years ago people had to go to sanatoriums to recover from tuberculosis."

"Yes, true, but many families also kept that a secret. What's your theory on all of it? Do you have any ideas why she left so suddenly without even saying good-bye?"

My theory had been in my head for years, but I'd never actually verbalized it to anybody. I blew out a breath and took a sip of wine. "What I've always felt," I said softly, "was that she'd probably just had it with motherhood. A young, single mom trying to raise a daughter on her own. Even though my grandmother helped a lot, I'm sure it was still pretty tough on her. Especially in the sixties and seventies. I remember telling kids in school that my father had died in Vietnam, and when they didn't question me further I never volunteered the information that my parents had never been married."

Saxton nodded. "Hmm, the stigma of being different. But she *did* come back after a few months, and it seems the main reason for the correspondence with your grandmother was to make sure you were doing okay—to check on *your* welfare."

"Yes, true. I've thought of that also."

"Do you remember how she was when she returned? Any difference in how she acted toward you? A change in her lifestyle?"

"That period in my life is pretty blurry, and it's hard to remember details from that long ago, but I'd have to say, no. I don't recall her acting any different at all. She resumed working in the chocolate shop, she was still very overprotective with me, still didn't show much affection. Don't get me wrong, she wasn't a bad mother at all. Actually, I'd have to say she was a very good mother. . . . It's just that I always felt something was missing from her. I can't explain it."

Saxton reached out and patted my hand. "I certainly hope you'll find your answers, Berkley. But more important, I hope they'll be answers that will make you feel good—both about your mother and yourself."

Before I had a chance to question exactly what he meant, we both turned to the sound of a male voice approaching our table.

"Hey, Saxton, how're doing?"

I looked up to see a man that had directed his question at Saxton but was staring at me. Tall, good looking in a relaxed sort of way, he appeared to be in his early seventies. With a silver ponytail caught at the nape of his neck with elastic, wearing cutoffs, tee shirt, and sandals, he reminded me of an aging hippie.

Saxton stood up to shake his hand. "Doyle, good to see you. I'm doing fine, and I'd like you to meet my new friend, Berkley Whitmore."

The man put his hand out to shake mine as I noticed he seemed to be scrutinizing my face.

"Nice to meet you," he said, with a hint of a Southern accent. "Are you visiting the island?"

"No, I recently moved here and opened the chocolate shop over on Second Street."

"Chocolate shop?" he questioned with surprise in his tone. "Where're you from originally?"

The man was pleasant enough, but I got the feeling that my line of business baffled him, and I laughed. "Yes, chocolate. That wonderful-tasting stuff that so many people crave. I'm from Salem, Massachusetts."

My statement brought silence on his part, and he only nodded.

"So," Saxton said, "are we still on for the fishing trip tomorrow? Doyle here is a top fisherman, in addition to being quite an artist. Many of his works are displayed at the Arts Center."

"Really? I'll have to get over there and see them."

"And you'll have to be sure to let me know what you think. Yeah, the fishing trip is still on. I'll meet you at seven at the City Marina," he told Saxton before switching his gaze back to me. "It was very nice meeting you, Berkley. I hope you'll enjoy living on Cedar Key."

"Thanks," I said, watching him walk away. "He seems like a nice guy. Is he from here originally?"

"Oh, yeah," Saxton told me. "Doyle Summers was born and raised here. A really nice guy, and we've become very good friends since I moved here."

Born and raised on Cedar Key, huh? I wondered if Doyle Summers might be able to assist in filling in some pieces to my puzzle. A local, in the same age group my mother was, and he might have known her during that summer of 1972.

7

On Thursday morning I was folding clothes that I'd removed from the dryer when I got a call from Jill.

"Hey, girlfriend," I said. "How's everything going up in Maine and how are my Bosco and Belle?"

"Everything's great and they're just fine. More to the point— any answers yet down there?"

Jill knew my story and the main reason why I'd relocated to Cedar Key. It was actually Jill who encouraged me to make the move. She was one of the few people I knew who had actually been raised in a family that resembled *The Waltons* television show. Her parents were loving, supportive, and forgiving, and she had maintained a good relationship with her two brothers and three sisters, something that I'd always envied. It was Jill who felt I needed to finally find out why my mother had left that summer, and it was Jill who listened to my stories and theories over so many years.

"No," I told her. "Nothing yet, but I have to admit that I haven't been trying that hard either."

"And why not?"

I smiled. Jill had always been a no-nonsense type of person. Honest and to the point, she'd always been a follower of the creed, *If not now, then when?*

"Well, I'm slowly getting to meet the locals. And...I don't know. Maybe this is a silly idea. Maybe nobody will remember my mother at all, and if they do, maybe they won't tell me a thing."

"Right," she said. "And if you don't start inquiring, you'll never know anything. Don't be like your mother, Berkley. She was a fearful person. The two most daring things she ever did in life were to leave home for college in California and then the trip she made to Cedar Key. Other than that, she never took chances."

Jill was right. It still astounded me that my mother had actually done those two things, because the rest of her life seemed to be spent worrying or procrastinating. I recalled how I'd try to talk her into traveling with me somewhere for a vacation. My grandmother would encourage the trip, my mother would say she'd give it some thought, but in the end her answer was always no, with unfounded excuses.

"She also made that trip to Cape Cod for a few months before she got sick last year," I said, knowing it was another attempt on my part to try and justify my mother's actions.

"Sure, and when you found those postcards and discovered that Cedar Key was a coastal town, you wondered if her going to the Cape could have been for her to recapture that summer. Face it, Berkley, you felt rejected because she left you and the secrecy about all of it only made it worse. You're *there* now, where she was, and now is the time for you to get your answers."

Once again Jill was right, and I knew that. "Well, I'm going to a knitting group at the yarn shop this evening. There'll be a few women there that have lived here all their lives, so maybe I'll begin to ask some questions."

"Very good idea. Listen, another reason I called is because I wanted to tell you that I'll be shearing the alpacas next month. Any chance you'll make a trip up here for that? I'd love to see you again."

"Gee, I don't think next month will be possible. I really need to be here for a few months during the busy season to get my shop established."

"Yeah, I can understand that. How's business going?"

"Pretty well for the first weekend, and next month is the Arts Festival, so that should be a great weekend for business. But I'm told that September and October are fairly quiet here on the island, so I'll probably come up to Maine then."

"Oh, good. So besides Chloe, have you made any other new friends?"

I immediately thought of Saxton Tate III, and I was pretty sure that having two glasses of wine with him a few nights ago constituted the fact that we were now friends.

"Well, there is this guy . . ."

I heard Jill laughing across the line. "Leave it to you, Miss I'm Not Interested in a Relationship, and yet you have men drawn to you like a magnet. I should be so lucky."

I joined her laughter. "Yeah, right. And I never actually said I wasn't *interested* in a relationship. It's just that none of them have ever worked out for me."

"Hmm, gee, and of course that has nothing to do with the fact that you're so compulsive and won't settle for anything less than Mr. Perfect."

"First of all, I'm not compulsive. All of us have quirks, and maybe I have a fair share of those, but . . . hey, why should I *settle* anyway? I'm happy with my lifestyle. You never hear me complaining about that. And you know as well as I do that there was never a lasting connection with any of the guys that I've dated."

"All true, and I'm just teasing you, so tell me about this new *friend*."

"Well, his name is Saxton Tate the third and . . ."

Before I could go further, Jill's laughter echoed across the line again. "You *are* kidding, right? That's not *really* his name!"

I smiled as I recalled my identical reaction the day he had introduced himself. "It is, and it fits him. He's British, fifty-eight years old, and he's an author, not to mention he's pretty good looking."

"Wow," was all Jill said.

"He's very nice and easy to talk with. He came into the shop, bought some chocolates, and then invited me out for some wine Tuesday evening. We got to know each other better, and I do like him as a person—as a friend."

"Interesting."

"What's that supposed to mean?"

"Just ... interesting. I'm pretty sure I know about every guy you've ever dated, and this is the first time you've ever used those two words to describe one. *Nice* and *friend*."

I smiled as I digested what Jill had said. She was right. Saxton *was* nice, and I already considered him a friend.

"Okay, Ms. Pearson, I guess interesting might be correct, but you can retire cupid's arrow because I seriously doubt this will ever go beyond friendship."

"Famous last words, and I have to get going and get some work done. Call me next week with some updates—on everything."

I heard the line disconnect and shook my head. Jill was my best friend, but it didn't mean she knew me better than I knew myself. Did it?

After I finished the laundry, I cleaned up the kitchen and then began filling trays with chocolate clams to take downstairs to the shop. Placing each one precisely one eighth of an inch apart, I recalled what Jill had said about me being compulsive. I liked things orderly, yes. And I also liked everything done in a timely fashion, but compulsive? I didn't think so.

At six-thirty that evening I walked into the kitchen to get my knitting bag from the chair and noticed that my plant was looking a bit droopy. This plant was special to me. It had belonged to my grandmother for as long as I could remember, and before she died she had entrusted it in my care. I had no idea what kind of plant it was, but it had sat in the kitchen of our chocolate shop. Medium size, it resembled a bonsai plant and was in a bright orange terracotta pot. Although we never told our customers, my grandmother always clipped off a bit of the leaves to add to the chocolate she was preparing. Not only did I not know what kind of plant that it was, I also had no idea why she added that ingredient to our chocolates. Whenever I'd question her, she'd smile and say, "Berkley, it's magic. Pure magic." As a child, I was always delighted with her answer, and as an adult, I had stopped asking the question but never failed to also add it to my chocolate recipe.

I filled a small pitcher with water and wet the soil before touching the leaves. Silly, I know, but that plant always made me feel extra close to my grandmother.

I then got my knitting bag and headed to the yarn shop.

I arrived to find quite a few women already seated on the sofas and chairs. Dora saw me and grabbed my arm to pull me closer to the group.

Clapping her hands together, she said, "I want everyone to meet our newest member. This is Berkley Whitmore, who opened the chocolate shop down the street, and she'll also be providing us with some wonderful alpaca yarn from Maine that you'll be able to purchase."

I recognized Flora, Corabeth, Liz, and Betty from our meeting earlier in the week, and the four other women seated across from them smiled and introduced themselves.

"Chloe called and is on her way," Dora told me. "She had to go to Gainesville earlier and should be here shortly. Have a seat and join us."

I settled myself in a cushy chair and glanced around at the various knitting projects the women were working on. Gorgeous cable sweaters, an entrelac baby blanket, and a few scarves with intricate lace patterns. I reached into my tote and brought out the tank top I was making for myself in an apricot-colored yarn of pima cotton. I thought it would add to my wardrobe for the coming summer.

"So are you settling in well?" Liz asked me.

"Yes, I am. I love my apartment, and business was good at the chocolate shop last weekend. I think I'm going to really like it here."

"Here we are," I heard Chloe say, and everyone looked up as she walked in with her aunt. "I got stuck in traffic in Gainesville and then swung by to pick up Aunt Maude."

"Hi, everyone," Maude said, pulling up a chair beside me. She patted my hand. "Oh, it's good to see you here, Berkley. I'm glad you could join us."

"Me too," Chloe said, settling herself on the sofa. "I went to get my beauty treatment today and ended up spending three hours at the spa." She held out her bright red manicured nails while lifting her legs in the air so we could inspect her matching toenails peeking out from gold sandals. "But it was worth it."

"Very pretty," I told her, and realized it had been at least twenty years since I'd gotten my nails done professionally.

Flora waved a hand in the air. "Well, at my age that would be a total waste of time."

"Oh, I don't know about that," Betty said, as her knitting needles clicked away. "I got a manicure and pedicure last year for my granddaughter's wedding and I rather enjoyed it."

"Speaking of weddings, does anyone know if Grace is coming tonight?"

"I don't think so," Chloe told us. "I spoke to her this morning and she said she was going to spend a quiet evening at home with Lucas."

Liz let out a chuckle. "Yeah, if I had that Frenchman at home, I'd do exactly the same thing," she said, bringing forth laughter from the other women.

"I'm sure she's keeping him quite entertained with all those wedding shower gifts we gave her," somebody said.

Chloe laughed and nodded. "We had a nice shower for my sister, and some of the gifts were a bit risqué," she explained, "in addition to some lovely lingerie. Too bad you weren't here for that. It was a lot of fun."

"Yes," Corabeth said. "We were terribly sorry to hear about the loss of your mother. Had she been sick for a while?"

"Actually, my mother had never been in the best of health, but it was only a few months before she died that doctors discovered she had hemochromatosis."

"Goodness," Dora said, looking up from her knitting. "I've never heard of that. What is it?"

"It's a form of iron overload disease, and it's inherited," I explained. "It causes the body to absorb and store too much iron. Healthy people usually absorb about ten percent of iron contained in the food eaten, but people with hemochromatosis absorb up to thirty percent and over time they absorb five to twenty times more iron than the body needs."

"I read something about that," Betty said. "So it's a fatal disease?"

"Well, it doesn't have to be if it's diagnosed before any organ damage is done. Unfortunately, that wasn't the case with my mother. It can be very tricky to diagnose because the symptoms mimic many other diseases. For instance, my mother developed arthritis around age fifty, and she was treated for that the rest of her life. Doctors tend to focus on the conditions caused by hemochromatosis like arthritis, liver disease, heart abnormalities, thyroid deficiency, and those kinds of things."

"Wow," Chloe said. "What a shame. So there are really no definitive symptoms? How about blood tests? Couldn't they diagnose it with that?"

I nodded. "Yes, a blood test would determine if the iron level is too high, but the disease is considered rare and doctors may not think to test for it."

"And what if it was diagnosed early?" Corabeth questioned. "Is there a cure for it?"

"No, there's no cure. However, there is a simple treatment. Phlebotomy. Just removing blood the same way it's drawn from donors at blood banks. Based on the severity of the iron overload, a pint of blood is taken once or twice a week for several months to a year or longer. Once the levels return to normal, then maintenance therapy is started, which involves giving a pint of blood every two to four months for life."

"My goodness," Maude said. "I had never heard of this either. Do you know if you have it, Berkley? Have you been tested?"

I nodded. "My mother's doctor highly recommended that I go through the genetic testing not only to see if I had it but also to determine if I was a carrier. Because sometimes if it's only inherited from one parent, you don't necessarily have hemochromatosis, but you can be a carrier and pass it on to your children. But I tested negative on both counts. Thank God."

"And why isn't everyone just routinely tested during an annual physical?" Liz questioned.

"Hmm, that would be great if that could be done, but I'm afraid that as with most things in health care, it has to do with money.

Early detection and treatment would be very effective, and many researchers, educators, and advocacy groups have suggested widespread screening. But a simple, inexpensive, accurate test for screening doesn't exist. The genetic test does provide a definitive diagnosis, so I was fortunate to have good health insurance that covered that."

"Gosh, such a shame," Dora said. "To think that if your mother had known she had this . . ."

"Exactly, and the thing is, when I think back, she had the classic symptoms of the arthritis and fatigue. She was fairly active, but she always complained of being tired. After so many years of complaining about it, everyone just thought she had low energy. What's really disturbing, though, was the cause of death on her death certificate—cirrhosis of the liver." I let out a deep sigh and shook my head. "My mother barely drank her entire life. Sure, she'd have a glass of wine or gin and tonic now and again, but a drinker? Not at all, and yet that was the cause of death, because hemochromatosis destroyed her liver."

"I'm really sorry to hear about all of this," Maude said. "But thank you for sharing it with us, Berkley. I think you're doing a great service to your mother by sharing your knowledge and allowing people to be aware."

I nodded. "There is an American Hemochromatosis Society, and strange enough, it's located right here in Florida, in Lake Mary. But of course, I didn't even learn about it until after my mother died."

Dora stood up and patted my shoulder. "I think it's time for some of the delicious monkey bread that Corabeth brought this evening. The coffee and tea should be ready to enjoy with that."

"I'll help you serve," Chloe said.

No, I hadn't shared about my mother being here in Cedar Key. And no, I wasn't any closer to solving my puzzle. But I did feel a sense of *completeness.* I hadn't realized that I'd had a need to share any of this part of my mother's story—but I now knew differently.

8

I had just finished cleaning the shop when I looked up to see a young girl standing outside the door. Damn. Most likely a customer, and the floor that I'd mopped was still wet. It was only nine-thirty, a half hour before I was due to open. She was looking toward Second Street and not inside the shop, so maybe she wasn't a customer.

I went into the back room to check on my stock for the weekend, but when I returned just before ten she was still there. I flipped the sign to Open, unlocked the door, and opened it, causing her to jump.

She swung around and faced me. Tall and painfully thin, she looked like she could use some chocolate for the calorie value alone.

I sent her a smile and said, "Sorry if I startled you. Were you waiting for me to open?"

"Yeah," was all she said as she entered the shop.

I saw her glance at the gems on the table before she focused her attention on the display case filled with chocolate.

"What can I get you?" I asked.

She flipped a strand of her long honey-colored hair over her shoulder. "Oh, I'm not here to buy anything. I was, ah . . . wondering if maybe you needed somebody to help in your shop?"

"You mean like a job?" I questioned, and she nodded. "Oh, I'm afraid not. I just opened recently, and I'm not busy enough to hire any staff. Do you live on the island?"

She looked to be about sixteen or seventeen, so I wondered why she wasn't in school.

"We just moved here. We live out on Twenty-four. I could really use a job, though."

"Wouldn't it interfere with your school studies? I'm Berkley, by the way," I said, extending my hand.

"Oh, I'm not in school anymore," she said, returning the handshake. "My name is Paula. Do you know of anybody else in town that might be looking for help?"

I knew the economy was bad across the country, and I also had a feeling that this girl wasn't out of school by choice. "What type of work are you looking for?"

"Anything," she said without hesitating. "I can do cleaning or work a cash register. I tried the restaurants, but they didn't have any waitress jobs."

There was a sense of eagerness about her along with a hint of desperation.

"So you live here with your family?" I questioned.

"My mother and my younger sister. We're staying at the Low-Key Motel. For now."

A family of three living at a motel? I knew there was more to her story, but I didn't want to keep prying.

"Gosh," I said, letting out a deep sigh. "I wish I could help you, but I'm not in a position to hire anybody just yet. Have you tried the yarn shop down the street?"

She shook her head.

"Well, I honestly don't know if they need any help. But Miss Dora and Chloe own the shop. You might want to pop in there and check."

A smile crossed her face along with a hopeful expression. "Gee, thanks. I appreciate that. Can I tell them that you sent me?"

I laughed. "Sure. You can tell them you stopped by here and I don't have any work right now."

"Thanks again," she said, and turned to go.

"Oh, hey, Paula. Wait a sec. You said you have a younger sister?" I went behind the counter and slipped on a plastic glove as I removed some chocolates from the case to fill a small box. "Here," I said, passing it to her. "On the house, and welcome to the island. I bet your sister might like some chocolate."

"Really?" she said as her hand slowly reached across the counter. "Thank you. That's really nice of you."

"And check back with me now and then. I might eventually end up needing some part-time help."

"I will. Thanks again."

I watched her walk out the door and felt a stab of sadness. Here I was trying to search for answers, but this young girl seemed to be looking for survival.

Shortly before five I locked up the shop and headed down the street to Yarning Together. Flora had given me a pattern the night before for a pullover sweater, and after I got home I discovered that I'd misplaced my number eight needles. I was also curious if Paula had stopped by there to see about work.

"Hey," Chloe said, turning from the cubbyhole where she was arranging scrumptious colors of yarn in rainbow shades. "Done for the day?"

"Yup, and I need a pair of size eight needles."

"Hi, Berkley," Dora said, coming out of the back room. "Size eight, huh? Right here." She pointed to the revolving stand. "Bamboo? Circular or straight? Take your pick."

"Thanks." I removed a pair of the Addy circular needles. "I like these. I'm not sure you actually knit faster with them, but that's what the label says."

Dora laughed as she rang up the sale. "Guess it's what you get used to."

"Did you have a girl stop by here today looking for work?" I asked as I passed her the cash.

"We did," Dora told me. "That's a sad story."

I should have known that somebody in town would have the information. I was quickly learning that news spread fast in small towns. "She stopped by my shop, but unfortunately I don't have any work to give her."

Dora passed me the bag and nodded. "We're going to see what we can do for her. I told her to give me a few days and maybe I can come up with some odd jobs. She lives with her mother and sister out at the Low-Key on Twenty-four. They came here from the Orlando area. Flora works at the Food Pantry, and she met the mother there a couple weeks ago when they first came here. The mother's divorced, but seems she had a pretty good job for a company in Orlando. They owned their own house, but then the company downsized, she lost her job, the ex-husband took off for parts unknown, and then the bank foreclosed on the house."

"How did she end up here? Does she have family here?"

"No," Chloe said. "Flora told me that she's originally from Chicago, but her parents are both gone and there's nobody to help them. She'd been here a few times with her husband when they first got married and knew she could keep their travel trailer somewhere on the island and it wouldn't be too expensive."

"Right," Dora said. "They were staying in a motel in Orlando, but that got way too pricey for them. It was tough on the kids too, going to school from a motel room. So they drove the travel trailer here, and I think Carol and Pete are giving them a weekly break at the RV space."

I shook my head. "So the three of them are living in a small travel trailer? No wonder the older girl is looking for work. I guess she's not in school?"

"No, she quit," Chloe said. "Her mother begged her not to, but she's almost seventeen and she said she wanted to help with the finances and get a job instead."

"What a shame. Now I feel even worse that I had nothing for her."

"Well, I'm going to speak to Monica," Dora said. "She just mentioned the other day that with the triplets getting bigger she could really use a pair of extra hands and might consider hiring a babysitter. Actually, she called it a *nanny*. In my day, they were babysitters."

I laughed. "Oh, that would be great. Paula struck me as a re-sponsible girl, and if she has a younger sister, she's used to kids."

"Right. So hopefully this will work out for her. Well, time to close up, Chloe," Dora said, walking to the door to flip the sign.

Chloe glanced at her watch. "Yeah, it's almost five-thirty. Hey, Berkley, I'm heading over to the Pickled Pelican to grab some din-ner. Wanna join me?"

I had planned to have some leftover lasagna, but the escargot and a salad that I knew was on the restaurant menu tempted me. "I think I will. Sounds good."

"Dora?" Chloe questioned. "Why don't you join us?"

"Oh, thanks, but no. I have to get Oliver home for his dinner."

At the mention of his name, the dog lifted his head and looked at Dora questioningly.

"Yes, Oliver. You put in a good day at work. Time to go home and rest. Not that you don't get plenty of resting here all day."

Chloe and I laughed as we left the shop and headed to Dock Street.

"That sure beat leftover lasagna," I said when we finished dinner.

"My chicken was excellent too." Chloe took a sip of wine and glanced across the railing over to Atsena Otie. "Such a pretty night to eat outside."

My eyes followed a flock of pelicans as they swooped to the water, catching their own dinner.

"Yup. And I never get tired of looking at the scenery here." I let out a deep sigh. "I can understand why my mother came here," I said before I even knew what was coming out of my mouth.

I saw the look of surprise that covered Chloe's face across the table. "What? Your mother came here? So you *have* been here be-fore?"

I shook my head and took a sip of my cabernet. "No. I was never in Cedar Key until last year. That was my first trip here." I avoided looking at Chloe as I rolled my paper napkin in a ball. "Ac-tually, I wasn't quite honest with you when I met you at the coffee café." When she remained silent, I went on. "It's a long story, but my mother came here back in 1972. For the summer."

"Oh," Chloe said. "Without you?"

I nodded. "Right. Without me. I stayed with my grandmother in Salem."

"Did she come here for work?"

"I have no clue why she came here," I said and then proceeded to fill Chloe in on my story.

"Wow. So both your mother and grandmother would never tell you why she came here? It all sounds so mysterious. I mean, gee, there had to be a reason, and it doesn't make sense that even when you got older they refused to talk about it."

"Exactly. None of it ever made sense to me."

"And the only way you finally found out *exactly* where she went was from the postcards she sent to your grandmother? That's amazing."

"Yup. If I hadn't found those postcards after my mother died, I never would have known that this is where she came that summer."

"Why was it such a secret, I wonder. Do you have any idea why she would have come here without you?"

I laughed. "Yeah, a million ideas but no answers. I wondered if maybe she was pregnant—as unlikely as that scenario was. I thought maybe she just didn't want to raise a kid anymore, came here, thought better of it, and then went back to Salem. I also wondered if maybe she was ill, but when I got here last year and saw there were no hospitals or even a doctor on the island, I knew that couldn't have been why she came."

"How about the postcards? No hints there as to why she ended up here?"

"Nope. None. Just short messages from my grandmother telling her that I was doing okay. And my mother only wrote back updates on the weather here or that she was fine. That's pretty much it."

"So you're really here to try and find some answers."

I nodded. "Yeah. Sometimes I think I don't even have a right to know. That it was my mother's life, not mine. They used to tell me that too, my mother and grandmother. But as I got older, I realized that her leaving me for an entire summer had affected me in many ways."

Chloe reached across the table and patted my hand. "I can understand that. Well, then, we'll see what we can find out. There's enough locals still here that lived on Cedar Key the summer that your mother was here. So we need to start talking to them."

I squeezed Chloe's hand as I felt the moisture in my eyes. She had said *we*. For the first time I was going to have some assistance trying to put the pieces together.

9

When Saxton walked into my shop the following morning, I was surprised again at the reaction I had when I saw him. I felt fluttery and even a bit giddy. Yes, like a teenager with her first crush. I firmly believe that each of us gives off a certain amount of energy when we encounter particular people. And I was beginning to feel that when my energy combined with Saxton's the level was pretty high.

"Hey, good morning," I said, feeling a huge smile cross my face.

"And a good morning to you as well," he said as that dimple in his chin deepened.

"So what can I do for you?" I asked, and then realized what a dumb question that was. Obviously, he was here for his usual ration of chocolate.

"Well, I'd like my chocolate," he said, proving me right. And then he went on to say, "But I was . . . wondering . . . ah . . . if you had any plans for this evening?"

Plans? Meaning a *date* type of plans?

All of a sudden my throat felt like sandpaper. I swallowed and shook my head. "No. No plans for tonight."

Saxton's smile increased. "Oh, good. Well . . . I was wondering if maybe you'd like to join me for dinner. At my place."

At his place? Oh, yeah, this was definitely a date.

"You cook?" was all I could think of to say.

His deep laughter filled the shop. "Let's just say, I try. I thought I'd grill some steaks and we could eat out on the deck."

"That sounds great," I said, and then added, "But I don't know where you live." I felt flustered in addition to the fact that everything I said seemed to sound stupid.

Saxton didn't seem to be affected by my lack of intelligent sentences. "The pink house over on First Street."

Oh, wow! I loved that house. I'd passed it so many times since moving to the island and always wondered who lived in that gorgeous house overlooking the water.

"Great. I know exactly which house it is."

"Okay. Well, why don't we say seven? That'll give you a bit of time after you close the shop."

"Sounds good."

We stood there for a few seconds smiling at each other until it hit me the man had also come for his chocolate.

"Right," I said, reaching for a box and proceeding to fill it with his usual request.

I had chosen to wear a pair of black cropped pants with a white cotton sweater that I'd recently finished knitting. Gold sandals completed my outfit, and I leaned closer to the mirror to apply some mascara to my lashes. Adding a bit of blush and lipstick, I smiled at my reflection. My hair was a simple style, but I liked it, and I also liked the overall appearance I saw looking back at me. It had been a while since I'd had a bona fide date and taken extra time with clothes and makeup.

I walked over to the window and stroked the top of Sigmund's head. "Be a good boy," I told him before walking into the kitchen to get the almond cake I'd baked to bring for dessert.

On the short walk to Saxton's house I found myself excited at the prospect of spending the evening with a man who appealed to me. It had been three years since I ended the relationship with Rodney, and although I'd had other offers for dates I preferred being alone. But there was something about Saxton that made me think being with the right person could be a very enjoyable thing.

I saw the pale pink house farther down the street and smiled. Not a small structure, but not too large for one person. I could understand why this house had appealed to him. Referred to as a stilt house, it was positioned above a cement pad, and stairs to the side led up to a deck that had an unobstructed view of the water all the way to the horizon.

As I began climbing the stairs I heard the soft strains of a piece of classical music coming from above. When I reached the top, I paused and allowed myself to breathe in the fresh salt air as my gaze took in the Big Dock across the water to my left and the large expanse of water in front of me.

"Hey, you're here," I heard Saxton say, and swung around to see him coming through French doors holding a bottle of wine and two wineglasses.

"Yes, and I was just taking in this gorgeous view that you have. It's amazing."

"Thanks. Yeah, I enjoy it a lot," he said, glancing at the dish in my hand.

"Oh, I made an almond cake. I thought it might be nice for dessert."

Saxton placed the wine and glasses on the patio table. "Great. Come on in. We'll put it in the kitchen and I can show you around."

I followed him through the French doors into an open area that consisted of combined family room, dining area, and kitchen. All of it surrounded by glass. Another set of French doors led out to the deck from the kitchen. Skylights above and windows looking out the side and front of the house, with the sight of water everywhere, made me feel like I was on a boat.

"Oh! This really *is* amazing," I said, placing my cake on the counter that separated the kitchen from the family room.

Lola came running from another part of the house, barking and tail wagging, to greet me.

"Hey, there, girl," I said, bending down to give her a pat. "You sure have a nice home."

Saxton laughed. "Yeah, we both like it. It's comfortable and perfect for us."

That was when I noticed the chintz sofa and two cushy chairs, all positioned perfectly to take advantage of the water view. Newspapers were flung at the end of the sofa, and a stack of magazines on an end table looked ready to topple over. Three pairs of shoes lay abandoned by the front door, indicating they had been removed, tossed off, and left there.

"So this is the family room," Saxton said, gesturing with his hand. "And as you can see, I have a small dining area off the kitchen."

I followed him to the right and saw a round oak table filled with assorted papers, envelopes, ink pens and . . . two plants that had long ago stopped giving off oxygen.

Just as I wondered where Saxton found the space to actually have a meal at the table, he said, "You'll see I'm a bit untidy, but I have a cleaning girl that comes in weekly to dust, vacuum, and that kind of stuff."

I wondered how the poor girl could get to the surface in order to clean, but remained silent.

"And here's the kitchen," he said, waving an arm to the right.

No doubt that it was a designer kitchen with stainless steel fridge and stove surrounded by gorgeous oak cabinets, but the piled-up bags of chips, cookies, and more envelopes and papers detracted from the beauty of it.

I followed him to the end of the hallway, where he led me into a large room on the right overlooking the water. A cherrywood L-shaped computer station dominated the space in front of the large windows, with file cabinets and bookcases flanking the other three walls. Again, books, papers, and magazines were piled haphazardly on all of the available space.

"Very nice," I said quietly. And it was. The entire house was gorgeous, and it certainly wasn't dirty. It was just . . . cluttered. Cluttered and a disorganized mess.

Walking back to the hallway, I followed Saxton into a large master bedroom. Yes, the bed was made, but a couple of shirts had been tossed across the navy blue comforter and both night tables were filled with ink pens, pads of paper, and various other items. The two bureaus were the same, as well as the desk in the corner. In the other corner was Lola's bed, where she was now curled up.

I wasn't a neat freak. Really, I wasn't, but the thought of living in such chaos made me shudder. I itched to grab some plastic garbage bags, sweep through the house, and discard all of the clutter.

But instead I forced a smile and said, "It's such a nice house," as I thought, *and it's such a shame it isn't more organized.*

"I'm glad you like it," Saxton said, totally oblivious to my honest reaction. "Let's go on the deck and have some wine before dinner."

Good idea. At least the patio table had some room to put wineglasses and plates.

I watched Saxton uncork the bottle of cabernet and fill two glasses, and I found myself noticing that although some of it had dribbled onto the table he made no effort to wipe it up. Was I being overly picky? Probably. But gee whiz, it really didn't take a lot of effort to be organized and neat.

Saxton passed a glass to me and touched the rim with his. "Here's to you finding your answers," he said.

I looked up and focused on his handsome face. The clutter I'd observed a few minutes before was forgotten. "Thank you. Cheers."

He pulled up a chair across from me and smiled. "Did you have a busy day at the shop?"

I took a sip of wine and nodded. "Yeah, it was pretty steady. Didn't you go fishing with Doyle again this morning? How'd that go?"

"Oh, we did pretty well. I caught quite a few mullet. And that reminds me, Doyle has invited you to join us for a boat ride sometime. Have you ever been out there to Atsena Otie or North Key?" He flung his hand toward the water.

"No, never, and I'd love to go."

"Great. He said to ask Chloe if she'd like to go too. You gals pick the day and we'll do it."

"Sounds like fun. A Monday or Tuesday would probably work best for us since our shops are closed on those days."

I was surprised that an hour had passed over two glasses of wine as we chatted along in companionable ease.

"Well," Saxton said, getting up. "Time for me to get those steaks on the grill."

"Can I help with anything?"

"Sure. If you'd like to set the table, that would be great. Come on, I'll show you where everything is."

I got the table set with mismatched plates and silverware just as Saxton removed two rib eye steaks from the grill.

"Smells wonderful," I said.

He went back into the house and came out carrying a tray with a bowl of potato salad and French bread, along with two pillar candles and holders.

I removed the bowl and bread from the tray while he lit the candles and then poured more wine.

Sitting down and placing the paper napkin in my lap, I said, "This looks great. Bon appétit."

"And to you," he said, and smiled.

The steak was cooked to perfection, the potato salad was delicious, and the French bread was warm and crusty. He might have a cluttered house, but he was a good chef and host. I heard the soft music drifting outside and looked across to where the lights on Dock Street now reflected on the water, and smiled. This had been a very enjoyable evening. Being with Saxton was easy and relaxing. There was no fumbling for topics to talk about or feelings of boredom. All of it simply felt right. And comfortable.

We continued conversing right through dessert and coffee, and I was shocked to glance at my watch and see it was after eleven.

"Let me help you clean up," I said. "And then I have to be going. What a great evening it was. I really enjoyed it."

"No, no. I have the dinner dishes in the dishwasher. All that's left are these coffee cups. I'll get these inside and then I'll walk you home."

"Oh, you don't have to do that," I told him as I followed him inside with my empty mug.

He turned around and flashed me a sexy smile. "True. But I'd like to. Besides, we'll take Lola and she'll enjoy that."

* * *

We stood by the gate to my courtyard as Lola sniffed the pavement.

"Thank you so much for a lovely evening, Saxton. It was nice."

"It was, wasn't it?" he said.

And before I realized what was happening, I felt his lips on mine. Gentle, with just enough pressure to cause my stomach to feel like it was in a free fall. I felt his hand on the back of my neck pulling me closer. When we broke apart, both of us were breathing heavily.

"Very nice, indeed," Saxton whispered. "I'll see you soon, Berkley."

And with that he turned and headed back down D Street with Lola trotting along beside him.

10

It had been less than two weeks since I'd opened my shop, and as I sat spinning fiber for Yarning Together, I knew that I'd been pretty fortunate. My business was doing well, both with yarn and chocolate. I was making new friends daily. I loved the small town feel of Cedar Key. And I also might have a romantic partner in my life.

After dinner at Saxton's house the previous Saturday, he dropped by the shop on Wednesday for his refill of chocolate. I'd been kept plenty busy on my two days with the shop closed. Cleaning both my apartment and the shop, spinning fiber, knitting, making more chocolate clams, and updating orders from my website. But when I saw him walk through the door shortly after I opened, that giddy feeling returned and was magnified when I recalled his kiss.

"And how are you this bright and glorious morning?" he questioned with a smile.

Was this man always so upbeat and happy?

"I'm good," I told him as I decided that, yes, he probably had an overabundance of happiness genes. "And you?"

"Great. I wanted to let you know that if you and Chloe are free next Monday, Doyle said it would be a good time to go for that boat ride. The tides will be just right."

"That'll work. I asked Chloe and she said she'd be free next week either Monday or Tuesday."

"Well, good. Then it's a date. We'll meet you at City Marina about eight Monday morning."

So did this mean I wouldn't see him outside the shop until then? Without waiting to give it any thought, I blurted out, "I was wondering...I'd like to repay that dinner you did last week. Any chance you'd like to come to my place this Saturday evening?"

A huge smile crossed Saxton's face and without hesitating, he said, "That sounds good. What time?"

"Oh, well...ah, I close at five. So let's say seven?"

"Perfect, and I'll bring the wine. White or red?"

I had no clue what I'd even be cooking, but said, "Red would be good."

"Okay, and now I'll have my usual box of chocolate."

After Saxton left I confirmed what I'd been thinking earlier that morning. I was pretty darn fortunate. I'd see Saxton for dinner in two days and then a boat ride on Monday. *Not bad, girl,* I thought, *especially for somebody who had no interest in getting involved romantically.*

Before I reopened my shop after lunch, I went across the street to the coffee café and was pleased to see both Chloe and Grace sitting there.

"Hey," Grace said. "Join us for coffee."

I pulled up a chair after telling Suellen my order.

"How's everything with you guys?" I asked.

"Well, it seems my sister is leaving us," Chloe said.

"Leaving? Are you moving away?"

Grace laughed. "No, no. But Lucas and I have made a decision to spend the summer in Paris. His cousin has offered us his apartment there and we're going to take advantage of that."

"Oh, wow," I said. "Well, good for you. What a great opportunity that'll be."

"That's what we thought. We'll be leaving the end of April and will be back sometime early October. Lucas wants to take me around different parts of France while we're there, and we'll probably get over to Italy as well."

"Yeah, can you believe it?" Suellen said, putting my double latte in front of me. "Talk about a dream vacation."

"Oh, no." I looked up at Suellen. "Does this mean you're out of a job for the summer?"

She shook her head. "Not at all. They trust me to keep this place running while they're gone."

"Of course we do," Grace said. "We're fortunate to have you."

"And how about the bookshop?" I questioned. "Will you have to close that?"

"No. We were lucky there too. Lucas spoke to Corabeth and asked if she'd like to run it, and she was thrilled. She's such a huge reader and book person; she'll be great in there with the customers. So he's going to start training her soon and teach her about the ordering and everything, and I'm sure she'll do fine."

"I think she will too," Chloe said. "That really worked out well, but Aunt Maude and I are going to miss both of you."

Grace reached out to squeeze her sister's hand. "I told you. You both need to come over there for a visit. There's an extra bedroom in the apartment, and we'd love to have you."

"You really should," I told Chloe. "After all, France is where your heritage is. How long has it been since you've been there?"

Chloe raised her eyebrows and shrugged. "At least a few years. Before Parker and I divorced. Our son, Mathis, works there, so we went over to visit him."

"See," I said. "All the more reason to go. You can visit your son while you're there."

Chloe nodded. "Hmm. Maybe I'll give it some thought. Hey, don't forget that Dora is having the knitting group tonight rather than Thursday this week. You're going, aren't you?" she asked, looking at the three of us.

"Yup, Suellen and I will be there," Grace said.

"Me too, but I have to get going and reopen my shop. So I'll see you there at seven."

* * *

"And so," Dora said, knitting away on the beautiful pink sweater that she was making for Monica's baby, "I was really happy to hear that my niece has hired Paula to help her with the triplets four days a week."

"That really worked out well," I said. "I'm sure that family can use the extra money."

"Right." Dora placed her knitting in her lap. "I wanted to talk to all of you about something. I had an idea and could use your help."

"Sure. What is it?" Liz kept knitting away but glanced up at Dora.

"Well, the Arts Festival is next month, and I thought maybe we could get a vendor's booth. To sell some scarves."

"Scarves?" Corabeth questioned.

Dora nodded. "Yeah. I was thinking that perhaps Chloe could come up with a fairly simple design. Something that might resemble waves in the water. We could do them in a pretty shade of blue and use different types of yarns to get a different effect. We'll call them the Cedar Key scarves and I think we could easily charge twenty dollars each, and then I thought it might be nice to donate the money to Paula's family."

"Oh, that's a great idea, Dora," Chloe said. "And yes, I'd be more than happy to do a design for a pattern."

"You mean just *give* them the money?" Raylene questioned, causing everyone to look in her direction. She shifted in her chair. "Well . . . I just mean . . . that's charity. Do you think they'll accept that?"

"Raylene Samuels," I heard Dora say in a tone I wasn't used to hearing from her. "It is *not* charity. You know darn well we help each other on this island. How many times have we done fund-raisers with dinners and whatnot to help those in need? This would be no different and shame on you for thinking otherwise."

I saw a crimson flush creep up Raylene's neck.

"Well . . . yes. You're right," was all she said before she resumed her knitting with head bent.

"Count me in," Betty said.

"Oh, absolutely. Me too," Corabeth told Dora.

"And I'm not leaving for France till late April," Grace said. "So I'll have plenty of time to get some scarves knitted."

Maude nodded. "I'll gladly help."

"Same here," Flora replied.

"I think that's a great idea, Dora," I told her. "And I'd be more than happy to participate."

A huge smile crossed Dora's face. "That's wonderful. I knew I could count on most of you."

"Oh, for goodness' sake," Raylene sputtered. "I'll help too, of course."

"That's kind of you," Dora said. "I'm sure the family will appreciate it. Now, time for our snack. Berkley brought some blondies tonight."

"Oh, I haven't had those in ages." Corabeth shot me a smile.

"And I'll help you serve," I said, getting up and heading toward the back room.

"That Raylene is so nasty," Dora whispered. "But at least we'll get a few scarves out of her."

I chuckled as I began placing the squares with chocolate chips and nuts onto a platter.

As we sat around eating and sipping coffee, I decided the time had come for me to see what I could find out from this group about my mother.

When there was a lull in the conversation, I cleared my throat. "Um . . . there was something that I've been meaning to ask all of you," I said, and felt everyone's eyes on me as I looked down at my mug. "One of the reasons that I moved to Cedar Key was because I did want to live in a small town . . . but I also had another reason." All of a sudden that reason seemed scary to me, and I had to admit that as much as I wanted to know the answers, I was concerned about what I might find out. I looked up and saw Chloe nod, giving me the bit of encouragement that I needed. "Well . . . see . . . my mother . . . she actually came here back in 1972. For the entire summer."

"Really?" Flora said in surprise. "Were you with her?"

"No. I wasn't. And that's part of the reason why I'm here now." I went on to explain my story and about the postcards.

"So that's how you discovered that it was actually Cedar Key that she came to?" Corabeth leaned forward in her chair. "My goodness, that's quite a mystery to grow up with, isn't it? Your mother and grandmother refused to talk about it and now you're looking for answers."

"Exactly. Her name was Jeanette Whitmore, and since many of you have lived here all of your lives . . . I thought perhaps you could help me to discover some of those answers."

The room was silent for a few minutes.

"Jeanette Whitmore," Flora said thoughtfully. "And you say it was 1972?"

I nodded, but nobody in the group seemed to show any recognition when they heard my mother's name.

"Gosh," Dora said. "So many people have come and gone from this island over the years. It's hard to keep track. But if she was here for a whole summer, I would think she had to work someplace. Do any of you recall employing a young woman by that name?"

Heads began to shake and my confidence at finding answers quickly evaporated.

"No, but many days I can't remember what I had for breakfast," Flora said, causing the women to chuckle. "So we'll all think about this. Jeanette Whitmore, and she would have been twenty-seven years old."

"Do you have any pictures of her?" Dora asked.

I let out a deep sigh. "As silly as it sounds, no. We never owned a camera, and my mother hated having her photo taken. I was shocked to discover that after she died, when I was going through her things, the few pictures that I recalled we had were no longer around. She must have thrown them out. I really don't know."

Corabeth nodded. "Some families just didn't save photos. But that's a shame."

"Oh," I said, as I had a thought. "My aunt in Atlanta might have some. I can give her a call and find out. She's supposed to be coming to visit me in a few months."

"That's a good idea," Chloe said. "And in the meantime, maybe all of you could put your thinking caps on. It just might come to you that you did know her."

"And sometimes it's better to let sleeping dogs lie," I heard Raylene mutter under her breath.

She could be right—but I hoped that she wasn't.

11

Ten minutes before I was due to open the shop on Saturday morning I was arranging a fresh batch of my signature clams in the display case when I heard the doorknob rattling. I looked up to see Raylene Samuels and let out a groan. God, this woman was so unpleasant. I hated to begin my workday with her, but I knew she'd continue to rattle that doorknob until either it fell off or I opened the door. I chose the latter.

"Good morning, Miss Raylene," I told her while forcing a smile to my face.

"I've yet to discover what's good about it," she said, following me inside.

"Well, maybe another supply of chocolate clams will perk you up."

"I seriously doubt that, but I do want a pound."

No please. No thank you. No manners whatsoever. Yup, Saxton had been right. This woman was a piece of work.

I slipped on a glove and began filling the box when the chimes rang and I looked up to see Mr. Carl walk in.

" 'Mornin', Berkley," he said, a smile covering his face. "And a good morning to you as well, Raylene."

"If you think so," she said, not even bothering to cast a glance in his direction.

"Oh, I do," he told her. "I always say that any morning that I wake up on this side of the grass is a good one." He chuckled, and I joined him.

I put the seal on the box and looked to see that the sour expression on Raylene's face hadn't softened at all.

"Here you go," I told her, and repeated my phrase even though I knew that no nice reply would be forthcoming. "I hope you'll enjoy them."

She passed the cash across the counter, took the box, turned around, and walked out the door.

I stood there shaking my head at Mr. Carl. "You'd think it would be much easier to be nice than nasty," I told him.

"Oh, I don't think Raylene means to be nasty. It's just her way, ya know. I think that deep down inside . . . why, she might be just as sweet as those chocolates."

The man was joking, right? Either that or he just liked to see the good in people. Even if they didn't harbor one ounce of it.

Not wanting to get into a discussion on personalities, I shrugged and said, "So what would you like today, Mr. Carl?"

I had another busy Saturday with both locals and tourists and by the time five o'clock came, I was more than ready to rush upstairs to prepare for my dinner with Saxton.

By six-thirty I'd managed to shower, change into a clean pair of shorts and tee shirt, put together a hamburger casserole that was now in the oven, and mix up a batch of coleslaw. The no-knead bread was tightly wrapped in wax paper waiting to be sliced.

I stood gazing around the living room and let out a deep sigh. Everything in its place. A tray with two wineglasses sat on the coffee table. I'd placed a platter of cheese and crackers beside it. Pillar candles flickered on the end tables and the sound of Enya's mystical Celtic music filled the room. My eyes strayed to the urn on the credenza.

"Yes, Mom," I said. "We're entertaining tonight, so behave yourself."

I had walked over to rearrange my cluster of crystals next to the urn when I heard the knock on the door; I opened it to see Saxton standing in the hall holding a bottle of wine in the air.

"For us," he said, a huge smile covering his handsome face.

"Great, come on in." I gestured for him to have a seat. "I have the wineglasses right there."

"Nice place," he said, as his eyes scanned the room.

"Well, it's a bit small but perfect for me. I have a bedroom, kitchen, and bath, and that's all I need. Dinner will be ready in about a half hour, so you can uncork the wine and we can have a glass," I said, pointing to the corkscrew next to the wineglasses.

Saxton nodded as he continued to glance around the room. "I see you're a very neat person. You must have thought my place was a dump."

I laughed. "Well . . . I can't live in clutter, if that's what you mean. I like everything where it belongs."

Saxton began uncorking the wine. "So you're a rigid kind of woman."

Rigid? What was that supposed to mean? That was the first time somebody had used that adjective to describe me. "Um . . . no . . . I wouldn't say that exactly."

Saxton laughed as he filled the glasses. "I didn't mean that in a derogatory way. But you strike me as a woman who doesn't often let her hair down, if you know what I mean."

I accepted the glass he passed me as I paused to consider this. "Well, I wouldn't say that. And no, I'm not sure what you mean."

Saxton touched the rim of my glass with his. "Carpe diem. Here's to seizing the moment."

I nodded and took a sip.

"Do you ever do something *just because?* Just because it strikes your fancy and might be a spontaneous fun thing to do?" he asked.

Sitting beside him on the sofa, I felt a bit of annoyance that what was supposed to be an enjoyable evening was beginning to feel like a session with a shrink.

"Well . . . ah . . . yes," I replied as I racked my brain to try and recall such an incident. "Moving here. Moving to Cedar Key was pretty spontaneous."

"Was it?" Saxton asked. "You said you came here mostly to find some answers about your mother. So you actually did have a specific reason for relocating here."

I thought about this for a few moments. "Yeah, you could be right. But that doesn't mean I'm *rigid*." All of a sudden that five-letter word sounded nasty to me.

Saxton reached for my hand and gave it a squeeze. "I didn't mean to get you upset. It's just that sometimes it's good to let go, be loose, and enjoy the moment."

"Oh, you mean like leaving piled-up newspapers around and having shoes and clothes everywhere? Would that make me less rigid?"

Saxton threw his head back as his laughter filled the room. "Touché! That wasn't quite what I had in mind." He took a sip of wine. "Have you had any luck finding somebody who knew your mother?"

Smart man. Since we were obviously headed toward a tiff, better to change the subject.

I watched him reach for a slice of cheese and shook my head.

"No. I told the women at the knitting group my mom's name, but it didn't seem to ring a bell with anybody."

"It'll probably just take time for somebody to remember her. This is very important to you, isn't it? Finding out why she came here?"

"It is. Even if I find some answers it won't change anything. I mean, my mother came here, stayed the summer, went back to Salem, and life went on. But I just feel, in here," I said, tapping my chest, "that I need to know her story. It's like something has been missing all of my life in my relationship with my mother, and maybe by knowing why she left . . . it'll help me to understand better."

Saxton nodded. "I see what you're saying. And I applaud you for having the strength to do this."

"Strength?" I said with surprise. "Why would you think it required strength to try and find some answers?"

He took a sip of wine and then let out a deep sigh. "Well, many times the answers aren't pleasant. But you accept this and still, you're willing to forge ahead. That requires strength on your part."

Okay, so this man had now redeemed himself. He might feel that I'm rigid, but he also complimented me by saying that I had a strength I wasn't at all sure I possessed.

"Thank you," was all I said as I stood up. "That casserole's ready to come out of the oven. Give me five minutes and we'll be all set to eat."

Saxton took the last sip of wine in his glass and then smiled. "That was a delicious dinner, Berkley. Thank you. I really enjoyed all of it, and you're quite the chef."

I laughed as I stood to remove the dishes from the table. "Not really. Just basic home cooking. Let me get these dishes washed and then we can have dessert and coffee."

Saxton stood to help and followed me to the sink. "I'll dry," he said. "Where's your dish towels?"

A man willing to help in the kitchen? He had definitely redeemed himself.

"Oh, right there," I said, pointing to the closet. "Third shelf on the left." I heard him chuckle and turned around. "Something wrong?"

"No. Not at all." He had opened the closet door and stood staring inside.

My sight took in what he was seeing. Each shelf perfectly arranged with dishcloths, dish towels, tablecloths, linen napkins—each item perfectly folded, lined up, according to color and size.

I joined his chuckling. "Hmm, you mean to tell me that your linen closet doesn't look like that?"

In answer he came toward me, pulled me into his arms, and kissed me. "You're special," he said. "Very, very special."

"And you," I whispered, "are a very good kisser. Very, very good."

Following the kitchen cleanup and a slice of my almond cake, we were sitting next to each other on the sofa enjoying our coffee.

"This was nice," Saxton said. "Not just the dinner—but being with you. I enjoy your company."

I smiled and shifted to better see his face. "Thank you, and I like being with you too."

"I've been thinking," he said as I saw his expression grow serious. "I've been giving some thought to maybe contacting my daughter."

I remained silent to allow him time to continue.

He took a sip of coffee. "Resa probably doesn't even want to bother with me. Why would she? It's been thirty years, and not only did I make no attempt to contact her, I willingly allowed her to be adopted by Muriel's husband."

"You thought you were doing the best thing," I said softly.

He nodded. "True. But many times a child doesn't see it that way. She easily also could have considered it a rejection."

He was right. Didn't I still feel a nagging sense of abandonment because my mother had left me with my grandmother that summer?

"So, I don't know," he said. "I'm having mixed feelings about contacting her, I guess. How would you feel? What if your father hadn't been killed in Vietnam and he now tried to contact you?"

I blew out a breath of air. "Wow, I've never once considered that scenario. Well . . . ah . . . yes, I think I'd like to get to know him. You know, find out if we had any similar interests, did we look alike, that sort of thing."

"Really?" He stood up and smiled. "That's good to know. So you're saying that you'd probably forgive him for being out of touch for so many years?"

I stood up and reached for the coffee mugs to head to the kitchen. "Well, I'm not sure about forgiving. That can be a difficult thing to achieve sometimes, but yeah, I do think I'd like the opportunity to at least meet him and try to get to know him."

Saxton nodded. "Right. And maybe the forgiveness would follow."

"Another cup of coffee?" I asked.

"That would be great. Excellent coffee, by the way."

I smiled as I poured two more cups. "I grind my own beans," I told him as I walked back into the living room.

Saxton laughed. "I should have known. What's this?" he asked, pointing to a circular stained glass piece hanging on my wall. "It's a

Wheel of the Year, isn't it?" Removing a pair of reading glasses from his shirt pocket, he walked closer to get a better look.

"I'm surprised that you know what it is," I said, coming to stand behind him and passing him the mug of coffee.

"You seem to forget—I'm from England. Where Wicca was popularized in the 1950s and early 60s. This is an exceptionally nice piece."

I looked at the vibrant shades of blue, gold, green, and other colors depicting the annual cycle of the earth's seasons.

"It belonged to my mother. Except for me, it was one of the few things she brought back from being a student at Berkeley."

"I once wrote a mystery novel about a stolen Wheel of the Year, so I did quite a bit of research about them. As I recall, these are the eight festivals throughout the year referred to as Sabbats. I believe that term originated from Judaism and Christianity and is of Hebrew origin."

"That's right," I said, impressed with his knowledge. "The festivals themselves have historical origins in Celtic and Germanic pre-Christian feasts."

Saxton reached out a finger to touch the midsummer part of the wheel where *June 19–23* was etched into the glass. "The time of year that I came to earth," he said quietly.

"Really? Your birthday is in June?"

"June twentieth, the summer solstice. At least this year it will be, but most years it's on June twenty-first. I've always admired the Wheel of the Year. It shows time as cyclical and the progression of birth, life, decline, and death as experienced in human lives."

I nodded. "And this is echoed in the progression of the seasons."

Saxton removed his glasses and turned around. "And so . . . do you practice Wicca as a religion?"

I shrugged before answering. "Not really, although I do believe in some of their views and theories."

He took a sip of coffee and nodded. "And your mother? Obviously she must have had the same views to bring this back from California?"

"She did and so did my grandmother."

"So you weren't brought up with organized religion?"

I laughed. "Oh, but I was. Catholic Church and even Catholic school for eight years, but when I reached high school, all three of us stopped going. I'm not really sure why. All I know is that we seemed to drift more toward being spiritual rather than religious. My grandmother used to go every single day, rain or shine, down to Derby Wharf. She'd sit on one of the benches there overlooking the water and claim that was her *church*."

Saxton smiled. "Your grandmother sounds like a wise woman."

"She was," I said as a strong feeling of nostalgia washed over me.

Saxton glanced at his watch and took the last sip of his coffee. "I really hate to leave, but I'm afraid I have to get home to take Lola out. I very much enjoyed this evening, Berkley. Very much. You're not only special; I think you have a bit of mystery that I've yet to discover."

I laughed as I walked him to the door. "Oh, I'm not sure about that."

He placed his hands on each side of my face and kissed me. As I reached up to encircle his neck I knew he was *every* bit as special as he thought I was.

12

I was putting the last of the items into the picnic basket when Chloe knocked on the door.

"Come on in," I hollered as I placed potato salad and coleslaw on top of the fried chicken, biscuits, and blondies.

I looked up when I heard her laughing. "What's wrong?"

"Good Lord. We're only going out to Atsena Otie for lunch, aren't we? Looks like you have enough food there to last a week." She held up her own picnic basket. "And along with the food I'm bringing, we could probably survive longer."

I joined her laughter. "Well, I know Saxton has a healthy appetite and maybe Doyle does too. So we don't want to run out of food."

Chloe settled her basket on the table. "I don't think there's any chance of that. Anything I can help you with?"

I looked around the kitchen. "Nope, I think I'm all set."

"Great. Let's get this stuff loaded on the golf cart and head over to the marina."

I spotted Saxton on the pontoon boat as soon as Chloe pulled into the parking lot. We grabbed our picnic baskets and headed down the walkway to the slip.

"Hey there," he hollered, reaching over to give us a hand. "Welcome aboard."

"Good morning," Doyle said, standing up from the cooler where he'd been arranging water bottles and cans of soda. "Great day for a boat ride. Thought I'd take you gals up around North Key, out toward the airport, and then we'd head back to Atsena Otie for lunch."

"Sounds great," I told him as I settled myself on the leather seating beneath the bimini.

"It sure does," Chloe said. "And thanks so much for inviting me."

Chloe sat beside me as Saxton untied the ropes tethering the boat to the slip. Doyle sat behind the wheel and started up the motor. He expertly put the boat in reverse and positioned it to head toward the channel.

He was right. It was a perfect day for a boat ride. As we cruised under the bridge toward the channel the wind teased my hair as the sun warmed my skin.

Picking up speed, Doyle headed out, and I glanced across the water toward my hometown.

"Looks different from this perspective, doesn't it?" Saxton said.

I nodded as I saw his house on First Street, and we curved around where the Beachfront Motel now stood empty. Another example of the poor economy our country was experiencing. Guests at the Faraway Inn sat in the pavilion and waved to us as we cruised past.

Doyle shifted in his seat to face us. "There's a nice beach at North Key. We'll stop there for a bit."

I looked over to my left. "Isn't that Seahorse Key?" I asked. "Could we make a stop there too?"

Doyle shook his head. "No, I'm afraid not. It's a wildlife refuge and bird sanctuary. There's a three-hundred-foot buffer zone around the island and it's closed to the public from March first through June thirtieth. That protects the nesting birds from human disturbance."

"That's really great," I said. "But what about that lighthouse there? Nobody uses it?"

"Oh, no, it's used," Doyle informed me. "Since 1951 the lighthouse has been leased to the University of Florida. It's used as part of the Seahorse Key Marine Laboratory. The lighthouse itself serves as a dormitory with six bedrooms and twenty-six bunk beds. See the boat dock over there?"

I looked to where Doyle was now pointing and nodded.

"The laboratory is located near there."

"During Seafood Festival weekend in October, it's open to the public," Saxton said. "Maybe Doyle will take us over there in the fall."

Doyle nodded. "Yeah, we could do that. It's definitely worth visiting."

"Great," I said, and gave him a smile. I liked this fellow. He had an easy way about him, and I could understand why Saxton enjoyed his company.

After Doyle pulled the boat onto the shore, the four of us got out to walk the beach on North Key. We spent quite a bit of time searching for driftwood, shells, and whatever else the tides had brought in. Heading back to the boat, I stopped for a few moments to breathe in the salt air as Chloe, Saxton, and Doyle walked ahead. There was something primal about being on this barrier island surrounded by the Gulf of Mexico. I looked up and saw puffy white clouds floating by, and was suddenly overcome with an intense feeling of my mother's presence. Closing my eyes for a moment, I felt her spirit surround me. Odd, since this was the first time I'd experienced this sensation since she'd passed away four months before. When I opened my eyes, I saw that Chloe and Saxton were back on the boat and Doyle was standing nearby waiting for me.

I jogged toward him and saw a smile on his face. "Like it here, do you?" he asked.

"I do. I almost feel like a castaway. It's so peaceful and calm here."

He nodded. "That it is," he said, before heading to the boat.

By the time we reached Atsena Otie, the four of us agreed we were ready for lunch. After Doyle had positioned the boat along the shore, Chloe and I set to work filling the table with plates and food.

I felt Saxton's arm around my shoulder and smiled as the boat gently swayed.

"Well, now . . . you two ladies are welcome to join us sailors anytime when you bring food like that."

Doyle placed bottles of water on the table and nodded. "I agree. That sure does look good, and when we're finished Saxton and I will take you around the island."

I settled myself on the seat beside Saxton while balancing my plate. "Is it safe to walk in there?"

Doyle laughed. "Well, there are snakes of course, but there's a trail and we'll stick to that."

"This is my first time visiting Atsena Otie also," Chloe said. "I heard there's a cemetery in there."

"There is. A small one, but there's still a few stones. The remains of the Faber Pencil Mill are also there. During its peak in the 1880s, the mill employed about a hundred people."

I took a bite of chicken and nodded. "Oh, I'd read about that. I got a book at the bookstore on the history of Cedar Key. You're a great historian, Doyle. Saxton told me you were born and raised here."

"Actually, I was born in Bronson, but when I was just a baby my folks came to Cedar Key. Been here ever since. My parents ran a restaurant over on Dock Street. My dad and I were fishermen and provided all the fresh seafood for the customers."

"Has the island changed much since then?" Chloe asked.

"Oh, not that much. Certainly not like other Florida towns," he told her, and then directed his gaze at me. "And you're originally from Salem, Massachusetts? Your family still up there?"

"No, I'm afraid I was the last one. My grandmother passed away over a year ago and then my mother in November."

He nodded his head before lifting his water bottle to his mouth. "What brought you here? Had you visited here before?"

"My first time visiting Cedar Key was last spring. I was looking for a small town to relocate." I took a bite of potato salad, waiting for Doyle to say something else, but when he didn't, I continued. "I had never been here before last year . . . but my mother had been." I went on to once again share my story.

When I finished, Doyle remained silent for a few moments. "I see. And how do you feel about that?"

"You mean about her coming here and leaving me behind?"

"I mean about the fact that she never told you *why* she came here."

I shrugged. "It was certainly her right to never mention the reason. I do understand that. But none of it ever made sense to me."

"And you're trying to make sense of it all these years later?"

"I suppose so," I said, but had the distinct feeling that Doyle Summers considered me a snoop. "Wouldn't you want to know if it were you? Sometimes the not knowing can build resentment." I heard the defensive tone in my voice.

He nodded. "Very true. I'm not judging you. I was just curious."

Chloe effectively changed the subject by asking more questions about Atsena Otie, but Doyle had left me wondering if perhaps I should let well enough alone.

By the time he'd steered his boat back to the marina later that afternoon, my doubts had disappeared. If at all possible, I was going to find out what I could about my mother and the reason she had fled to Cedar Key. I strongly felt that if I was meant to know, the information would be revealed. And for now—all I could do was let go of it.

It had been a great day, spent in the company of people I liked. But the highlight of the day was when we returned to the marina and Saxton invited me for dinner on Friday evening.

"I'll pick you up about seven," he said. "We'll go to the Black Dog first for a glass of wine and then walk over to the Island Room. Would that be okay?"

Okay? That would be more than okay. "Perfect," I said, as I climbed into the golf cart beside Chloe.

⚮ 13 ⚮

By the time that Arts Festival weekend arrived the following month, the women in the knitting group had managed to make fifty scarves to sell at our vendor's table—and every single scarf sold, which gave us an even one thousand dollars to present to Leigh Sallenger and her two daughters, Paula and Paige.

Since Monica employed Paula, it was decided that she would be the one to invite them to the yarn shop on Thursday evening. Monica only told them that the knitting group had a surprise for them.

All of us were assembled when Leigh arrived with her two daughters. The look of surprise on her face with the number of women gathered told us that she had no idea what was going on.

"Come in, come in." Dora greeted them at the door with a smile and then went around the room introducing us.

"First of all," Dora said, "we want to give you an official welcome to Cedar Key. We're aware of your situation and know it must be difficult for you financially. Therefore, we took it upon ourselves to have a little fund-raiser for you. All of us knitted scarves that we sold during Arts Festival weekend."

The expression on Leigh's face showed confusion.

"Right," Chloe said, extending an envelope to Leigh. "And

here's a check for the amount of the sales. We hope it will help you a bit with living expenses."

Leigh remained silent as she reached for the envelope, opened it, saw the check, and burst into tears.

Paula and Paige peered over their mother's shoulder and looked at us with the same confused expression their mother had displayed.

Dora put an arm around Leigh's shoulders as Chloe passed her a tissue.

"I'm overwhelmed," Leigh said, attempting to compose herself. "I think this is the nicest thing that anybody has ever done for me." She blew her nose and gave a weak smile. "But... you don't even really know me. Why would you do such a kind thing?"

Dora laughed. "Well, that's what we do, I guess. We try to take care of those that have less. Even though we don't know you very well, we knew you could use some help. It isn't much, but we do hope it'll help a little."

"Oh, my goodness. You have no idea how much this will come in handy and how much I appreciate it. I begged Paula not to leave school during her senior year, but she insisted." Leigh reached for her daughter's hand and gave it a squeeze. "Because of my divorce, I'm afraid both girls have suffered, but we're determined to make a new life for ourselves."

"And from the looks of it, you will," Chloe said. "Divorce is never easy and sometimes it's more difficult for some. But I heard you now have a job waitressing at the Pickled Pelican."

Leigh nodded. "Yes, I was very grateful for that and it certainly helps. Paula will be starting classes soon to get her GED, and if things go well, maybe she'll be able to attend Santa Fe Community College to receive a degree."

"Oh, that's great," I said. "Do you know what you might want to major in?"

Paula gave us a shy smile. "Well... I'm thinking about childhood education. My mother would like to ..." She shot a glance toward Leigh as if looking for permission to share some news, and I saw Leigh nod. "She'd like to maybe open a day care center here on the island."

"Oh, that would be wonderful," Monica said. "Sign me up. With triplets, I'll be your first customer."

The room broke into laughter.

"I'm not sure it will happen, but that's my goal. It's something that I know I'd enjoy doing and hopefully something that would be beneficial for the town. And Paula would be my assistant."

"I do believe that type of service would be very beneficial for many young couples with children. With the economy down, I know of many young mothers that would love to supplement the family income, but they have nobody to care for their children." Dora patted Leigh on the back. "So I say good for you, and if there's anything we can do to help make this happen for you, just let us know."

"Thank you so much," Leigh said, tears glistening in her eyes as she held up the check. "And thank you so much for this. I hope you know how much we appreciate it."

Dora nodded and smiled. "Okay, and now it's time to socialize. Help yourself, ladies," she said, pointing to the table behind her that held assorted cakes, cookies, tea, and coffee.

After getting one of Dora's lemon squares and coffee, I seated myself beside Leigh on the sofa as the room erupted into chatter.

"You have two great daughters. Paula had come to my chocolate shop looking for work, and I felt bad that I had none to offer her."

"Oh, you're the owner of the chocolate shop. Thank you so much for the chocolate you sent home for Paige. She really enjoyed that treat. And yes, my girls are great. I don't know what I'd do without them. As tough as it's been, I'm convinced I made the right decision getting away from my ex."

I thought of my own mother and the decision she'd made not to marry my father. I couldn't help but wonder once again what her reasons may have been.

"Physical abuse on a spouse is the one thing I knew I could never tolerate in a marriage," Leigh said. "I knew that abuse could easily be directed at the girls. My only option was to leave and file for divorce."

I still marveled at the difficult decisions women faced, and somehow most of them had the strength to make the right decision and go forward.

I reached over to pat her hand. "And you certainly did the right thing," I assured her.

Walking home from the yarn shop, I let out a deep sigh. The evening had gone well, and it had been nice getting to know Leigh Sallenger and her two daughters. There was also a feeling of satisfaction in being able to give back.

I was greeted by Sigmund when I entered my apartment.

"Hey there, fella." I leaned over to scoop him up in my arms. "You're such a handsome boy."

I placed Sigmund on the sofa and walked into the kitchen to grab a bottle of water from the fridge. Walking back into the living room, I glanced at the urn resting on the credenza and proceeded to open the rolltop desk, removing the tin box containing the postcards.

Settling myself on the sofa, I began sifting through them. Pictures of Dock Street were on the front of some, looking much the same as Dock Street still looks over forty years later. I flipped one over. From my grandmother to my mother. Addressed to:

JW PO Box 456 Cedar Key, Florida.

Berkley is fine and I hope you are the same.
Tourists to the shop are keeping me busy this summer.
We both miss you. Much love.

All in all, a pretty generic message. Most of the others contained similar sentences. None of them contained a salutation or a signature. But it was my grandmother's handwriting, and there was no doubt the exchanges were from her.

Had I missed my mother? I vaguely recalled that yes, I had.

Blurred memories returned of me questioning my grandmother as to where she was. That answer never came. Instead I was told, "She'll be back soon." But *soon* had stretched out to include an entire summer without my mother, and it was that sense of aching and loneliness that still gnawed at me.

I picked up another postcard sent from my mother.

> *Dear Mom, I'm doing okay. As well as can be expected.*
> *People are kind to me. Job going well.*
> *Much love to both of you. "J"*

The message was like a secret code of sorts. For somebody without further information, it was difficult to decipher its actual meaning, but reading it this time, two things jumped out at me: As well as can be expected? What did that mean? What had happened to cause her to indicate all had not been well? And I noticed that she did actually mention a *job*. So she was working while living on Cedar Key. But where? For whom?

I let out a deep sigh and took another sip of water. Was I crazy for thinking that I'd ever solve my mother's puzzle? Probably. But a deep, gut feeling told me to keep going. To keep trying as much as I could to find answers, while at the same time not understanding exactly what those answers might do for me.

As I was replacing the postcards the phone rang, and I felt a smile cross my face when I heard Saxton's voice.

"Hey, Berkley. Hope I'm not disturbing you."

"Not at all. What's up?"

"Well . . . I wanted to share something with you. I took a chance this evening. I've written to my daughter."

I heard the uncertainty in his tone. "I think that's a good thing," I told him. "You found her address?"

"Not exactly. I'm sending it addressed to Resa but at the address I have for Muriel, and I'm hoping she'll get the letter to our daughter."

As silly as it sounds, a sliver of jealousy coursed through me. It was one thing to contact his daughter. But did he have to use his ex-wife as the vehicle to make that happen?

Shoving aside the momentary jealousy, I said, "I think that's great, Saxton, and I really hope you'll get a friendly answer from Resa in return."

"Me too. Hey, any chance you could join me for dinner tomorrow evening? I'm craving some of those great burritos at the Blue Dessert."

"Oh, gee. Tomorrow evening is the surprise going-away party for Grace at the yarn shop. I'm sorry."

I was positive I heard disappointment when he said, "I understand," as a thought came into my head.

"Hey, I have an idea. I've been wanting to have a little thank-you dinner for you and Doyle taking us out on his boat. How about if you ask him if he's free next Friday and I'll ask Chloe. Nothing fancy. But it might be fun."

His voice now had a definite sound of happiness. "Great idea. I'll get with Doyle tomorrow and give you a call after I speak with him."

As I prepared for bed with my usual ritual, I felt a smile cross my face. For the first time since my mother had left me that summer, I felt that perhaps even if I never discovered her secrets, there might be another reason why I was meant to also make my way to this island.

14

The month of May arrived on Cedar Key, touching the senses of both sight and smell. Brightly colored flowers and trees were in bloom with their sweet fragrance mingling with that of clams at low tide. Something that the locals referred to as *Cedar Key perfume*. More boats could be seen offshore. Early mornings and late evenings the sound of air boats pierced the otherwise quiet of the island.

After only two months in Cedar Key, I was beginning to truly feel I was *home*. For the first time in my life I had a sense of belonging. Of being precisely where I was supposed to be—of being in my element.

Many things accounted for this. The warmth and welcome that the community displayed toward me. The success of both my chocolate shop and my yarn business. But most of all, it was the interest and fondness that Saxton showed to me. Being with him felt right. It was *easy,* which was something I hadn't always felt in previous relationships. With Saxton, I didn't feel like I had to work at making it work. It just did. That saying *just be* came into my mind a lot, making me realize that probably for the first time, I could just be myself—and that was okay.

I headed down Second Street on my way to the post office filled with a feeling of satisfaction. That sense of contentment evaporated when I saw Raylene Samuels walking toward me.

"You're open today, right?" she demanded.

"I'm afraid not. Closed on Mondays and Tuesdays. I'll be open tomorrow, Raylene."

Fully expecting a torrent of verbal abuse, I was more than surprised when I only got a sniff and a mild retort.

"Oh," she said. "Well, yes, I suppose you must have time off. Right then. I'll be looking for my chocolate bright and early tomorrow morning." And with that, she walked off.

I felt my eyebrows rise as I shook my head and smiled. "Maybe there's hope for her yet," I said out loud.

It was known to all who resided on Cedar Key that the post office was the meeting place every morning about ten, and this morning was no exception. I weaved my way inside, nodding and saying hellos, as I made my way to my letter box. When I unlocked it, I was pleased to find a postcard from Grace and Lucas. The Eiffel Tower adorned the front of it. Gathering the rest of my mail, I made my way back down Second Street to the coffee café.

"Hey, there," Suellen greeted me. "Your usual?"

"That would be great," I told her, settling down at one of the tables as I proceeded to sift through my mail. The postcard from Paris told me Grace and Lucas had arrived in the City of Light and were having a great time settling in for the summer.

Suellen placed my latte in front of me and I passed her the postcard. "Oh, how nice," she said. "Grace called me yesterday morning. I miss her already, but I'm so glad they went."

I nodded. "I know. Me too. It must be great to be there with the love of your life."

Suellen laughed. "I wouldn't know."

"Aren't you dating somebody that lives in Tampa?"

"Oh, Mitchell? Yeah, we've been dating for a while now, but with him down there and me up here, it's a bit of a transient relationship. He owns a dog grooming business in the Tampa area, so that makes it difficult for him to get away a lot. And I have my job here." Suellen shrugged. "Hey, I'm happy the way things are. It works for me."

"What works for you?"

I turned around to see Chloe joining us at the table.

"Good morning," I said. "Have a seat."

"Thanks. What are you two talking about?" she asked, sitting across from me.

"My love life," Suellen said. "I was telling Berkley that whatever it is that I have with Mitchell, it works for me."

Chloe laughed. "Yeah, I know what you're saying. Same with me and Cameron. He's a nice guy, he really is, and I enjoy the time we spend together, but . . ."

"But?" I questioned.

Chloe flipped a strand of hair behind her ear. "But I'm perfectly happy with the way things are. A companion for dinners or events, but nothing too involved."

I nodded. Despite the fact that I fully agreed with them, I also wondered—is that what I wanted with Saxton? Not much more than a companion?

"Can you get me a regular coffee?" Chloe said. "I haven't had my quota this morning."

Suellen laughed. "Coming right up."

"So what are your plans for the rest of the day?" Chloe questioned.

"Oh, the usual. Cleaning my apartment, cleaning the shop. Doing some spinning. Probably some knitting. Oh, I almost forgot. I'm having a little dinner at my place this Friday to thank Doyle and Saxton for taking us out on the boat. I hope you'll be able to make it."

"Friday evening? Sure. Count me in. Doyle's a nice guy, isn't he? You'd think some female would have snagged him by now. How old is he, do you know?"

I laughed. "He's very personable. I'd say he's probably early seventies. Why? Do you have your eye on him?"

Now it was Chloe's turn to laugh as she shook her head. "No, no. Not me. I'm happy keeping company with Cameron. I'm just surprised Doyle doesn't have a lady friend in his life."

"Well, Saxton says that everybody has a story, so I'm sure that Doyle does too."

Chloe smiled. "Yup, that sounds like the author in Saxton. Speaking of which, have you had a chance to read any of his books yet? They're really good."

"I read the first one and loved it, and actually I'm going next door shortly to get his second one."

After finishing coffee and conversation with Chloe, I wandered into the bookshop and saw Corabeth behind the counter.

She looked up and smiled. "Good morning, Berkley. Looking for anything in particular?"

"Yeah, Saxton's second novel."

Walking over to one of the bookcases, she pointed. "They're all right here."

"Thanks. How do you like running the bookshop?"

Corabeth's face lit up. "Oh! I just love it. You know, there's just something about a small bookshop that I've loved since I was a young girl."

"I know what you're saying, and this one is extra nice."

Corabeth nodded. "It is. I understand that those e-readers are convenient and certainly decrease space needed for print books, but for me, nothing will ever replace the feel of a book in my hand."

"My sentiments exactly," I said, and caught sight of a table display with Lacey Weston novels. "Are you getting aggravation from Raylene on that display?"

"Actually, no. She popped by yesterday, glanced at the table, sniffed, and proceeded to ask if the book she'd ordered had come in." Corabeth laughed and shook her head. "I guess she figured she'd tried her best to get that poor author banned, but it didn't work in this shop. I know I'm probably wrong, but she seems to be mellowing a bit lately. I wonder what could account for that."

"Strange. I bumped into her this morning and was pleasantly surprised with her attitude. It did seem a bit less nasty."

It wasn't until later that afternoon when I was in my kitchen pruning my plant that I recalled my conversation with Corabeth, which made me remember customers to our shop in Salem. As I clipped little pieces of the leaves, I recalled some of the regulars to our shop.

Mrs. Potaski, a Polish woman who visited our shop for chocolate twice a week. She showed up one morning all excited and told my grandmother she was convinced it was the chocolate witches' hats that had changed her husband from a grumpy old man into a very pleasant spouse. She laughingly accused my grandmother of putting special potions into her chocolate.

And Mr. Pelletier, another faithful customer. I was assisting my grandmother the day that he came in and proclaimed it had to be the chocolate. Over the past few months that he'd been purchasing it for his wife, her romance meter had notched up a couple of levels. My grandmother had laughed and said, "Ah, but chocolate has very special properties. I don't think most people realize that."

But now I recalled bumping into Raylene that morning and what Corabeth had said about her. Could it just be the chocolate? Silly, of course it was. Unless—I snipped off another leaf and held it to my nose. It did have a very distinct aroma. Something that I couldn't describe and had never smelled in another plant. And after it was ground with the mortar and pestle, it was always an essential ingredient used by my grandmother, and now me, for the making of our chocolate.

Maybe I needed to start paying more attention to my regular customers. I thought of Ava Wells. She had begun coming to my shop the week I opened. Mid-thirties, she lived out by the airport. Her husband was a professor at the university, and I recalled hearing something at the knitting group about her. How sad it was that after ten years of marriage she still had not become pregnant, and the couple was still desperately wishing for a child. Apparently, there was no medical reason as a cause.

What was it she'd said the other day? Something about feeling confident that my chocolate just might work the trick. Surely, she couldn't have meant that my chocolate would actually assist her in getting pregnant, could she?

I let out a deep sigh. So many things in this life were unexplainable. Most of which people chalked up to *coincidence*. But was it?

15

Mr. Carl was my first customer when I opened the shop on Friday morning.

"Beautiful day, isn't it?" he greeted me.

"It certainly is," I said. "May is a beautiful month here on the island."

"That it is. I'll have my usual, Miss Berkley."

After I boxed his chocolates and took his cash, he remained standing on the other side of the counter.

"Anything else I can get you?"

He shuffled from one foot to the other, cleared his throat, and said, "Well, I was wondering . . . that is, I'm really out of practice . . . and . . . how does a man ask a woman out these days?"

Oh, my goodness. This man in his late seventies was asking *me* for dating advice?

"Hmm, well . . . I don't think the proper procedure for that has changed much over the years," I told him. "I would say, just ask her."

"Oh, no, I couldn't do that. I mean, what if she said no?"

If the woman in question was who I thought it was, poor Mr. Carl was taking a risk and probably headed straight for a major disappointment.

"Well, yes. That's always a possibility. So maybe you need to take it slow. You know, get to know her a bit better."

"Oh, I know her mighty well as it is."

"Yes, well . . . what exactly did you have in mind for taking her out?"

"Maybe a dinner. You know, one of them early bird specials that they have in Gainesville. Then we'd be back to the island before dark."

Good thinking. Driving on SR 24 in the dark could be a bit dicey with deer sometimes running across the road.

"Okay. That makes sense. Well, is there someplace this woman goes where you could kind of . . . just show up? This would give you a chance to have some conversation with her. You know, spend some time with her in a social atmosphere before you ask her to go out with you."

Mr. Carl thought about this for a few moments and then snapped his fingers. "Yeah, the lunches."

"The lunches?"

"Sure enough. The Senior Lunches over at the church that they have every day. I haven't gone to those in years, but I know that she does."

"Well, there you go," I told him. "Going there might be just the thing to break the ice for you."

A huge smile crossed Mr. Carl's face. "Thank you, Miss Berkley. I think I'll mosey on over there for lunch today. Thanks again."

When he turned to leave the shop, I could have sworn I saw an extra zip in his step.

I shook my head and laughed as I recalled the quote, *In the spring a young man's fancy lightly turns to thoughts of love.* Perhaps Alfred, Lord Tennyson should have left out the word *young.* When it comes to love, there are no restrictions on age.

Chloe was the first to arrive for dinner. She placed a Tupperware cake plate on the counter.

"My contribution. Pistachio cake."

I lifted the cover to take a peek. "Yummy. It looks great.

Thanks, Chloe. The guys should be here shortly," I said at the same time there was a knock on the door.

This time Saxton didn't have just a bottle of wine but also a beautiful bouquet of spring flowers, which he passed to me.

"Thank you so much," I said, inhaling the wonderful fragrance. "Welcome, Doyle. Come on in."

He passed me a covered bowl. "I thought we might enjoy some of my mullet dip with crackers before dinner."

"How nice. Thank you."

"I'll put these in water for you and you can get the crackers," Chloe said, as she reached into my cabinet for a vase.

"Have a seat," I told Saxton and Doyle. "The corkscrew is on the coffee table."

Chloe placed the vase in the center of the set table and joined us in the living room.

"Nice place you have here," Doyle said, looking around. "It's changed a bit, but not much."

I looked at him with surprise. "Oh, you've been in this apartment?"

He laughed. "I guess growing up here, I've probably been in most of the houses and apartments at one time or another."

Chloe had spread a cracker with mullet dip and took a bite. "Delicious. Seems there was a man on the island that was famous for mullet dip years ago."

Doyle accepted the glass of wine Saxton passed to him and nodded. "That would be Saren. Saren Ghetti. Born and raised here, and he was also an artist. And actually, this here is the recipe that Saren shared with me years ago."

"Oh, Saren," Chloe said. "That was Monica's grandfather, right?"

"Yup. He passed away a couple years ago. Was in his late eighties."

"Right. Grace had told me the story. Now there's a love story that endured over time and probably into eternity."

I took a sip of wine and nodded. "Yes, I remember you telling me that story. Sybile was Monica's grandmother. Although they never married, from what I heard, what Sybile and Saren shared came full circle in their later years."

"Right," Doyle said. "Saren had loved her most of his life, but she spurned him at age eighteen when she left the island to seek her fortune in New York as a model. But years later she returned and in a roundabout way, they were reunited before she died. At least they had that bit of time together before she was gone."

I was sure I detected a note of wistfulness in his tone. Maybe Saxton was right—everybody had a story.

My lasagna, salad, and garlic bread proved to be a hit. The four of us were relaxing with coffee on Chloe's porch.

"Thank you so much for a great dinner," Doyle said. "I really enjoyed that."

"My pleasure. We really enjoyed the day out on your boat."

"Well, then, we'll have to do that again. Maybe go up the Suwannee next time."

"Oh, that would be fun," Chloe said. "And can't you go from here by boat over to Shell Mound?"

Doyle nodded. "Yeah, you can. Shell Mound is one of my favorite places. We'll go sometime."

He now directed his attention to me. "How're you doing trying to solve your puzzle?"

I took a sip of coffee and shook my head. "Not very well, I'm afraid. Nobody can seem to recall a Jeanette Whitmore that spent a summer here. I do think, though, that there was a particular incident that caused her to come here."

"Why do you say that?" Saxton questioned.

"Well, I was going through the postcards again the other evening, and in one of them she said she was doing as well as could be expected. As well as could be expected. That makes me think something had happened which caused her *not* to be well."

"Hmm, like maybe she was ill? You'd mentioned before you thought perhaps she was sick when she came here," Chloe said.

"I had briefly thought that, but she also mentions that her *job* is going well. If she was ill, I don't think she'd be working here. And that's another thing—what kind of job did she have? Who did she work for?"

"Yeah, you have a point there," Saxton said. "If she worked here on the island, you'd think somebody would recall that."

Doyle leaned over to take a refill from the coffee thermos. "Not necessarily. We have many people who come here briefly, they pick up a bit of work, and then they're gone. You had mentioned your mother's sister. Was she any help to you?"

"Not yet. She's supposed to come next month to visit me, but I haven't heard back from her. I didn't want to ask a bunch of questions on the phone. I figured I'd wait till she gets here. But to be honest, I'm not sure how much help she'll be. Once she left home she didn't stay very close to my grandmother or my mother. Her husband was in the military and they were always traveling around the world."

Saxton nodded. "Yeah, that's a shame. If families don't stay in touch, sometimes a family member ends up losing a significant part of their history."

I knew he was thinking of his daughter.

"True," Chloe said. "I'd been estranged from my aunt and my sister for quite a few years. When we did finally reconnect, I was amazed at some of the things that I found out. We never really ever know somebody completely, but when we lose touch, it's even less."

"I agree," I told her. "I always felt that something was missing with my mother. Except for that summer that she was gone, we were together a lot, and yet . . . more and more I feel like I probably never knew her at all."

"The most mysterious part of human nature, isn't it?" Saxton said. "I've always believed that we're very complex creatures. The picture we project to the public may be entirely different from the person that we are inside. I think that's why I enjoy writing my novels—it allows me to attempt to discover what, exactly, we're all about."

I smiled. "I think you're right. Look at that author Lacey Weston. Nobody knows who she is. Only that she writes erotic stories, and yet people like Raylene Samuels can judge her very harshly."

Doyle nodded. "You know what they say—never judge a person until you've walked a mile in their shoes."

I wondered if the discovery of my mother's secret and the reason she came to Cedar Key might cause me to end up *judging* her.

∾ 16 ∾

June first is the official start of hurricane season in Florida. I noticed that much of the talk on the island during that month involved debates on the predictions from meteorologists. Overall, everybody agreed that Cedar Key had a fifty-fifty chance of being hit until the season officially ended on December first. With this fact generally accepted, it was forgotten and conversation in the coffee café, post office, library, and other gathering spots shifted to the economy, politics, local gossip, and fishing.

Just when I didn't think I'd hear from my aunt I received a phone call from her in mid-June.

"Berkley, I'm so sorry not to get back to you sooner," she told me. "I was all booked and confirmed to come visit you next week, but I'm afraid I've had an accident."

My annoyance was replaced with concern. "Oh, no. Are you okay?"

Stella Baldwin laughed across the line. "Well, I guess that depends. You'd think at sixty-eight, I'd have more sense. I signed up for salsa dance classes. The first two went really well. By the way, those male instructors are pretty hot. Anyway, I was wearing my fancy pair of those really high, strappy heels and, well...I... slipped and took a tumble."

I was beginning to see that there was more to Stella Baldwin than I was aware of. Salsa dancing? Stiletto heels?

"And unfortunately, I ended up in the hospital with a broken leg. I'll be in a cast for the next eight weeks or so."

My hand flew to my face. "Oh, my goodness. I'm so sorry to hear this. Are you still in the hospital?"

"No, I'm now in a rehab facility for a while. I think I'll be going home by next week, but then I'm afraid I'm facing some physical therapy when the cast is removed."

So much for finding answers about my mother, I thought, and then felt guilty for only thinking of myself.

"Is there anything that I can do? Maybe I should come up there?"

My aunt's laugh came across the line again. "As much as I'd love to see you, no, no. That's not necessary. There's truly nothing that you could do. I've already hired a companion to be with me constantly when I go home. I just feel terrible, though, about having to cancel my trip to Cedar Key. But I'm hoping you'll allow me to come in October or November, when I should be back on my feet again. Literally."

"Oh, of course. Any time would be fine. I hope you're not in too much pain."

"No, the pain is minimal, so that's a plus. It's just darn annoying knowing my social calendar has gone down the drain. Although the bridge club assures me that we'll meet at my place while I'm laid up. But no golf for me, and my daily exercise class is out of the question. My book club said we could meet at my house also, so that was nice of them. But I guess this is the end of my salsa dancing days, I'm afraid."

I shook my head and smiled. Bridge? Golf? Book club? This aunt of mine was a social butterfly and had a social agenda that put me to shame.

"Well, give me your address and I have your home phone. You probably don't go on the Internet; otherwise, we could also exchange e-mail addresses."

"Oh, but of course I go on the Internet. I'm very involved in quite a few chat rooms. Actually, I've met a few gentleman friends via those chat rooms."

Yup, Aunt Stella was a definite surprise to me. I didn't dare ask if she'd actually met them in person. We exchanged information with the promise to keep in touch. Hanging up the phone, I was hit with the thought of how very different my mother and my aunt were. My mother had always isolated herself from both people and events. My aunt sounded like somebody who stayed constantly active. Even a broken leg didn't seem to faze her very much—except for the limits it now put on her socializing. I smiled as I jotted a note to call a florist the following week and have flowers delivered to my aunt's home.

The hot and humid days of June and July morphed into August, when the mornings and evenings showed promise of the cooler air to come.

Saxton and I were spending most of our free time together with dinners, day trips into Gainesville, a movie in Crystal River at the mall, and always enjoying each other's company.

I was just settling down to get some spinning done for recent orders I'd received when the phone rang.

"What're you doing?" Saxton questioned.

"I was just about to start some spinning. Why?"

"Well, put the spinning aside. Let's drive over to Manatee State Park and take a dip in the springs."

I laughed. "Oh, I can't. I'd like to, but I can't."

"And why not?"

"Well . . . uh . . . I have to get this spinning done. Then I have to vacuum and do a bit of cleaning. And I really should get some more knitting done on the Christmas gifts I'm working on. I also . . ."

Saxton interrupted me. "You don't *have* to do any of those things. What you *need* to do is be more spontaneous. It's a gorgeous day. I've packed us a picnic lunch, and you need to take advantage of the moment. Lighten up, Berkley. Come with me and Lola."

I recalled how he'd once referred to me as rigid, and felt annoyed. I didn't think it was being *rigid* because I had a schedule. And I kept to that schedule.

Silence filled the line as he waited for my answer, and my annoyance gave way to concern. Was I being inflexible? Did it really matter if I cleaned today or tomorrow? I knew I had plenty of time to fulfill the orders and get my knitting done.

"Well . . ." I said, and cleared my throat. "I suppose . . . I suppose I could go."

Without hesitation, Saxton said, "Great. Be out in front of your shop. I'll pick you up at twelve noon." And with that, he hung up.

I placed the phone on the table and glanced over at my mother's urn. Had she ever once been spontaneous in her life? I always thought she had been when she took off for that summer—but the more I thought about it, the more I began to wonder if perhaps she had been forced to leave Salem. For whatever reason.

Sitting at the picnic table, I looked up as Saxton took a bite from the chicken salad sandwich he'd prepared. The summer sun was producing a golden bronze to his skin, making him look even more handsome.

"After we eat, we can go back in the water, if you want," he said.

I smiled. "That was fun. The water is so nice." Not to mention that I'd felt like a kid again, swimming, getting splashed by Saxton, like I didn't have a care in the world. He had been right. I did *need* to come here with him. I looked up at the huge leafy trees providing shade above us and let out a deep sigh.

"Happy?" he asked.

Happy? I'm not sure I've ever given that emotion much thought. I had always gone through my life, day to day, with the usual ups and downs. But thinking about this day, from the moment Saxton had picked me up, I realized that yes, I did feel happy. And happy was something that I always seemed to feel when I was with him.

"I am," I told him. "I am sincerely happy, so thank you for forcing me to come with you."

He laughed. "Oh, don't say that. I'd like to think you came because you wanted to."

"I did, but you gave me the push that I needed. So thank you. It's beautiful here, isn't it?" I looked around at the trees, picnic tables, and the walkway surrounding the springs. On a Tuesday, there were only a handful of people around.

"Yeah, I love it here, being outdoors. As a matter of fact . . . I'm planning a trip to the Georgia Mountains in the fall."

I felt my heart drop. He was going away? Momentarily, all of the old feelings of loss and abandonment came over me. "Oh," was all I could manage to say.

"Ever been there?" he asked.

I shook my head. "No, never have."

He smiled. "Good. I thought you might want to join me, and I could introduce you to that area."

He was asking me to go with him?

When I remained silent, he said, "I'll rent a two-bedroom cabin, so you'll have your own space."

I was taken completely by surprise, both by the fact that he wanted me to go with him and that he offered to get two bedrooms. Since our relationship hadn't progressed beyond some very heated kisses, I guess that did make sense.

"That sounds great. When are you going?"

"I was thinking early to mid-October. Are you free?"

I nodded. "I think so. Oh, I was planning to get up to Maine to visit my alpacas in the fall. But . . . maybe I could postpone that trip. And I really should be here for Seafood Festival weekend. That's a busy time for merchants on the island."

"Okay, that's being held the third weekend, so we could go the week before for about four or five days."

My happiness suddenly jumped a few notches and I felt my face break out in a huge smile. "That would be great, Saxton. I'm really looking forward to it."

"Great," he said, standing up and reaching for my hand. "Let's get this stuff back in the car and walk around a bit with Lola."

We spent the rest of the afternoon walking around, talking and taking a final dip in the springs before heading back to Cedar Key.

As Saxton approached the Number Four bridge, I looked out the window at the sun beginning to set in the western sky. Pelicans dipped and soared. The water shimmered as boats bobbed here and there. There was something special about this place. My mother came to mind, and I wondered if after coming here she had found what she might have been looking for. But actually, I still wasn't sure if Jeanette Whitmore was going *toward* something or *away* from it.

≈ 17 ≈

With Labor Day weekend approaching, the talk all week had been about a hurricane churning in the southern Gulf. It was the main topic of conversation wherever I went. Some experts predicted this one would be a direct hit on Cedar Key. Emergency Management went into increased preparation, advising people to have an evacuation plan and supplies.

When I opened my shop on Wednesday morning, the sun was shining, temps were in the high eighties, and any sign of a hurricane was nonexistent.

I looked up as Mr. Carl walked in. "Well, I think we're gonna be spared again," he said.

I wondered if he had a direct line to Mother Nature.

"You think so?" I asked.

He nodded. "Yup. Oh, I'm not saying we won't get our share of wind and rain. But a direct hit? Nope. I think they're wrong."

"I sure hope so."

"You're all prepared though, right?"

"No, not really."

Mr. Carl shook a finger in my direction. "Oh, now, just because we probably won't get it doesn't mean you don't have to take precautions. Do you know how we're alerted if we have a mandatory evacuation of the island?"

I had no idea and shook my head.

"A three-minute siren blast. We have three outdoor community warning sirens. These were donated to the city, ya know, by Progress Energy through Levy County Emergency Management. So if you hear that blast, you have to already have a plan in place as to where you're going."

This was starting to sound serious. "Are there shelters off island?"

He nodded. "Yeah, there are, but don't you have a cat? You can't take your pets. The shelters are in Chiefland, Bronson, and Williston, at the schools. But no pets allowed. Your best bet is to book one of the pet friendly hotels in Gainesville."

I knew Mr. Carl meant well, but he was beginning to make me nervous. I looked up to see Saxton walk in and felt a sense of relief.

"I'm trying to instruct this here young lady on hurricane precautions."

"I just heard the latest update. Seems she's stalled pretty south of here. But we'll have to stay tuned to the weather forecasts and see what happens."

"You can't take pets to the shelter," I told him, even though I figured Saxton was most likely aware of this.

He nodded. "Right. There's hotels in Gainesville, but it probably won't come to that. Listen, I'm heading into Chiefland to Walmart. I need to stock up on supplies. Do you need some things?"

Born and raised in New England, I knew hurricanes were something that paid very sporadic visits to that area. But this was Florida and a whole different story.

"I have some candles," I said, knowing that was far from sufficient.

Saxton shot me a smile and nodded. "Okay. Don't worry. I'll handle it. I'll be back later this afternoon."

Just as I was preparing to close the shop at five, Saxton walked in.

"I'm back," he said. "I have the golf cart loaded down with supplies for you. Maybe you could give me a hand unloading?"

"Sure. I was just about to lock up."

When I followed him around the corner and saw his golf cart, I gasped.

"What on earth are all those bags?"

He laughed. "Everything you'll need to survive a hurricane. Come on," he said, placing a few bags in my hand. "We'll get everything upstairs."

It took us two trips to unload. I stood gazing at my kitchen table and floor and shook my head. "Don't you think you went a bit overboard with the shopping?"

Saxton began removing items. "Not at all. Here," he said, passing me a package containing a flashlight. "And here's batteries to go with it. Did you have a flashlight?"

"Hmm, no. Thank you."

I proceeded to rummage through the bags to find more candles, matches, a case of bottled water, canned soups, crackers, chips, canned tuna, and an assortment of other food that required no cooking.

"I really appreciate this," I said. "But I don't eat canned tuna or some of these other items."

"You will if we lose power and you're hungry enough. I've stocked up on charcoal too. I have a gas grill and just refilled my propane tank, so if we're without power too long I can fix us a steak or something."

Us? Was he planning to ride out this hurricane with me?

"Was there anything you didn't think of?" I asked, marveling at his shopping ability.

"I hope not. I heard the latest update on the car radio. They've increased Kara to a category two, but she's still down by Naples, doing minimal damage. Mostly high winds and heavy rain."

"Well, guess I should get this stuff put away," I said, reaching for some canned items.

"I'll give you a hand, and then maybe you'll join me for a glass of wine at the Black Dog and dinner at the Pickled Pelican?"

"Sounds like a plan. Thanks."

*   *   *

Thursday morning brought cloudiness to the island and a gentle breeze. But coming around the corner to Second Street I looked around, and except for a few locals here and there, Cedar Key was exceptionally quiet. I decided to postpone opening the shop and headed across the street to the coffee café.

"Hey," Suellen said. "All set to hunker down for Kara?"

"With Saxton's help, yeah. I'll have a latte."

"Well, everyone's getting their ducks in a row. We're going to close the coffee shop and bookshop early and start putting sandbags out front, just in case we get some flooding. You might want to do the same. Lucas has plenty of extra sandbags in the back if you need some."

I was definitely a novice with this hurricane stuff. "Oh, gosh, I never even thought of my shop. I'll take you up on your offer. I may as well close early too. I doubt there'll be much business today."

We both looked up as Chloe walked in and joined us.

"Hey," she said. "Whew . . . just finished getting the sandbags in front of the yarn shop. Dora and I decided to not open today. By the way, she's going to Gainesville to stay with her daughter."

"That's a good idea," Suellen said. "Her house is pretty close to the water on Andrews Circle."

"Are you staying at your places?" Chloe looked at both of us. "And could I have my usual coffee when you get a chance?"

"Sure," Suellen said, heading behind the counter. "Yeah, my house isn't on the water. I think I'll be okay. How about you?"

"I'm going to go over and stay with Aunt Maude. With Grace and Lucas away, she has Annie and Duncan there with her and could probably use my help with the dogs."

"Oh, that's good." Suellen placed a mug of coffee in front of Chloe. "Not to mention the company. I'm sure Maude will appreciate you being there. How about you, Berkley? Will you be staying in your apartment?"

"Yeah, Saxton made sure I have everything in the way of supplies, so I guess I'll be okay."

"His house is right on the water too. Even though it's on stilts, he could still get some damage."

"Oh, really?" I said, and looked up to see both of them staring at me. "What?"

"Well, everyone kind of looks out for everyone else here when a storm is coming." Chloe took a sip of her coffee. "It might be nice to invite Saxton to stay at your place. You're on the second floor and should be okay there."

Invite Saxton to spend the night at my house?

"Oh . . . I . . . ah . . . never thought of that," I stammered.

Suellen laughed. "You're a grown woman. It just might be a neighborly thing to do."

"True," I said, taking the last gulp of my coffee. "Well, guess I'll go open the shop for a few hours for my regulars. Will you still be here around three? I'll come back and get those sandbags."

"Yeah, Corabeth and I decided to close around three, so I'll see you then."

I walked outside and was surprised to see a television crew setting up with cameras and a reporter with mic in hand. The van parked across the street told me it was CNN news. Good Lord, did they think Cedar Key was going to be swept away with this hurricane? I nodded to the reporter and headed to unlock my shop.

Shortly after opening, the male reporter I'd seen outside came in.

"Hey," he said, in that overly friendly anchorperson manner. "I'm Steve and I'm with CNN. I wonder if I could interview you?"

I had never been overly fond of the media. I understood it was their job to cover newsworthy events, but I also felt that many times they went overboard and trespassed into people's personal lives.

"I seriously doubt I'd have anything very important to say," I told him.

He laughed and gave a shrug of his shoulders. "Well, I'm just wondering if you're planning to stay on the island or evacuate."

"Gee, I must have missed the siren blast," I said, annoyance creeping into my tone. "I'm not aware that we're under a mandatory evacuation. It isn't even raining out."

I must have hit a chord because Steve now had a sheepish expression on his face. "Oh, no . . . I didn't mean that it was mandatory. I just wondered if you were planning to leave."

"Well, I'm not sure if you've ever been to this town before. But we're pretty resilient people here. I'm not from here originally, but that resilience seems to rub off on you. So no, I'm not planning to leave—unless we're forced to."

"Right. I was also wondering if you knew the bookshop owner."

"Lucas? Yes, I know him. Why?"

"Lucas?" he said, and I saw confusion cover his face. "Oh, I thought the woman in there was the owner."

"No, that's Corabeth Williams. She's in charge while Lucas is away till next month."

"Oh, I see." He began inching his way toward the door. "Okay, I guess I was mistaken. Thanks," he said, and walked out.

I shook my head. What was that all about?

❧ 18 ❧

By the time I'd finished placing the sandbags along the doorway edge of my shop, large drops of rain were hitting the pavement.

I ran around the corner and raced upstairs, attempting to avoid getting drenched. But the sky had opened quickly and even a short distance caused me to be soaked. I had just finished changing into dry clothes when the phone rang.

"How're you doing?" I heard Saxton ask.

"Good, now that I'm dry. Boy, that rain came really fast. Just running around the corner I got soaked. I got all the sandbags in front of my shop just before it started."

"Oh, you should have given me a call. I would have helped you."

The word *help* reminded me of what Chloe and Suellen had suggested earlier. "That's okay. It didn't take long, but I was won-dering . . . well . . . that is . . . Chloe and Suellen thought because your house is on the water . . . uh . . . you might want to come over here with Lola."

I heard Saxton's laughter come across the line.

"Ah, this was Chloe and Suellen's idea, huh?"

"Well . . . yeah. They thought of it but . . . it might be a good idea."

"So are you saying you'd like me to ride out this hurricane with you?"

I smiled. "Yeah, I guess that *is* what I'm saying."

"Then I accept your invitation. That's very nice of you. Plus, it's always better to have company during a hurricane—makes one less nervous, you know?"

As if *he* was nervous about a hurricane.

My smile increased. "Great. Come on over whenever you're ready. I have a roast chicken that's going into the oven shortly."

I opened the door to Saxton's knock and let out a burst of laughter. Good Lord, this man must have been a Boy Scout and still followed the motto *Be Prepared*. He was loaded down with what appeared to be bedrolls, a couple bags, and Lola on the end of a leash.

"Come on in," I told him. "You couldn't possibly have thought of more things that I needed here?"

Saxton put his load on the floor and smiled. "Well, I brought a couple of bedrolls, and of course Lola here needs her bed, and . . ." He reached into one of the bags. "No hurricane is complete without a couple bottles of good wine," he said, placing three on my coffee table.

I leaned over and kissed his cheek. "You're a wonder. With everything else you brought, I'd say we'll be okay. Dinner will be ready in about an hour. The latest update I heard on the radio was that Kara had been downgraded again to a Cat 1, but she's moving up the coast."

"Right, and we just might luck out and be on the best side of her."

"Well, the first line of business is introducing Lola and Sigmund, I guess."

"Lola's used to cats, so that'll probably help."

I went and retrieved Sigmund from my bedroom. "Now, I want you to be a gentleman," I crooned in his ear. "We have guests and you need to behave."

Saxton still had Lola on her leash, and I put Sigmund on the floor. We watched as my cat sauntered over to Saxton's dog. Some sniffing followed, and after a minute or two, Sigmund looked up at me as if to say *You woke me for this?* He turned around and returned to his spot on the bedroom windowsill.

I laughed. "Well, I guess that went well. You can take poor Lola off her leash."

I could hear the wind picking up outside. "Why don't you flip the TV on while I check on our dinner?"

As I peered into the oven, the aroma of roast chicken and baked potatoes filled my nostrils. I stabbed the fresh green beans with a fork and turned the heat down a bit.

"A glass of wine before dinner?" Saxton asked.

"Sounds great," I said, curling up on the sofa where Lola immediately joined me. "You're a real cutie," I told her while stroking her wiry fur. "Gee, I hope this hurricane won't do too much damage to the island," I said as I accepted the glass from Saxton.

"The worst of it is supposed to arrive here during the early morning hours."

"Well, according to Mr. Carl we'll be spared anything too bad. He stopped in just before I closed to make sure he had his supply of chocolate."

Saxton nodded. "Those locals usually know what they're talking about. Did he ever end up asking Miss Raylene out?"

"Nah, not yet. The poor man needs a boost to his self-esteem. He sees her a few times a week at the Senior Lunches but still hasn't taken the step to ask her out."

"Working his way up to it, I guess." Saxton reached for my hand. "I was nervous about asking you out that first time, so I can sympathize with him."

I shifted on the sofa to face him better. "You were?" I asked with surprise. "Why on earth were you nervous?"

"Well . . . I was attracted to you the first time I looked up from the pavement and looked into your face. So I would have been terribly disappointed if you'd rebuffed me."

I smiled as I recalled that day five months before when I returned from lunch to find Saxton sitting outside of my shop waiting for me to open.

"Then I'm very glad that I accepted."

"Me too." He took a sip of wine.

"Still no word from your daughter?"

Saxton shook his head. "It's been about five months now, so I may never hear from her."

"Are you prepared for that possibility?"

He nodded. "Yeah, I am. When I mailed the letter I knew it might be a futile attempt to have a relationship with her, but . . . I wanted to try."

"Exactly," I said, placing my wineglass on the table. "I just hope you're not disappointed."

"I feel the same way about you searching for information about your mother. I know many people would say we should leave well enough alone . . . but . . ."

I squeezed his hand. "But sometimes that's just not possible. By the way, how's your new novel going? I'm almost finished with your second one and I love it."

Saxton ran a hand through his hair. "Slow. I'm grateful that my deadline isn't until March first, but I do have to get moving on it. I've been doing some research for it, and I'm sure once I actually sit down and focus I'll get the rest of it finished."

"Maybe we're spending too much time together and it's taking away from your work."

He leaned over to touch his lips to mine and gave me a wink. "Never. Not ever."

I smiled and stood up. "Okay, give me a few minutes and I'll have everything on the table."

"Can I help?"

"No, I'm all set. Just try and catch another weather update."

I had put the final bowl on the table when Saxton walked into the kitchen. "Smells great."

"Good. Have a seat and we can start."

"Is Chloe staying in her apartment?" he asked.

I shook my head and went on to give him an update on the whereabouts of my friends.

"That's a good idea that Dora went to Gainesville. I wouldn't want to see her alone at her house."

We exchanged easy conversation over dinner, Saxton helped in

the cleanup, he fed Lola, and then we settled on the sofa with coffee. The rain was now coming down in torrents, and the wind had
increased.

"Sounds nasty out there," I said. "But at least we have power."

"Yeah, the last update still said we'll get the worst around three
or four in the morning. Hey," he said, getting up to rummage
through his duffel bag, "how about a game of Scrabble?"

"Good idea, but I'm not sure how fair it'll be playing with an
author."

Saxton laughed. "Ah, word master that I am, huh?"

When we finished the game, he reached for his cell phone. "I
have to give Miss Maybelle a call. To check on her. Only be a second."

I listened as he asked how she was doing, was there anything she
needed, and if so, to be sure to call his cell.

When he hung up, I inquired as to who Miss Maybelle was.

Saxton smiled. "Oh, you haven't met Maybelle Brewster yet?
She lives out by the airport. She's quite a gal—was a Copa Girl
back in the fifties. She lives alone, and whenever there's a hurricane
or bad storm a lot of us check on her. The airport bridge has the
potential for flooding with heavy rain, and we want to make sure
she's not stuck at her house."

"What? She was really a dancer at the famous Copacabana in
New York?" I mean, it was nice that locals checked on her and just
another example of community and caring on the island. But a for-
mer Copa Girl here in Cedar Key?

Saxton laughed. "Yes, she really was. She's quite a character. She moved here in the sixties when her dancing days were over.
Doesn't talk about it much, but I'm sure she has quite a story.
You'd know her, if you saw her around town—even at eighty, she's
still quite a glamorous woman."

I made a mental note to find out more about her. I had always
been intrigued by the style and allure of those famous showgirls.

I was surprised when the clock on my mantel struck twelve.
We'd been sipping wine and playing Scrabble for hours, and the
evening had disappeared. I stifled a yawn.

An apologetic expression crossed Saxton's face. "You must be really tired. You can go to sleep, you know. I'm just going to bunk out here on the carpet with my sleeping bag."

The thought of leaving him didn't appeal to me.

"Oh, well . . . actually I was going to go throw on a pair of sweats and tee shirt and make myself some herbal tea. Would you like some?"

"Sure. That sounds good."

"I'll be right back," I said, and headed into the bathroom. After closing the door, I proceeded to change and brush my teeth and then rejoined Saxton.

When I returned to the living room, I noticed that he'd shut off two of the lamps, leaving only the small dim one on. He'd also arranged the two sleeping bags side by side on the carpet in front of the sofa. Lola had already claimed a spot at the bottom of one of them, ignoring her bed.

"Just going to put the kettle on for tea. Would you like cookies or anything to go with it?"

Saxton settled himself on the sleeping bag with Lola and shook his head. "No, thank you. Just tea will be fine."

Waiting for the water to boil, I glanced out the kitchen window. I could see sheets of rain whipping down from the streetlight. The wind was increasing and the sound reminded me of a gothic movie filmed on the coast of Cornwall. The sign across the street on the Historical Museum was thrashing back and forth. But all was calm and cozy in my apartment, and best of all—Saxton was here to relieve my uneasiness.

"It's looking worse out there," I said, as I passed him a mug and sat down next to him.

"Thanks. I imagine the next few hours will be the worst."

"Music," I said, jumping up again. "We need some soothing music." I went over to my CD player and pushed the button. Pachelbel's Canon filled the room.

"Ah, perfect choice," Saxton said as I rejoined him.

Sitting cross-legged, I said, "I've always loved the piece."

"Another new thing I've discovered about you. You like classical music?"

"I do. My mother and my grandmother always listened to it, so I guess you could say I was brought up with it. Oh, my mom loved all those hippie songs from the sixties too, so we had a mixture of music in our house."

"When I'm working on a novel, I always have a piece of classical music playing softly. Somehow it seems to stir my creativity."

We finished our tea and Saxton reached for me, pulling me close with his arm around my shoulder. I felt him run his fingers through my hair before he turned my face toward his. His lips found mine, and when we broke apart we both let out a deep sigh.

"What do you want in life, Berkley?" he asked.

His question caught me off guard. "What do I want? I'm not sure I know what you mean."

"Well . . . do you hope to be married some day? Do you want children? Do you think you'll always live here in Cedar Key? Or do you have other long-range plans?"

He was asking questions that I couldn't recall anybody else ever asking. I thought about it for a few moments.

"Do I want to be married? I'm not sure I've ever given that a lot of thought, to be honest. I mean, I've been alone a lot." I snuggled closer into his chest. "I know I love being with you. But I also know that couples don't have to be married to share a deep and meaningful relationship."

I felt Saxton's head nod against the top of my head.

"And children?" I blew out a deep breath. "I love children, but it's never been a burning desire for me to have my own. Again, it isn't something that I feel pressured about. Besides, I'm forty-five and I guess each year I realize there's less of a possibility."

"And you're okay with that?"

I nodded. "Yes. I think I always have been. What about you? You've only had one daughter that you barely know. Would you want to start a family now?"

"I wouldn't be averse to that happening, but like you, I guess I'm content with where my life is right now." He reached for my hand and began stroking his thumb up and down along the top. "And do you think you'll stay here?"

Without hesitating, I said, "I do. I love this town. I love the people and the sense of community. My shop is doing well and so is my mail order yarn business."

"So those are the things that would keep you here?"

"And you," I said, squeezing his hand. "You would keep me here."

I heard the smile in his tone. "Good. I was hoping you'd say that. I wanted to ask you something else . . ."

I heard his voice turn serious and sat up to look at him.

"This is probably silly . . . and there's probably no reason to even discuss it. But . . . do you consider what we have to be an . . . exclusive relationship?"

"Exclusive?" I asked, not understanding his meaning.

"I guess what I'm trying to say is, would you be interested in dating anybody else?"

"Oh," I said, his meaning becoming clear. "Oh . . . no. Not at all. Why would I, Saxton? I love being with you. I love what we share—the fun, the laughter, good times." I stopped myself from saying that I also thought that I was falling in love with *him*.

He leaned toward me and I felt his lips on mine as his arms went around me. This time when we broke apart, we were both breathing heavily.

"I'm happy to hear you say that," he whispered against my hair, his voice husky. "Very happy. Because I feel exactly the same way."

I curled back into his arm and leaned my head against his chest. Before I knew it, I had dozed off. A loud crash outside caused me to jump, and I realized that the room was completely black. I felt Saxton beside me and heard him say, "It's okay. I'm right here. Sounds like something went flying outside."

I rubbed at my eyes and sat up straighter. "Why isn't the light on? What time is it?"

"Four-thirty, and we lost power about an hour ago."

I'd been sleeping for over three hours—and in the dark.

"Go back to sleep," he said. "It's okay."

"No, I can't. I have to have . . ." I stopped myself before sharing one of my idiosyncrasies with him.

"Have what?" he asked, and I heard the curiosity in his tone.

"It's just that . . . I always . . . sleep with the light on." There, I'd said it.

But he didn't laugh at me. Instead he fluffed up the pillow in back of my head. "Why don't you lie back down? I'm right here next to you. It'll be okay. Really."

I let out a deep breath and nodded. I slid down to position myself and felt Saxton stretching out beside me. He reached for my hand, and that was the last thing I remembered before drifting off to a relaxed and easy sleep.

19

I awoke to the feel of kisses on my cheek and Lola peering down at me. Smiling, I turned my head and saw Saxton peacefully sleeping and realized that his hand was still clutched in mine. It was light out and the sound of rain and wind was gone.

I tried to readjust my position carefully so as not to wake him, but his eyes shot open. He looked over at me, a huge smile covering his face.

"Good morning, beautiful," he said as he placed a kiss on my forehead. "Looks like we survived Kara."

I smiled and relinquished his hand to stretch my arms above me. "We did, and I have you to thank for that."

Saxton rubbed his eyes and yawned. "I'm glad you think so."

"I can't believe that I slept as well as I did. But I feel terrible. You didn't sleep much at all, did you?" I had a feeling that he had been on guard in case I woke in the dark.

"No, no. I did catch a few winks. How about some coffee? Looks like the power is back on." He got up to shut off the lamp and stretched.

"Great," I said, getting up to join him. "I prepared it last night, so you just have to flip the switch. I'll get into the bathroom first, if that's okay."

"Sounds good," he said, heading into the kitchen while I headed toward the bathroom.

I emerged following a quick shower, teeth brushed, wearing shorts and a tee shirt, to the wonderful aroma of Maxwell House.

He passed me a mug.

"Thanks," I said. "Your turn. I left clean towels out for you."

"Perfect. Oh, and by the way, don't be alarmed when you look out the window."

I walked farther into the kitchen and glanced out. "Oh! My God!" I exclaimed. I looked down onto SR 24 and Second Street to see water covering the entire street, looking more like a pond than a means for transportation. A few rowboats went past with people pushing oars back and forth.

"It's okay," he said, and I felt his arm go around me. "This has happened before with severe storms. Unfortunately, it was high tide during the height of the hurricane. But the water will begin to recede pretty quickly and we'll have our streets back."

"Do you think the chocolate shop got flooded?" I asked. I couldn't believe what I was seeing outside my window.

"You may have gotten some flooding. Do you have a shop vac? We'll get it all cleaned up as soon as the water recedes." He kissed my cheek. "I'm heading into the shower. At least we have our power back."

I smiled. Ever the optimist.

"You're right. How about a muffin with coffee?" I asked as I realized that, no, I did not have a shop vac.

"Definitely," he said, before heading for the bathroom.

Saxton was right. By early afternoon the water covering the streets was gone and we decided to venture outside. As we came out of my courtyard onto D Street, I saw a crowd of people in front of the bookshop.

"Wonder what that's all about," I said as we headed in that direction.

Most of the people congregated were locals, but some were visitors who had been on the island when the hurricane struck. I saw Mr. Carl in the crowd and went toward him.

"What's going on? Is everything okay?"

"Yeah, Miss Corabeth's inside with that reporter and Officer Bob. Nobody allowed in there right now. Seems that reporter is accusing Miss Corabeth of being that Erica writer. I think he was harassing her, so she put out a call to Officer Bob."

"Erica writer?" I asked with confusion. "What on earth is that?" All of a sudden, it hit me. "Do you mean *erotica* writer?"

He nodded. "Yeah. You know, those books that Raylene was complaining about."

"Are you serious?" Saxton said, shaking his head. "Where the heck did the reporter get that idea?"

"I heard something about his girlfriend working for the *New York Times* and she gave him a tip. He didn't come here to cover a hurricane—he came to interrogate poor Miss Corabeth. Imagine accusing her of something like that."

I now felt quite justified in my dislike of that reporter the day before. And he didn't even purchase one piece of my chocolate.

"Well, that's just plain crazy," I said as Suellen came up to join us. "What's going on?"

I filled her in, and disbelief showed on her face.

"That reporter must be kidding," she said. "Corabeth's no author. So Officer Bob is inside? Maybe I should wait to open the coffee café."

"Good idea," I said as I looked across the street to my chocolate shop. "Well, guess I'll go inspect my damage. You don't happen to have a shop vac, do you?"

"I do, and as soon as I can get inside and clean up, I'll let you borrow it."

"Thanks," I said as Saxton and I crossed the street.

I put my key into the lock and opened the door. Puddles of water covered the floor, but other than that, the shop looked the same.

"Not too bad," I said. "I guess we were fortunate."

Saxton nodded. "And when Suellen brings over the vac, we'll get the puddles cleaned up. Why don't we walk around town and see if anybody needs help."

"Good idea," I said as we walked out and I relocked my door.

Heading down Second Street we saw merchants sweeping water out of their shops, putting wet items on the sidewalk to dry, but for the most part there was no serious damage. We walked over to City Park, where branches and palm fronds littered the ground. The ocean still looked pretty choppy, but with the sun now shining it didn't look quite as menacing. We headed over to Dock Street and saw the same type of cleanup was going on. Everyone seemed to have things in order, so we headed back to my shop. By now the crowd had dispersed in front of the bookshop, but it was closed and the door was locked. We walked next door and went into the coffee café, where a few people were gathered. Suellen was busy filling orders and gave us a quick wave. She came over to our table a few minutes later.

"What the heck was that all about next door?" I asked.

Suellen shrugged. "Beats me. It seems that reporter was pretty insistent that Corabeth is the erotica author Lacey Weston."

"That's insane," I said. "Corabeth isn't even an author. Is she?" I looked at Saxton like he was supposed to have the answer.

He laughed. "Not that I'm aware of."

"What did Corabeth say?" I asked. "And what happened to the reporter?"

"When I came in here, I heard Corabeth denying it. She said she had no idea what he was talking about. Officer Bob made the reporter leave the island. Said if he didn't, he'd charge him with harassment."

I shook my head and laughed. "So is our little town going to be on CNN?"

"I doubt it. He didn't get a story, so I guess that's the end of it."

But that wasn't the end of it. The following week we were all gathered at the yarn shop for our evening of knitting when Corabeth walked in.

Everybody looked up, stopped talking, and ceased knitting.

She took a seat, removed a beautiful pale green cotton sweater from her bag, knitted a couple of stitches, and then laid it in her lap.

"I suppose you gals want the details on the commotion at the bookshop last week?"

"Well . . . no. Not if you don't feel the need to share . . ." somebody said, while somebody else said, "Yeah, I'm dying to know what that was all about."

Corabeth cleared her throat. "Okay. Well, the truth of it is . . . I've spoken to my publisher and . . ."

"Publisher!" Raylene interrupted. "You mean to tell me *you're* Lacey Weston and you *do* write that smut?"

Completely ignoring Raylene, Corabeth went on. "And my publisher feels the cat is now out of the bag and yes. . . . My pen name is Lacey Weston and I'm an author."

A collective gasp filled the room as questions were tossed at Corabeth faster than the speed of light.

"An author? Why didn't you ever tell us?"

"How long have you been writing?"

"I can't believe we never knew your secret."

"Does Lucas know who you really are?"

Corabeth raised her hand in the air. "Give me a chance and I'll tell you everything." She took a deep breath. "I've always enjoyed writing. And years ago I began writing erotica for my own entertainment. I knew it was becoming more popular in the book industry and it also didn't have the stigma that it did years ago. So, on a lark, I decided to send one of my manuscripts off to a publisher in New York. Imagine *my* surprise when about five months later, I received a letter from them offering me a contract."

Dora chuckled.

All eyes were focused on Corabeth as she continued her story.

"And those contracts kept coming, my sales skyrocketed, and before I knew it, I was a *New York Times* bestselling author."

"But why the pen name?" Chloe questioned.

Corabeth laughed. "Not everybody likes the fact that erotica is in bookstores." Her glance strayed to Raylene, who'd managed to remain silent. "I discussed it with my editor, and we both agreed that perhaps a pen name might be best."

"I'll be darn," Liz said. "All those books of yours that I read... and I never knew it was *you*."

"You read them?" Raylene said, surprise in her voice.

"Sure I did. They're good. Maybe you should broaden your own reading horizons."

Raylene sniffed and resumed her silence.

"So is that why sometimes you were holed up in your house and couldn't make the Garden Club meetings or other events? You were busy writing?" Flora leaned forward in her chair.

"Exactly. When I was on deadline, it got a bit tricky trying to make excuses why I couldn't join the rest of you."

Dora laughed and shook her head.

Needless to say, I was absolutely stunned with this news. Prim and proper Miss Corabeth, satisfying the sexual appetites of women around the world.

I joined Dora's laughter. "Well, I say bravo to you! But now that your secret's out, will it affect your writing career?"

"No, I wouldn't think so, and my editor said it might even give it another boost. I have another novel coming out in the spring, so I guess only time will tell."

"Well, I'll be first in line to get one," Betty said.

"Not if I get there first," Flora retorted.

"Well, you sure had us fooled," Raylene snapped. "Here I thought you were a churchgoing woman."

"Maybe you'll want to get a copy for you and Mr. Carl to read together," Flora said, causing a deep crimson blush to creep up Raylene's neck. "Who knows how it might spice up your life."

"What a thing to say.... As if ... I wouldn't ..."

"Oh, Raylene, lighten up, for goodness' sake." Betty leaned over and patted Raylene's arm. "We're just joking with you."

"Yes ... well ... I would hope so," she stammered.

But I couldn't help but notice that her normal nasty remarks were missing. Was it really possible that Raylene Samuels was beginning to mellow a bit?

"Well, my goodness," Dora said, standing up. "Life is just filled with surprises, isn't it? I think we should take a break now and have some pastry and coffee."

Yes, I thought. *Dora's right. Life is filled with surprises, but learning about Corabeth made me realize even more how little I probably knew about my own mother.*

20

By mid-September the gossip and surprise had died down about Corabeth Williams and she carried on as usual. That's one thing about a small town. You don't have to wait very long for the next bit of gossip to surface, and people move on to something else.

I had skeins of yarn spun and ready to deliver to the yarn shop. Just before I headed out, my phone rang and I answered to hear Jill's voice.

"Hey there, girlfriend," she said. "You must be really settling in because I don't hear from you much anymore."

Jill was right. In the six months that I'd been living in Cedar Key our phone calls had dwindled to only once every few weeks, when at one time it was almost daily.

I plunked onto the sofa as a wave of guilt came over me. "I know and I'm really sorry. But I've been pretty busy, and then we had the hurricane here and , . ."

Jill laughed. "I'm not scolding you. I just miss you. I saw on the Internet that thankfully you didn't get too much damage on the island."

"I miss you too, Jill. And no, we were really lucky. A bit of flooding, a couple of trees down, but no major damage."

"Great. And how's the puzzle coming along? Anything yet on your mother?"

"Not a thing. As you know, I did share my story at the knitting group, but nobody can seem to remember her."

"And your aunt? Has she been any help?"

"Well, I told you about her accident, so she wasn't able to come here in June. I really don't want to question her on the telephone, but when I spoke to her last week she said her leg is about back to normal and she hinted about coming here for Thanksgiving."

"That's great. I hope eventually you'll get some answers. Okay, enough chitter-chatter—and Saxton Tate the third? What's the latest update there?"

I laughed. "I like him, Jill. I like him a lot."

"Hmm, I can hear that in your voice."

"Actually—" I hesitated before going on. "I really did want to get up to Maine, especially to see Bosco and Belle, but . . . Saxton's asked me to join him next month for a few days in the mountains of Georgia . . . and . . ."

Jill laughed. "You silly girl. Let's see—trip to Maine to see alpacas or romantic getaway with good-looking guy. Duh! Berkley, you don't have to make excuses. Go! Go and have a great time. Besides, I've been giving some thought to getting out of here for Thanksgiving and maybe heading to a little island off the west coast of Florida."

I sat up straighter and punched my arm into the air. "Yes! Really? You think you might come for Thanksgiving? Oh, Jill, that would be super."

My friend laughed across the line. "Yup, there's a good possibility that'll happen. So don't give it a second thought. Go to Georgia with Saxton Tate the third—but I'll never forgive you if you don't give me an in-depth report when you return."

After she hung up, I sat there holding the phone in my hand and smiled. Every woman needed a best friend like Jill—and I was lucky enough to have one.

I walked into the yarn shop to see Dora putting a brightly colored scarf around Oliver's neck.

"Well, doesn't he look spiffy," I said, leaning over to give him a pat. "How're ya doing, Oliver?"

Dora smiled. "Oliver is going to school later today."

"Oh, another obedience class?"

"No, no. Oliver is actually going to *school*. The Cedar Key School. He's now going to officially be part of the Pages and Paws program."

"What's that? I'm not familiar with it."

Dora adjusted the knot on Oliver's scarf. "Oh, it's a new program based on the national one, Reading With Rover. That program originated in Washington State. Well-behaved dogs are brought to schools, libraries, and bookstores so that children can read to the dogs. It builds the child's confidence and fosters a love of reading. Many children find it difficult reading out loud in a classroom, but with a dog next to them listening, it makes it easier. Dogs don't judge if you read slow or have a problem pronouncing a word. I feel it's a very worthwhile program, so I wanted to volunteer and Oliver was accepted."

"That's wonderful. And I agree, sounds like a great program." I reached over to give Oliver a pat on his head. "Gee, it makes me almost wish I had a dog."

"Well, if you're serious, there's sure plenty at the Levy County Humane Society that could use a good home."

I filed the thought away and changed the subject. "I have some more skeins of yarn here for you," I said, reaching into my bag.

"Oh, very good. We've run out of your last delivery. They're selling so well, Berkley. Knitters just love hand-spun and hand-dyed yarn."

I smiled as I watched her arrange the skeins on a table that held a sign proclaiming YARN BY BERKLEY.

"I'm glad. It's a pleasure doing business with you." I noticed that Oliver had retreated to his cushion in the corner of the shop. "He's so well behaved, Dora. Did he have to have any special training to be in that reading program?"

"Well, he had to have extensive obedience training. We had to make sure that he was socialized, especially with children, and he passed all the tests. And of course, all of his injections have to be up to date, and the vet gave me a certificate to give to the school. Today is just a trial run. We're going over so Oliver can meet some of the children and we'll see how they interact. If this goes well, then he'll be put on a schedule for once a week and be with a child that will read to him."

"I'm really impressed. This is a win-win program. I can see where it would boost a child's confidence with reading, but I'm sure the dogs involved will also feel productive. I wonder if Saxton is aware of this program. Lola is also very well behaved."

"Oh, you should mention it to him. It's a fairly new program, so they're looking for more volunteers."

"I will. Well, time to open my shop. Have fun this afternoon at the school."

Just before I was going to close the shop for lunch, the chimes rang on the door and I looked up to see an unfamiliar woman walk in. Tall, slim, and dressed like a fashion model out of a sixties *Vogue* magazine, this woman without a doubt *had* to be Maybelle Brewster. She wore a stylish two-piece beige linen suit with jacket and skirt, beige pumps, celery green lace gloves that matched the filmy scarf cleverly wound around her neck, and a small pillbox hat perched atop her perfectly coifed white hair. This may have been Maybelle Brewster, but there was no way she could be around eighty, as Saxton had said. This woman was utterly stunning and could easily have passed for somebody in her sixties.

"Hello. I'm sorry I haven't gotten in here sooner," she said, extending her gloved hand.

Gloves and a hat—accessories that had been abandoned by the time I was born. She reminded me of the old-fashioned magazines my grandmother used to have around the house.

"I'm Maybelle Brewster and a friend of Saxton's. Any friend of Saxton's is a friend of mine, so I wanted to finally get in here and welcome you to the island."

I smiled as a whiff of Chanel No 5 drifted toward me. No doubt about it—Maybelle Brewster was a relic of a fashion era that no longer existed.

"How nice of you. It's a pleasure to meet you, and thank you for the welcome. Saxton told me about you the night of the hurricane. I'm glad you didn't have any damage at your house."

"Oh, Safe Harbor has been very blessed. When I bought that house back in the sixties, somebody told me the house was positioned perfectly to avoid any flooding or damage, and all these years later that still holds true. I'm right on the water, but I've always been safe there. So what did Saxton tell you about me?"

She lifted her head a fraction as a smile crossed her face.

"Oh . . . just that the locals checked on you during storms because the airport bridge could flood and they wanted to be sure you were okay."

She nodded. "Yes, I'm very fortunate to be surrounded by such caring and genuine people. You mean to tell me that Saxton didn't reveal what my career was before I came to Cedar Key?"

I laughed. "Ah, yes, he did happen to mention that you had been a Copa Girl."

Her laugh joined mine as she waved a gloved hand in the air. "It seems to be my claim to fame here on the island, but I'm sure you're too young to know what a Copa Girl was."

"Oh, but that's not true," I gushed. "My grandmother had saved a lot of magazines from the fifties and sixties, and I used to love to pore over them when I was a teen. The girls who danced and sang at the Copacabana were quite famous. I had always longed to wear some of those costumes and jewelry, and I wondered what it must have felt like to be so sophisticated and alluring."

Maybelle nodded as her expression turned serious and a faraway look came into her eyes. "Yes, those were very exciting days, they were. But the fame didn't come without a price." She cleared her voice. "Now then, I'd like three pieces of chocolate, please."

Three? Seemed like she rationed herself with chocolate the same way that Saxton did.

"Certainly," I said, reaching for a plastic glove and small box. "Which would you like?"

She pointed to the truffles from Angell and Phelps and explained, "I could devour pounds of chocolate, so I'm very careful. My weight, you know."

I shot a quick glance at her still-perfect figure and wondered if at age eighty I'd still be concerned with a scale and my dress size.

Ringing up the sale, I passed the box across the counter. "Thank you so much. I hope you'll enjoy them."

"Oh, I plan to savor them. It was so nice meeting you, Berkley."

She turned to leave and then paused. "So you were enchanted with the Copa Girls, were you?"

I nodded.

"Well, then, perhaps you'd like to come out to Safe Harbor sometime. You might enjoy seeing some of my old costumes and photographs. Bring Saxton with you. We'll have tea."

And with that, she left the shop.

⮾ 21 ⮾

The following week Saxton called to invite me to lunch at the Red Onion in Gainesville.

"Oh, I'd love to," I told him. "But is there any chance I could make a quick stop at Yarnworks?"

Saxton laughed. "That's like taking coals to Newcastle, but sure. Something you need and can't find at Yarning Together?"

"Actually, I'd like to get back to needlepoint for a while. I love my knitting, but it's nice to work on something different every now and again. I haven't done needlepoint in years and I know they carry it at Yarnworks."

"Sure. That's fine, and I'll pick you up about noon."

"Thanks for waiting while I ran into the yarn shop," I told him as we enjoyed a Cobb salad. "I know I'll like doing the needlepoint butterfly that I bought."

"Good. Well . . . I wanted to tell you . . . I've heard from Resa."

My head popped up to gauge his expression, which appeared to be neutral. "Oh, that's wonderful. Isn't it?"

He took a sip of ice water and then nodded. "I think so. The letter was rather generic. She is married, as I thought. Her husband is Jake. Dr. Jake Campbell, to be precise. He's a pediatrician in Seattle. They have no children, and Resa works for a software company."

"Oh, that's it? Well, it sounds like she's doing well. Did she mention anything about getting together with you?"

"Just briefly said she's giving it some thought. She'll get back to me."

I could hear the disappointment in his tone. "Well, that makes sense. You have to understand you haven't been in contact in, what? Thirty years? I'm sure she has a lot to think about. But I think it's a good sign that she answered your letter."

"You do?" His voice sounded hopeful.

I nodded. "Yes, definitely. If she didn't want to bother with you at all, she wouldn't have replied back. That would have been the end of it. But she's probably taking it slow and trying to decide where to go from here. Do you plan to write her back?"

"I think I will. The last book that I wrote—I dedicated it to her. Maybe I'll send her an autographed copy."

"Great idea. I would think that would please her. I mean, after all, her father is a well-known, successful author."

"Yeah, and a man who stayed out of touch. But you're right. I'll give her the time that she needs. At least this was a start."

"Exactly," I said and hoped his relationship with his daughter could be what he hoped for.

Mr. Carl was my first customer when I opened the shop, and I noticed that he seemed to have an extra zip in his step when he walked in. In addition to that, his blue eyes had an increased sparkle.

"What's up, Mr. Carl?" I asked as I arranged the crystals on the table in a more orderly fashion.

"Beautiful morning, isn't it?" A huge smile covered his face. "Yes, indeedy, I love these cooler September mornings."

I had a feeling something more than the weather had brought about his burst of happiness.

"I think I'll take a box of your best chocolates. And ... could you wrap them up real pretty like? Maybe put a bow on top?"

"Certainly," I said. "A gift for somebody?"

"Yes, it is," and I heard the pleasure in his voice. "It's for Miss Raylene. I got around to asking her out—on a date. And she accepted."

I smiled as I began filling a box with truffles. "That's wonderful. Where are you taking her?"

"A fancy Italian restaurant in Gainesville. Do you think she'll like that?"

I pulled a piece of gold wrapping paper off the roll and nodded. "Oh, I'm sure she will. And with the chocolates, she'll be one happy woman."

"I sure hope so. Oh, and could you give me a pound of your chocolate clams too. No need to wrap those. They're for me. It's those chocolates, ya know."

I turned around to face him as I wrapped the box with white ribbon. "What do you mean?"

"Well, ever since I started eating those chocolates of yours— well, each day I seemed to get more confident with Miss Raylene, and finally . . . the other day, at the Senior Lunch, I just blurted it out. Came right out and told her I had a fondness for her and I'd like to accompany her to a lunch in Gainesville. And she said she'd love to. Now, doesn't that just beat all? It has to be your chocolate. I'm certain of it."

I smiled as I placed the bow on top of the package. "Hmm, so you think my chocolate has magical qualities?"

"I don't know much about magic or any of that. All I do know is that after a few months of eating that chocolate, why, I'm a whole new man."

I placed both boxes into a bag, rang up the sale, and passed them across the counter.

"Well, I'm very happy for you, Mr. Carl. When is this date scheduled for?"

"I'm picking Miss Raylene up Saturday morning about eleven. And I plan to give her the chocolates then. Do you think I should also get her a bouquet of flowers? Or would that be overdoing it?"

"Why don't you see how the date goes, and if it goes well, maybe have some flowers delivered to her. To thank her for a nice time."

He nodded his head emphatically. "Great idea. Thank you so much, Miss Berkley. You've been a big help to me and I appreciate it."

"My pleasure. Just be sure to give me a follow-up on that date," I told him as he turned to leave.

I stood by the door and watched him cross the street to the coffee café. Such a sweet man. And if he wanted to believe that it was my chocolate that had boosted his confidence, who was I to disagree?

The ringing phone pulled me out of my thoughts, and I answered to hear Flora's voice.

"Hey, Berkley. Do you have any plans for lunch today?"

"None at all. Why?"

"Because I'd like you to come over. I'm fixing up some soft-shell crabs. They just molted last night, so they're nice and fresh. I was up most of the night with them."

You have to babysit crabs? "Sure," I told her. "I can be over about noon."

A few hours later I walked up State Road 24 to Flora's house overlooking the bayou.

She opened the door with a warm welcome. "Come on in," she said as the aroma of garlic filled my senses.

Flora led the way through the small house out to a screen-enclosed porch with a great view of the salt marshes and water.

"How pretty," I said, taking a seat on one of the patio chairs.

"Yeah, I was always glad we could raise our kids in such a great spot. And now my grandson runs the soft-shell crab business that my husband started years ago."

There's a lot to be said for family continuity, I thought, and I felt proud that I was carrying on Gran's tradition with the chocolate shop.

I glanced down into the yard and saw tanks of water. "Is that for the crabs?" I asked.

Flora nodded. "That's where we keep them while they're getting ready to shed their shells. You need to grab them within three or four hours before the new shell hardens. That's why I was up with them all night. Once they back out of their shell, I remove them from the tank and they go into the freezer or refrigerator. How about a glass of sweet tea?"

"Sounds great," I said, standing up to get a better look at the glass tanks below me.

Flora poured from the plastic pitcher on the table.

"Thanks," I said, and took a sip. "Delicious." I might be a Yankee girl, but I'd quickly come to love the sweet tea the South was noted for. "This is quite a business you have going here."

"Oh, it was much larger during my husband's time. But my grandson gets enough of the crabs to sell to local restaurants, and we enjoy eating them too. Let me get our lunch," she said, heading back into the house.

"Can I help?"

"No, I'm all set," she hollered over her shoulder, and returned a minute later carrying a tray.

Flora placed a dish in front of me with crabs that had been sautéed in butter and garlic.

"And help yourself to some salad," she said, indicating the bowl before she sat down to join me.

I took a bite of the crab and smiled. "Oh, gosh, this is really delicious!"

Flora nodded. "Nothing quite as good as soft-shell crabs."

Neither of us spoke for a few moments as we enjoyed the delicacy.

"So, any luck finding something out about your mother?" she asked.

I took a bite of salad and shook my head. "I'm afraid not. Nobody seems to remember her being here. I did find out from one of the postcards she sent to my grandmother that she was working here though. She only mentioned a job, but didn't say exactly what she was doing."

Flora wiped her mouth with a napkin. "Hmm, there have never been that many jobs available on the island. Well, there's fishing and now clamming, but back in the seventies . . . beyond that, a young woman would have worked in one of the shops, done cleaning or maybe waitressing."

"I suppose she could have done any of those things, but wouldn't you think somebody would remember her?"

"Those employees came and went. And if it was just a summer job, all the more reason not to recall a person." Flora refilled her glass with sweet tea. "I do hope you'll find your answers, Berkley. Must have you feeling a bit lost to have a missing piece to your family history."

"Thanks, and yeah, it would be nice to finally understand why my mother came here."

"Any updates from Grace and Lucas? Are Chloe and Maude still planning to go to Paris?"

"Suellen heard from Grace the other day, and they're doing fine. They're down in the south of France for a couple weeks, traveling to different towns. Chloe changed her mind on going. Apparently her son is no longer working there. He got transferred to San Francisco, and Maude said they'd have to get somebody to look after the two dogs if they went, so they're not going. Both of them seemed fine with staying put here."

Flora laughed. "Yeah, Cedar Key has a way of doing that. Making one want to stay put."

I knew after finishing the crab and salad that I'd be having a light supper. This was confirmed when Flora brought out a funnel cake on a plate.

"Oh, that looks wonderful," I said, gazing at the puffed fried cake topped with confectioners' sugar. "Do you really use a funnel to make that?"

"We do. So the batter can't be too thick, because it has to fill the funnel, and then you release it into the oil in the skillet."

I took a bite and let out a groan. "This is *so* good, Flora."

"I'll give you a copy of the recipe before you leave."

Just a small thing, I know. Offering to share a recipe—but also another small expression of being accepted on the island.

22

A few days later I got a call from Saxton asking if I was free late Sunday afternoon.

"Well, I normally don't close the shop till five, but I can close earlier. Why? What's up?"

"Miss Maybelle called and asked if we could join her for tea around four."

"Absolutely," I said. "I'd love to."

"Great. I'll pick you up about three forty-five."

Saxton steered the golf cart over the airport bridge and took a right down a dirt road. He pulled into the driveway of the last house, which had an unobstructed view of the water.

"What a nice spot," I said, getting out and following him to the front door. "The flowers were really sweet of you, by the way." I nodded toward the large bouquet of vivid yellow and orange chrysanthemums.

Maybelle opened the door as soon as Saxton knocked, pulled it wide, and said, "Welcome, welcome. Oh, Saxton, you shouldn't have . . . but thank you." She accepted the flowers and gestured for us to have a seat in the small but cozy sitting room.

The cottage made me feel like I was stepping back in time. Ornate deep brown velvet furniture was arranged to flank the brick fireplace. Vintage lamps with satin shades and fringe perched atop pale pink marble tables. An exquisite oval shaped Persian carpet, in shades of beige and tan, covered the white tile floor beneath the furniture. Large framed paintings covered the pale yellow walls, and all of it was surrounded by glass windows on two sides from floor to ceiling.

"What a beautiful room," I said, as I seated myself in one of the cushy chairs.

"Thank you. It's my little sanctuary. Always has been. Let me get these in water and I'll just be a minute."

Maybelle walked around the counter, which separated the sitting area from a kitchen that looked like it could have been taken from a fifties television show. A candy red refrigerator and matching stove stood along one wall, while the other three walls had white cabinets with stenciled red strawberries along the edges. I smiled and couldn't help but feel that perhaps Maybelle was stuck in a time warp.

"Lovely," she said, placing the crystal vase on the counter. "Now I'll get our tea."

"Let me help," Saxton said, jumping up from the chair across from me.

He came back into the sitting room, placing a silver tray complete with silver teapot and Limoges cups, saucers, sugar, and creamer on the large marble coffee table.

Maybelle followed with another tray filled with bite-size sandwiches, scones, and pastries.

"Oh, my goodness," I said, leaning over for a better look. "This reminds me of afternoon tea at the Plaza."

"It is. Saxton, if you'll be so good as to uncork the champagne, we'll have a glass with the sandwiches."

I noticed a bottle of Veuve Clicquot chilling in a silver ice bucket on one of the end tables and heard a soft pop as Saxton expertly opened it. He filled three flutes, passed one to Maybelle and one to me, and then held his in the air.

"To the illustrious Miss Maybelle, as bubbly as the champagne and as sweet as the pastries."

She nodded, took a sip, and smiled. "Now then, help yourself," she said, passing me a plate. "We have strawberry and cream cheese sandwiches, these are smoked salmon, and those are cucumber, radish, and basil."

I was definitely beginning to feel I was back at the Plaza Hotel for my memorable tenth birthday. "I can hardly believe this," I said, reaching for one of the sandwiches. "My mother took me to the Plaza when I turned ten and I had the Eloise Tea."

"Really?" Saxton said, surprise covering his face.

"Ah, you were one of the lucky girls, weren't you? That's a memory that no little girl ever forgets." Maybelle delicately placed a salmon sandwich on her plate.

"Did you go there and have an Eloise Tea?" I asked, after taking a small bite of the strawberry and cream cheese sandwich that was every bit as tasty as I'd remembered it being.

Maybelle laughed. "I did, but not as a little girl." She took a sip of champagne and blotted her lips with a linen napkin. "I took my goddaughter there when she was eight."

"So she has a great memory just like I do," I said, fractions of a second before seeing the imperceptible shake of Saxton's head.

Awkward silence filled the room for a few moments, and then Maybelle cleared her throat. "I'm honestly not sure if Victoria remembers that event or not. Her mother, Dorothy, was my best friend since my Copa days, but when Victoria was about ten . . . well, we had a falling out."

"Oh, I'm sorry," I said.

"Yes. So am I. I adored that child, but it's been many years since we've been in touch."

It was obvious that whatever had caused the parting with her friend was a source of sadness for Maybelle.

"These sandwiches are just delicious," I said, in an attempt to change the subject.

"I'm glad you're enjoying them, and when we finish I'll show you some of my costumes as I promised."

Saxton reached for another sandwich and smiled. "And I think Maybelle has a story to go with each one of them."

"Had you always wanted to be a dancer in New York?" I asked.

Maybelle laughed, and I was glad that the mention of Dorothy and Victoria hadn't ruined her jovial mood. "Oh, my, yes. Always. By the time I was thirteen, I'd pretty much made up my mind that eight years of dance classes was going to be my ticket to fame. I left upper state New York and headed to the Big Apple the day after I turned eighteen. And I never looked back."

I'm sure there was a lot more to her story. It was obvious that she was a determined woman, and with her talent and motivation, she acquired whatever she set her sights on.

Conversation flowed about island stuff as we enjoyed the delicious scones, Devonshire cream, and raspberry preserves. The citrus flavor of the tea added to the overall experience.

Maybelle then brought out four of her costumes, covered in protective plastic. I sat beside Saxton on the sofa and momentarily felt like I was attending a Paris fashion show as I oohed and aahed over each one.

It was easy to understand how each costume set the tone and mood of each production. The combined texture, line, and shape of each garment must have been magnificent with the stage lighting.

I sighed as Maybelle brought out stunning gowns covered in beads, pearls, and jewels, along with white furs and stunning headpieces.

I had no doubt that she enjoyed every second of her display for us.

When she finished, she said, "Isn't that the wonderful thing about memories? They're with us forever. Now then, time for some pastries with a fresh pot of tea."

I was astonished when she brought out a platter filled with small squares of lemon tea cake and French macaroons. There was no doubt that Maybelle was back in her element and also that she had enormously enjoyed the baking and preparation for our tea.

When Saxton and I got back to my apartment four hours later, I let out a deep sigh.

"I hope she knows how much I enjoyed our time with her."

Saxton pulled me into an embrace as he kissed my forehead. "I'm pretty sure she does, and I'm glad you enjoyed it."

"Can I get you coffee, wine?"

He patted his stomach and smiled. "Oh, no, but thanks. They might call it *tea* but it's really a meal."

I laughed and joined him on the sofa. "I know. All of it was really wonderful. What a great person she is. So you know her pretty well?"

"Maybelle was one of the first people I met when I moved here. She had been reading my books for quite a few years, it seems. Used to order them special from England. So when she found out I had moved here, she wasted no time showing up on my doorstep to introduce herself as one of my biggest fans."

"No! Did she really?"

"Yes, she really did. Maybelle isn't shy. But she was so delightful that I asked her if she'd like to join me for a cup of tea on the deck. She accepted, and the rest is history. I consider her a very good friend."

"What *is* her history? Was she ever married? Any children? Do you know what caused that rift with her friend Dorothy?"

"Except for her Copa days, she doesn't talk about herself much. I do know she was never married, no children, but she did adore that goddaughter, Victoria. And no, she never told me why she and Dorothy parted ways."

"And Victoria hasn't been in touch with her either? Gosh, she'd probably be in her thirties or forties now, wouldn't she?"

"Probably, and no, she never saw or heard from Victoria again. Rather sad, and I'm sure it bothers her. By the way, I had no idea your mother took you to the Plaza for a birthday celebration."

I nodded. "Yeah, to be honest, although Maybelle said that's something a little girl never forgets . . . I hadn't thought about that in years. My mother and I took the train from Boston to New York. We certainly didn't stay at the Plaza. She had booked us into a small hotel for three nights. We did all the usual touristy things. Took the carriage ride around Central Park, went to the top of the Empire State Building, a boat ride around Battery Park, but the highlight was the Eloise Tea at the Plaza. I had read the Eloise book, and I strongly related to her. An only child, spent more time with a nanny rather than her mother, and a bit precocious, as I could be. I didn't have a nanny, but I spent a lot of time with my grandmother."

Saxton reached for my hand and gave it a squeeze.

"So you do have some nice memories of time spent with your mother."

I did, and wondered if it was *resentment* that kept me from thinking about them more often.

23

Two days later Saxton and I left Cedar Key and headed to the northeast Georgia Mountains. I knitted for much of the eight-hour drive as we kept up nonstop conversation.

Adding another skein of yarn to the emerald green cable sweater I was working on, I said, "Gee, I hope Chloe remembers to give Sigmund the ice water in the fridge. He likes his water nice and cold."

"That was good of her to offer to watch him while we're away, and you left her a list, so I'm sure she'll refer to it."

I nodded and kept knitting.

A little while later, I looked out the windshield and could now see mountains in the distance. "Oh, look. We must be getting close."

"Yup. We should be at the cabin within the hour."

After driving down a dirt road between Ellijay and Blue Ridge, we pulled up in front of the log home about five-thirty, and as soon as I stepped out of the car I inhaled the fresh, cool mountain air.

"This is great," I said, looking around. Huge trees were filled with leaves of yellow, orange, and red, and I could just make out a pond in back of the house.

Saxton came over, stood behind me, and wrapped his arms around my waist as he nuzzled my neck. "I think we'll enjoy our stay here."

I turned around and his lips met mine. When we broke apart, I wondered if we'd be utilizing both bedrooms after all.

Saxton took a deep breath and popped the trunk open with his remote. "We may as well take in one piece of luggage," he said, reaching for one of his bags.

"Good idea." I pulled out my black canvas bag containing toiletries before following Saxton up three steps to the deck.

He unlocked a double set of French doors and we stepped into a gorgeous living room with both a pitched ceiling and walls covered with honey-color wood. A cushy sofa filled with pillows faced a fieldstone fireplace that reached to the ceiling. I glanced at the paisley fabric club chair with matching ottoman and thought it would be a perfect spot for knitting.

"Very pretty," I said as Saxton led the way to a beautiful kitchen with cherrywood cabinets and granite countertops.

Another set of French doors led out to a screen-enclosed deck where I saw a wooden swing, a large hot tub, and a patio set, all of which overlooked a pond surrounded by trees.

"Bedrooms and bath must be down this way," he said, heading down a hallway.

I stepped into the first bedroom on the left and saw an oak four-poster king-size bed. Very nicely decorated and cozy. Off the bedroom was an elegant bathroom complete with Jacuzzi tub.

"Why don't you take this one?" Saxton said, and walked across the hallway.

"Oh, this is nice too." I stood beside him and saw this room also had a king-size bed and attached bathroom.

"Okay," he said, pulling me into an embrace. "I think the sleeping arrangements are sorted out. Let's get the rest of the stuff out of the car and then we can settle in."

We made two more trips and I placed the picnic basket on top of the kitchen counter.

"That'll do it. I'm glad I thought to bring our supper for tonight. Now we don't have to leave to go out to eat."

"You're a good planner," Saxton said as he removed three bottles of wine from a bag.

I smiled and nodded. "So are you. I'm going to get unpacked."

"Me too, and I'll have a glass of wine waiting for you when you're finished."

When I walked into the living room, not only was a glass of wine waiting for me, but Saxton already had the fire roaring.

"Oh, that looks great," I said, walking up beside him. I reached my hand out toward the flames. "Nice and warm too."

"Yeah, as soon as that sun goes down it begins to get pretty nippy here in the mountains. Here you go," he said, passing me a wineglass. "Here's to our first getaway together and here's to us."

I touched the rim of his glass with mine. "To us," I said before taking a sip. "This is very good. What is it?"

"It's a Barbera. Originated in the hills of Monferrato, in central Piemonte, Italy."

I took another sip and allowed the robust flavor to touch my palate. "I definitely like it."

"Good, I'm glad." Saxton took my hand, leading me to the sofa.

I curled up next to him and gazed at the flames flickering in the fireplace. The log house, the wine, the fire, but most of all Saxton, gave me a secure feeling—a feeling of permanence and stability.

"Thank you," I told him. "Thank you for inviting me here with you."

He kissed the top of my head. "I'm glad you agreed to come. I think we'll have a nice five days here."

"Where are we going tomorrow?" I asked, sitting up straighter. All of a sudden, I felt like a kid on a summer vacation.

"Anywhere you'd like. There's lots of great towns around and we can explore all of them. Murphy, North Carolina, is a short drive from here. A cute little place that reminds me of Mayberry R.F.D."

"Sounds like fun. Then Murphy it is."

We finished our wine and I headed to the kitchen. "Why don't you get some nice music going on that CD player and I'll set out our supper," I told him.

I reached into the basket and removed a cooked ham before popping a dish of scalloped potatoes into the microwave to heat. I found placemats, plates, and silverware and got the table set. After removing the scalloped potatoes, I placed a bowl of green bean casserole into the microwave and then lit the candles on the table. Stepping back to assess my work, I smiled. All of a sudden I felt like a proper housewife arranging a seductive dinner for her husband.

Strains of Vivaldi filled the room as Saxton joined me.

"Looks great," he said, placing a kiss on my cheek before we sat down.

It *was* great, and when we finished, Saxton helped with the cleanup.

"Maybe we can finish our wine on the deck," he said, tugging a black sweatshirt over his head. "But you'll probably need a sweater or something."

I grabbed an Irish knit sweater that I'd knitted years ago from my bureau drawer, and on the way out of my room, I paused outside of Saxton's door and peeked in. Good Lord! We'd only been in the house a few hours, yet his bedroom looked like a mini-tornado had swept through. Pants were flung across the bed, shirts and sweaters were stacked on the bureau, and one piece of luggage lay open on the floor, empty but not put away. I shook my head and let out a deep sigh. I might be falling in love with this man—but I wasn't at all sure I could cope with his messy lifestyle.

I joined him on the deck and sat beside him on the swing, reaching for the wineglass he held out.

"Thanks," I said as my body caught the synchronized motion.

After a few minutes Saxton put an arm around my shoulders. "Anything wrong?"

I debated whether to be honest or push aside my concerns. I went for honest. "Well...I was...kinda wondering....Is there any reason why you didn't unpack properly and hang up your clothes and use the bureau?"

He threw his head back laughing. Was nothing serious to this man?

"Ah, got a peek in my room, did you?"

When he didn't offer an explanation, I shifted to face him, waiting for an answer.

"Well, I'm on vacation," he said, as if that accounted for the condition of his bedroom.

I resisted telling him that based on the clutter I'd observed in his house, he must be on a permanent vacation.

"Does it bother you?" he asked.

"I guess it does. Otherwise, I wouldn't have mentioned it."

"Hmm, you really are a bit compulsive with orderliness, aren't you?"

"It doesn't have a thing to do with being compulsive," I said, annoyance lacing my words. "It has to do with simply being tidy."

He pulled me close as his lips touched mine. Damn. The man might surround himself with clutter, but he was a great kisser.

"I promise," he said, between nibbling on my lower lip, "I'll get . . . everything . . . straightened up . . . in there."

I nodded as I lost myself to the passion of his kiss.

When he pulled away, he buried his face in my neck. "Good thing," he whispered in my ear, "that we're not sharing the same room, huh?"

I smiled. After those kisses I wasn't so sure about that.

And a few hours later when I got into my bed—I was less sure.

❧ 24 ❧

I woke the next morning to the aroma of coffee and bacon filling my nostrils. Turning over, I glanced at the bedside clock. *Eight-thirty? God! I never sleep this late at home!*

After using the bathroom, I slipped into a pair of sweats and padded down the hallway to the kitchen. What greeted me caused a deep whoosh of air to escape from my lungs.

Saxton stood at the stove stirring something in a cast iron fry pan. The orderly kitchen of the night before now looked like a four-year-old had been let loose unsupervised. The counter was covered with bowls, utensils, a carton of eggs, milk, and other assorted items. The kitchen table held pages of a newspaper in disarray, and the sink was filled with enough plates and bowls to require two loads in the dishwasher.

Saxton looked up, saw me, and smiled. "Good morning, beautiful. Since you were still sleeping, I ran down to Blue Ridge and got us some things so I could make breakfast." He proceeded to fill a bowl with scrambled eggs from the fry pan, glanced at me again, and saw the look on my face. "Oh, don't worry about the mess. I'll have it all cleaned up in a jiffy. Go on out to the deck. I have the table all set for us."

He went to the coffeepot, filled a mug, and passed it to me after leaning over to place a kiss on my lips. "Here you go. I'll be right out."

I walked to the deck and let out a deep sigh. The sun was shining and just a hint of burning leaves filled the air. I sat down and took a sip of dark, rich coffee as I focused on my surroundings. Quiet. Peaceful. I felt another sigh escape me and glanced to the mountains that rose up to meet the blue sky.

"Hope you like scrambled eggs and bacon," Saxton said, coming onto the deck with a tray. "I also got some homemade pumpkin muffins." He started to sit down but jumped back up. "The juice. Got us some fresh apple juice."

When he finally sat down, I glanced across the table and felt a lump in my throat. All of a sudden, the disaster in the kitchen didn't matter. He had gone to all this trouble for me. *For me.* I knew without a doubt that he was one of the sweetest men I'd met in a long time. Reaching across the table, I squeezed his hand.

"Thank you," I said. "Thank you so much for this breakfast. It was a really nice thing to do."

"I just hope it's good." Saxton shot me a smile as he spooned eggs onto his plate.

I helped myself to bacon, eggs, and a muffin, and then took a sip of juice.

"This is really good."

"It's from the apple orchard in town, Mercier's. We'll have to go there. Great place to shop and get cider and apples."

Despite the mess in the kitchen, the bacon and eggs were cooked to perfection.

"I love these eggs," I told him. "What'd you put in them?"

Saxton laughed. "Ah, a good chef never gives away his recipes."

I joined his laughter.

"Did you sleep well?" he asked.

"I did. And I can't believe I slept so late. You should have woken me earlier."

"Why? You're on vacation. You get up early every morning at home, so I thought you could use a break."

"What time did you get up? You've already been downtown, shopped, and cooked breakfast."

"About six. I called Doyle to check on Lola. He said she's doing just fine staying with him. He'd never admit it, but I think he likes having her around. I've left her at his house a few times when I've had to go on book tours."

After I had cleaned my plate and even taken a second helping of the delicious eggs, I finished my second cup of coffee, stood, and stretched.

"That was really delicious, Saxton. Thanks again."

"I'm glad you enjoyed it. Well, let me get everything cleaned up while you shower and get ready, and then we'll head to Murphy."

"Oh, I'll help with the cleanup," I said, feeling a bit guilty for being so tough on him.

"No, no. I made the mess. I'll clean it up. Now scoot," he said, tapping my backside playfully.

When I reentered the kitchen it was like fairies had appeared in my absence. True to his word, Saxton had the kitchen back in shape.

He was hanging a dish towel on the rack and I walked behind him, slipping my arms around his waist.

"Good job," I said. "There might be hope for you yet."

He laughed and swung around to pull me into his arms.

His kiss mingled with the taste of toothpaste, and his aftershave had an intoxicating woodsy scent. This man was definitely hot, and at the moment, Murphy, North Carolina, was the last thing on my mind.

He broke away and cupped my face in his hands.

"If we don't stop . . . we may never leave this place for the entire day."

And that would be a bad thing?

"Right," I mumbled.

I gathered my tote bag and took his outstretched hand.

"Bringing along a picnic lunch?" he kidded me, pointing to my bag.

I smiled. "Hey, I'm a woman who's always prepared." I peeked inside my large black leather bag. "Camera, makeup, guidebook, sunglasses, two bottles of water, and knitting. Yup, I'm all set."

"You're a delight," he said, laughing, and I followed him out to the car.

Saxton had been right—Murphy was a cute little town that looked like a setting from a fifties television show.

The main street had older brick buildings, which had been restored to their original state, lining both sides. Located in the heart of the Appalachian Mountains, it was the county seat of Cherokee County.

As we strolled along holding hands, glancing in shop windows, I had to admit the town did remind me of a Norman Rockwell painting.

"There's a coffee shop across the street," Saxton said. "Feel like a cup and we can sit outside?"

"Sounds great."

When I entered the shop it was like stepping back to my childhood days in Salem. A hardwood floor, shelves stocked with jars of penny candy, a Formica soda fountain with stools, and a friendly proprietor with a huge smile.

"Welcome to Murphy," she said.

"Thanks," Saxton told her. "Can we get two coffees to go?"

"Absolutely. Where're you from?" she asked as she proceeded to prepare it.

Watching her get the coffee brought a smile to my face and made me realize it wasn't the fifties after all—she took two pods of coffee and inserted them into the Keurig coffee brewer.

"Cedar Key, Florida," I heard Saxton tell her.

"Well, here you go," she said, passing two cups across the counter as he paid her.

We found a table outside where we sat soaking up the wonderful autumn sunshine.

"You know," I said. "This might not be such a good idea, this vacation getaway. I could get used to this very easy."

Saxton laughed. "Good. That was the point. I'm on deadline for March, so when we get back I'll have to buckle down and get some writing done. But in the meantime, we'll enjoy it. Do you want to have lunch or do an early dinner?"

"I'm still full from breakfast, so an early dinner might be good."

"Great. We'll go into Blairsville later. There's a couple good Italian restaurants there."

By the time we got back to the cabin it was close to eight o'clock. I was loaded down with shopping bags with Christmas gifts I'd been able to find. The Essence of Rose in Blairsville had wonderful locally made candles that I knew Chloe and Suellen would love. And I found the perfect necklace for Grace at the shop next door. We had a delicious Italian dinner at Antoinetta's, and by the time I plunked onto the sofa and kicked off my shoes, I was ready to relax.

"Whew, this touristy stuff can be tiring," I said.

"How about a glass of wine? I have some Sangiovese."

"Sounds wonderful," I said, stifling a yawn.

Saxton uncorked the bottle, poured two glasses, and joined me on the sofa.

"Here's to a fun day." He touched his glass with mine.

I nodded and took a sip. "Delicious, and it was a fun day. I really enjoyed it. Where to tomorrow?"

He laughed. "You're a glutton for punishment, huh?"

"Well, I don't want to miss anything."

"Tomorrow we can hit Blue Ridge. Have lunch in town, you can browse the shops, and then we can go to the apple orchard."

"Sounds like fun. What time does the tour bus leave?"

Saxton leaned over and kissed my cheek. "Whenever you say. Sleep in and enjoy it while you can."

I had to admit that sounded mighty appealing.

"One of these evenings we have to take advantage of that hot tub out there," he said, waving a hand toward the deck. "You did bring a swimsuit, didn't you?"

"I did. Why don't we have dinner in tomorrow evening and just relax in that hot tub?"

"Good idea. We can get dinner to go at Taste of Naples, another great Italian restaurant."

Even though it was just after nine, I had a hard time keeping my eyes open. I took the last sip of wine and stood up.

"I hope you don't mind, but I'm wiped."

Saxton took the glasses and put them on the kitchen counter. "I am too," he said. "This mountain air is good for sleeping."

He walked with me down the hallway and paused outside my room. Leaning toward me, his lips brushed mine as he pulled me into an embrace.

"Good night, Berkley. Sweet dreams. I'll turn off the lights and check the doors."

I stifled another yawn and nodded. "Thanks again for a great day," I said, before walking into my room and closing the door.

25

I was awakened the next morning by the ringing of my cell phone and answered to hear Jill's voice.

"You weren't still sleeping, were you? Or *otherwise* engaged?"

I rubbed my eyes and saw the clock read 8:05. "Get your mind out of the gutter," I told her as I swung my legs to the side of the bed.

Jill's laughter came across the line. "Oh, Berkley, don't be such a prude. You're on a getaway with a handsome guy. What? You're sleeping in separate beds?"

"As a matter of fact, we are."

I heard the gasp from Jill. "No! Seriously?"

"Yes. Seriously," I said, heading to the bathroom. "Hold on. I need to pee."

I placed the phone on the bedside table and could still hear Jill chattering away.

A few minutes later, I retrieved the phone. "I'm back. What's up?"

"What's up? You tell me. You *were* joking about separate beds, right?"

"No, I was perfectly serious. The cabin is a two bedroom, two bath. I have my own space. What's wrong with that?"

"Well...uh...nothing. I guess. If that's what you want." I could hear the surprise in her voice.

Was this what I wanted? I honestly wasn't sure.

"Saxton booked a two-bedroom place," I told her, as if trying to justify the situation.

"Right. And it's certainly up to you if you choose to spend this time with him like a nun. I'm just surprised. I thought you told me that you agreed to have an exclusive relationship with him. Which I understood to mean that you were attracted to him—that there was a chemistry going on there."

I recalled Saxton's kisses. "Oh, there is. Definitely. I think I just need more time. I don't want what we have to just be about the sex."

Jill's laughter filled the line. "I don't think you have to worry about that, Berkley. You've known each other for seven months."

Hmm, she had a point.

"Anyway, I just called to see if you were having a good time and...to tell you that I'm definitely coming to Cedar Key for Thanksgiving. If that's okay with you."

I pumped my arm in the air. "Yes! Of course it's okay. Oh, Jill, that's great. I miss you and it'll be great spending time together next month."

"I was hoping you'd say that. I booked a flight into Gainesville, will rent a car there, and drive to the island. You said the airport is about an hour from Cedar Key?"

"Yup. Oh, no..."

"What's wrong?"

"Does this mean I'll have to cook a turkey?"

"Oh, God! You're right," she said, and I know she was remembering a past Thanksgiving when I'd offered to make the bird. The only problem was, I'd forgotten to ever turn the oven on.

I laughed. "Now, now. You said I was forgiven for that fiasco, and I promise to make sure I *cook* the turkey this time."

"Great. I'm flying in on Wednesday, the day before. I can't wait to see you."

"Same here. I'll call you next week after I get home. Love you."

I walked into the kitchen with the aroma of coffee greeting me again but no smell of bacon in the air and no Saxton. I peeked through the French doors and saw him engrossed in the newspaper. Filling a mug with coffee, I joined him.

"Good morning," I said, leaning over to place a kiss on his cheek.

He looked up and a smile covered his face as he pulled me close. "Good morning. Did you sleep well?"

"I did." I pulled up the chair beside him. "All this fresh mountain air is making me quite lazy."

"Well, I hope you're all rested because I thought maybe we'd grab a big breakfast in Blue Ridge, rather than lunch, and then go to the apple orchard."

"Sounds like a plan. I'll finish this coffee and hit the shower."

Saxton was right. I did love the Mercier apple orchard. We had fun strolling the aisles together, and I was amazed at all the various products they sold. All kinds of preserves, different varieties of apples for both eating and baking, and one entire room dedicated to Christmas decorations. Their bakery was to die for, and three pies ended up in our basket along with all the other items.

After we filled the trunk of the car with our purchases, Saxton checked his watch.

"We have time to take a drive over to Ellijay, if you want."

"Let's do it," I told him.

I also fell in love with this small town. A few streets for shopping surrounded a small park area with a fountain in the center of town. We found a great place to sit outside and have coffee before we walked along, browsing in shops.

By the time we got back to the car and headed out of town it was going on four o'clock.

"We may as well go to the restaurant now and get our dinner to go," Saxton said. "We can always heat it up later in the microwave."

* * *

"Oh, I almost forgot to tell you," I said, as I stretched out in the warm water of the hot tub. "Jill called me this morning and she's coming to Cedar Key for Thanksgiving."

"That's great. I'm sure you'll be happy to see her. Have you heard from your aunt yet? You said she might also be there for the holiday."

I reached for my glass of wine and took a sip. "Not yet. Oh, gee . . . I just realized . . . I was going to extend an invitation to Mr. Carl and Raylene too. So that would be six, and I don't have enough room in my kitchen to seat that many."

Saxton patted my hand. "Not to worry. We can have the dinner at my place. Between the deck and the dining room, I have plenty of room."

"Really? You wouldn't mind?"

"Not at all, and maybe we can invite Miss Maybelle too. Sometimes she likes to dine at the Island Hotel for Thanksgiving dinner, but we can ask her."

"That would be great. Thanks. I'm glad we finally got around to using this hot tub. I'm beginning to feel like Jell-O in here. It's *so* relaxing."

Saxton nodded. "Hmm, maybe I should get one installed on my deck. That is, if you promise to join me."

"I promise," I said, and as I turned my head his lips found mine.

"I like this," he whispered in my ear as his hand caressed my body. "Being with you like this."

"I . . . do . . . too," I told him as I tried to catch my breath. This man had a way of kissing that notched up my desire to a level I hadn't felt in a long time.

"I want you, Berkley," he said, his voice husky.

I knew it wasn't just the wine causing my body to react to his touch.

His kisses covered my nose, my cheek, my chin, before finding my lips again.

When he pulled away, he took a deep breath. "I didn't think I'd ever feel this way again. I wasn't sure I wanted to . . . but I've fallen in love with you, Berkley. I love you."

All the years of being alone, all the years of thinking I didn't want to be involved with somebody, instantly vanished. I allowed myself to be in the moment. To feel this man beside me, to feel the passion he aroused in me and to feel the magic of not only loving, but being loved in return.

"I love you too, Saxton," I whispered.

He stood up as he stretched out his hand. "Come on," he said, and then wrapped a fluffy bath towel around me.

I followed him into the house, down the hallway, and into my bedroom.

26

As soon as I opened my eyes the following morning, I knew something was different. Stretched out beside me was Saxton, and I heard the soft sound of his breathing. Turning my head slightly, I gazed at his sleeping face. He was one handsome man. And after last night I knew he was also one incredible lover. Gentle yet passionate. We had shared an intimacy I couldn't recall sharing with another man.

I let out a sigh and allowed myself to relive the moments of the night before. My fingertip stroked his cheek and I smiled as he began to stir.

Shifting onto my side, I felt his hand reach out, and he placed it on my thigh as he opened his eyes, a smile covering his face.

"Good morning, beautiful. I love you."

"Good morning, handsome. I love you too," I said as I relished waking to those words.

His fingers drew circles on my inner thigh, and I luxuriated in the act of making love with a man I not only loved but felt a deep connection with.

"Coffee could be a little late this morning," he whispered as he edged closer to me. "I hope you don't mind."

At the moment, coffee was the last thing on my mind.

* * *

Later that afternoon, we sat at an outdoor restaurant in Dahlonega, holding hands and having a hard time keeping smiles from our faces.

"After we eat, we can walk around the shops," Saxton said.

"It's most unusual for a man to enjoy shopping, you know."

The smile on his face increased. "Oh, I'm not sure I'd go that far. But I do enjoy being with you. Besides, you don't take hours on end in the shops like some women do."

"Well, I do know I want to stop at that chocolate shop we saw as we drove into town."

"Ah, you have to make a comparison to your chocolate and Angell and Phelps?"

I laughed. "Yeah, something like that. But I have no doubt theirs doesn't have the magical quality that mine does."

"I have to agree with that—everything about you is magical. I have a question for you though."

"Yes, I most definitely love you."

Now Saxton laughed and shook his head. "That's very good to know, and I love you too. But . . . I've never mentioned it . . . however . . . is there a reason you have that purple streak in your hair?"

I took a sip of ice water and shifted to see him better. "Before I answer that, I have a question for you. Why has it taken you so long to ask me that?"

"Well, I guess because . . . I honestly don't know." He let out another laugh. "And it isn't that I don't like it. It's part of who you are, so I guess I'm just curious."

"I'm not sure I have an answer for you. A few years ago after I broke up with the guy I'd been seeing, I wanted something different. Maybe I wanted to *be* different. I thought about a nose ring or a tattoo . . . but ended up deciding the purple streak in my hair was enough of a change."

Saxton squeezed my hand. "I'm glad that's the choice you went with."

"Gosh, tomorrow's our last day here," I said, as the waitress placed quiche and a cup of soup in front of me.

"Will you be sad to go home?"

I shook my head. "Not at all. This has been incredibly wonderful. I've loved every single minute, but... it'll be good to get home."

"And tomorrow we'll drive to Helen. It's a cute little Alpine village. I think you'll like it there."

I leaned over to kiss his cheek. "I've loved all of this... and especially you."

When we hit the Number Four bridge on Sunday afternoon, I let out a deep sigh. Saxton slowed the car to the requisite thirty miles per hour and I soaked in the view on both sides—shimmering blue water, patches of sawgrass, pelicans swooping—and I knew I was blessed. Not only did I live in a slice of paradise, but the man I loved was beside me.

We had mutually decided to spend the night at our own places. I had just finished unpacking when there was a knock on the door. Saxton changing his mind? But I opened the door to find Chloe with a casserole dish in her hand.

"Welcome home. I didn't think you'd want to cook, so I made you a tuna casserole. Nothing fancy but thought you might like it."

"That was so nice of you. Come on in. Did you eat yet or can you share some with me?"

"I was hoping you'd ask," she said, and followed me into the kitchen.

"I'll pop some biscuits into the oven to go with it. Wine? Tea?"

"Oh, a glass of wine would be good. Gosh, we were busy at the yarn shop today," she said, removing a cabernet from my wine rack.

"Busy is good." I placed two glasses on the table for her to fill.

"And guess who dropped by and will be starting the beginners' knitting class?"

I shook my head.

"Ava. Ava Wells. She's pregnant! Can you imagine? After all these years. Due in March, and she's over the moon. Says it's all due to your chocolate." Chloe laughed and passed me a glass.

"Get outta here! Really? That's great, but I doubt my chocolate had much to do with it. Here's to Ava," I said, lifting my glass in the air.

"Well, you'll have a hard time trying to tell her otherwise. She's convinced it was your signature chocolate clams that did it."

I thought of Mr. Carl and Miss Raylene, but refrained from saying any more. "Thank you so much for watching Sigmund for me."

"Oh, he's a sweetie. Very easy to care for. So I take it you had a good time?"

"The best. It gave Saxton and me a chance to really get to know each other. We're very compatible in almost every way."

"Almost?"

I laughed. "Well, he tends to be a bit untidy, but I think we can work through that."

"Keep separate living quarters?" Chloe chuckled and took a sip of wine.

I popped the biscuits into the oven and joined her at the table. "We haven't discussed living together, so I guess that's a solution."

"I take it this has climbed up to serious?"

I let out a deep sigh. "I think you could say that. I thought I had fallen in love with him before we went on the trip, and over the five days together we both admitted it to each other."

"That's great, Berkley. I'm really happy for you."

"Oh, before I forget. My friend Jill is coming next month for Thanksgiving. I'm not sure what your plans are, but I want you to know you and Cameron are invited too."

"Thanks, but we'll probably have dinner at Aunt Maude's with Grace and Lucas."

"How're they doing? Any update on when they'll be back?"

"November first. I have to admit, after six months, I'm really missing my sister. I'll be glad when they get home."

I removed the casserole from the microwave and the biscuits from the oven.

"Thanks again for supper tonight, Chloe," I said as I placed it on the table.

"My pleasure. Plus I missed you. So I figured we needed to catch up."

I took a bite of casserole. "Delicious. Yeah, there's something special about female friendships, isn't there?"

She nodded. "The thing is, I thought I had female friendships when I lived on St. Simons Island. But I know now they were only superficial. Women I knew from fund-raisers or the garden club or whatever. None of them were true friends. Not like I have here with you and Grace and Suellen."

I knew the feeling. Except for Jill, I had never had genuine friendships with women until I moved to Cedar Key.

"Are you and Dora all set for Seafood Festival next weekend?"

"Oh, yeah. By the way, will you have that yarn you mentioned? The skeins with different shades of green?"

"I'll finish spinning it tomorrow and definitely have it ready for you. That reminds me, I'd better give Angell and Phelps a call. I'll be needing more of their chocolate for the weekend."

"Looks like we have a busy week ahead."

After Chloe left, I got into my pajamas, curled up with Sigmund on the sofa, and knitted till bedtime. I was just about to shut off the lights and head to bed when the phone rang.

"Just wanted to call and say good night. I miss you, Berkley, and I love you."

"I miss you too." And I did. It would seem odd not falling asleep beside Saxton. "Are we still meeting for lunch tomorrow at noon?"

"Absolutely. I'll meet you at the Pickled Pelican. Good night."

"Good night, Saxton. I love you."

I got into bed, lay there for a few minutes, and then reached over and snapped off the light.

❧ 27 ❧

"She's what?" I said, and leaned across the table because surely I had just misunderstood what Saxton had told me.

He let out a sigh, ran his hand through his curls, took a sip of sweet tea, and nodded. "I know. I could hardly believe it either. I mean, God, I was thrilled that Resa agreed to come to Cedar Key. But with her mother? I certainly wasn't expecting that."

Obviously, neither was I. "So Muriel will be coming with her?"

"Apparently so," he said, and took another gulp of tea.

I couldn't account for it, but a ripple of jealousy spread through me. They had been divorced for years—why should her visit matter to me?

"I see. So when are they coming?"

"In two weeks. They arrive on November first for three nights. Muriel has already booked a room for them at the bed and breakfast. They're flying into Gainesville, will rent a car, and drive here."

I took a sip of ice water and nodded. "Well . . . I'm sure you're thrilled that you'll be seeing your daughter again. I know you'll enjoy that. Did she say why her mother was coming with her?"

"Resa said her husband couldn't take time from his schedule to accompany her and she didn't want to come alone, which I can understand. After so many years, it might be a bit awkward. I just hope the meeting goes well."

I did too. I really did.

"Listen," he said, reaching to take my hand. "I was hoping you'd join us for a dinner. I'd love for you to meet Resa and, well, we are a couple now. I thought I'd also invite Doyle so he can meet her."

Oh, great. Meeting his daughter was one thing—but the ex-wife too? I knew I should be a big girl about it, and said, "Sure. That would be fine. I'd love to meet your daughter."

He gave my hand a squeeze, causing me to feel a tiny bit guilty for my jealous thoughts.

"Okay, I'll book the Island Room for one of the evenings that they're here."

The child in me kicked in again. *Oh, goody,* I thought.

I returned home from lunch to find a message from my aunt on the recorder.

I dialed the number and heard her chirpy voice answer.

"This is Berkley. How're you doing?"

"Oh, ever so much better. I'm back on two legs again. But I guess my salsa dancing days are over. I'll just have to find another pastime, like I don't have enough already."

Her chuckle came across the line. "I wanted to let you know that I will be coming for Thanksgiving. I called and booked the Faraway Inn for Addi and me, and we're all set. I'm driving down on Tuesday, if that's okay with you."

"Oh, that's great. I can't wait to see you. Listen, I was wondering if you could do me a favor. Do you happen to have any older photos of my mother?"

"Hmm, gee, I'm not really sure. We weren't much of a photo-taking family. But I'll see what I can do. Any particular reason you want her photos?"

I smiled. "Oh, yeah, but it's a long story and I'll fill you in when you get here."

"Sounds intriguing. Well, I'll see you in about six weeks, but I'll be in touch before that."

On Thursday evening I walked into Yarning Together and was surprised to find it busier than usual.

Dora greeted me with a hug. "Come on in. We have five new additions to our group tonight."

I saw Leigh Sallenger with her two daughters fumbling with needles as Chloe attempted to teach them the basics of knitting. Across the room Miss Maybelle was sitting next to Maude, her lap overflowing with a soft cloud of beige cashmere in the process of becoming a gorgeous sweater. It was then that Ava Wells looked up, dropped her needles with a few rows of yellow stitches, and came running over to me.

"Did you hear my news?" she said, filled with excitement. "I'm pregnant! And all due to your chocolates."

"Oh, honey," Flora said. "I seriously doubt it was *all* due to those chocolates."

I joined the laughter that broke out. "I did hear, and I'm so happy for you. Whatever the cause. You're due in March?"

"Yes, and I decided the time had come for me to learn to knit. So Maude is helping me to make a baby blanket."

I leaned over to give her a hug. "That's wonderful, and congratulations. Both on the baby and learning to knit. I bet in no time at all you'll be making all kinds of beautiful things for that baby."

I grabbed an empty chair next to Suellen and brought out the lace socks I'd started that morning.

"Oh, nice," Suellen said, leaning over for a better look. "I love that pattern, and the ecru color makes them look vintage."

"Yeah, I found the pattern online at Ravelry. Thought they might be nice for winter, but not too heavy."

"So," she said as her voice dropped to a whisper. "What's this I hear about the ex coming to Cedar Key?"

"Chloe told you, huh? Yup. Seems Saxton's daughter is coming to visit but she's bringing mommy dearest with her."

"Uh-oh. Do I detect a hint of tension there?"

I shrugged. "I just don't understand *why* she'd even want to come. They've been divorced for years and out of touch."

"Hmm."

I looked over at Suellen. "What's that supposed to mean?"

"Well, Chloe said her recent husband passed away. So maybe she just wants to reconnect again. You know . . . for the daughter's sake. So I take it you have a problem with this?"

"I don't know. I'm just not real pleased that she'll be spending three days here with him."

"Yeah, but the daughter will be with them too, and aren't you going out for dinner with them? You'll be able to draw your own conclusions on the ex when you meet her."

"That's what I'm afraid of. She's probably going to be drop-dead gorgeous. Lived in New York for years and then Seattle. Those are pretty trendy places."

Suellen stopped knitting to look at me. "Hey, I don't think you're being fair to Saxton. You're not giving him any credit at all. He loves you. That's pretty obvious just by the way he looks at you. I don't think you have a thing to worry about."

I hoped Suellen was right and changed the subject. "That's really great that Leigh and her daughters are also learning to knit."

"I know. She said when they were here last spring they all fell in love with the different yarns. Paula now has her GED and will be starting college classes in January, so she thought knitting might be a nice break for her between studying. And Paige is at a good age to learn, so Leigh thought it would be a fun thing for them to do together."

"I didn't know that Miss Maybelle also knitted."

"Oh, gosh, yes. I guess she and Dora have been friends for years, and both of them have knitted since they were small girls. I'm glad she joined us tonight. She's such a sweetie."

I looked up as Dora was clapping her hands together.

"Ladies, Maude and I were just talking about Thanksgiving. Making sure that everyone has a place to go for dinner. I'll be having my entire family this year. I'm so glad that Sydney and Noah won't be in France again and my daughter, Marin, will be coming, along with Monica, Adam, and the children. And my good friend, Maybelle, just accepted my invitation."

"Oh, Saxton and I were going to invite you," I said. "But I'm glad you'll be with Dora. I'm having my friend Jill from Maine, and my aunt Stella will also be here. I'll be doing the cooking, but we'll eat at Saxton's house because he has more room."

"I've been invited to Maude's house for dinner," Suellen said.

Dora looked over at Leigh, who had remained quiet. "You're not able to cook a turkey dinner in that travel trailer, are you? What are your plans?"

"Well . . . we thought . . . maybe this year we'd skip the turkey dinner."

Without hesitating, I blurted out, "Absolutely not! The three of you will join us at Saxton's house. There's going to be plenty of food and plenty of room."

Leigh's face lit up. "Are you sure? We don't want to impose."

"It's not an imposition at all. We'd love to have you, and that's settled."

I looked over and caught the wink that Dora sent me.

"Good, and I think everybody else is accounted for. Oh, Raylene's not here tonight. Anybody know what she's doing for dinner?"

"Probably going to be with her sweetie," Flora said, and everyone laughed.

"Yeah, but she and Mr. Carl shouldn't eat alone. I'll check with him." *What's two more on the growing list,* I thought.

I had to admit that I was getting excited about having such a large gathering for Thanksgiving dinner. All of my years growing up, it had only been my mother, my grandmother, and me.

28

On the morning of November first I'd just unlocked the door of the shop to open for business and Saxton walked in.

Pulling me into an embrace, he said, "Good morning, beautiful. I missed you."

I laughed and put my arms around his neck. "You just saw me last evening."

"Much too long apart. We have to work on fixing that."

I pulled away and walked over to rearrange a few crystals that were out of order. "What time is Resa getting here?" I asked, purposely avoiding Muriel's name.

"They should be here around three. That's why I wanted to stop by, to tell you I'm taking them to dinner this evening at the Island Hotel, but I'll call you later after I get home."

"Oh, okay." Again, that ripple of jealousy appeared. Muriel would be spending the evening with Saxton. And I would not.

"Oh, before I forget. I didn't think you'd mind, but Doyle had nowhere to go for Thanksgiving, so I've invited him to join us."

"Sure. That's great."

Saxton walked over to give me another hug that was followed by a kiss.

"I love you, Berkley. I'll talk to you later," he said, and headed out.

I wished I could shake the sour feeling that had been nagging at me all morning, and looked up to see Mr. Carl walk into the shop.

"A bright and glorious morning to you, Miss Berkley," he said, causing me to smile. It was difficult being down for long around somebody like Mr. Carl.

"And to you," I told him. "How's it going?"

"Wonderful. Miss Raylene and I are headed to Gainesville in a little while, but I had to stop and get my chocolates. Wouldn't want to miss my daily dose."

A huge grin covered his face, followed by a wink. Which made me wonder if possibly my chocolate might have a tad of Viagra ingredients, and I laughed.

I boxed up his purchase and said, "Oh, what are you and Raylene doing for Thanksgiving?"

"I don't rightly know. We haven't really talked about it."

"Well, I don't want you to be alone. I'm cooking, but we're having the dinner at Saxton's house, and I'd like to invite you and Miss Raylene. I don't want you to be alone on a holiday."

"That's sure mighty kind of you. I'll talk to her about it and get back to you."

I smiled as he walked out the door. Okay, that's it, Berkley. Ten for dinner is the limit.

I closed the shop an hour early on Friday afternoon. Dinner reservations were for seven o'clock, and I'd spent two hours going through my clothes trying to decide what to wear. Just as I'd about given up hope, I heard Chloe at the door.

"Just came over to see . . . oh . . ." she said, staring at my shorts and tee shirt. "Not dressed yet? I thought the dinner was at seven. I wanted to see what you were wearing."

"It is," I said, almost on the verge of tears. "I have no idea what I'm wearing because nothing in my closet seems appropriate."

"Uh-oh. You need a girlfriend rescue. Come on," she said, grabbing my hand and leading me to her apartment and into the bedroom. "We're the same size, take your pick."

She flung open her closet door.

I momentarily thought I was in a department store when I saw all the dresses, skirts, and other items hanging neatly side by side.

"My God, I never realized you had so many clothes."

"Yeah, hardly wear any of them anymore. But I sure stocked up when I used to shop in Jacksonville and Atlanta. What's your pleasure?"

I laughed and walked over to begin an inspection.

Between the two of us we finally decided on an ankle-length, silky black skirt with a pale pink silk tank top. Black sandals completed the outfit.

I spun around in front of her mirror. "I feel ravishing," I said, laughing.

"You *look* sexy. Saxton will love it."

"Are you sure? It's all right to borrow this?"

"Of course it is. I'm glad somebody can get some use out of it."

I leaned over to give Chloe a hug. "Thank you so much. You're the best."

"Oh, and we can't forget this," she said, picking up a bottle of Chanel No 5 and giving a few sprays to my neck.

By the time I headed down Second Street to the Island Room, I truly *did* feel ravishing. That is, until I walked into the restaurant and met Saxton's ex-wife.

The three of them were already seated when I arrived. I shot a quick glance to Resa and saw a young woman of medium height and build, with a mass of dark curls falling to her shoulders. The resemblance to Saxton was amazing. But it was Resa's mother who caused my gaze to linger. Sitting beside Saxton, she looked like a fashion model from *Vogue*. Pale blond hair was pulled back into a French twist, and I could see she was wearing a sleeveless sheath dress of cobalt blue that contrasted perfectly with her hair. Makeup looked like it had been applied by a technician from Lancôme, and I caught a thick gold bracelet on the slim wrist she was waving in the air.

Saxton looked up, saw me, and rushed to greet me with a hug, which momentarily restored my equilibrium.

"Come on," he said, grabbing my hand and leading me to the table. "I want you to meet my daughter." He got ten points for not also including Muriel in the sentence.

"Berkley, this is my daughter, Resa."

She took me by surprise when she got up and came over to give me a hug.

"It's so nice to meet you," she said.

"Same here. I've heard so much about you, and welcome to Cedar Key."

"And this is Resa's mother, Muriel."

Another ten points for not referring to her as his ex-wife.

I reached out my hand in greeting and for a moment thought she wasn't going to reciprocate, but she gave me a limp shake.

"Yes, nice to meet you, Berkley," she said in an accent that sounded somewhere between haughty and condescending.

Saxton was seated at the head of the table and indicated the chair to his right.

"Doyle's running a little late but should be here shortly. I took the liberty of ordering a bottle of champagne," he said, reaching for the bottle in the ice bucket and then filling my glass.

I felt awkward and out of place, but I wasn't about to let it show.

"How do you like Cedar Key?" I asked, looking across the table.

"Oh, it's gorgeous," Resa said. "It must be wonderful to live here all the time."

"What exactly do you *do* here?" Muriel questioned.

"Do? Well, I own a chocolate shop and I have a knitting business on the side, so I'm kept pretty busy. But there are all kinds of activities going on at various clubs..." I knew this information sounded pretty dismal to somebody that looked and spoke like Muriel. "So really, one can be as busy as they'd like to be or not."

"I see," was all she said, and I was saved from any more questions as Doyle approached the table.

Introductions were made. He sat beside me and patted my hand. "How's everything with you, Berkley?"

"Good. Thanks."

"So are you enjoying your stay here so far?" he asked both women.

"I just love it," Resa said. "I can see why my dad wants to live here. It must be a great place to be a writer."

Muriel remained silent.

"Yes, it's a great atmosphere. And Doyle is an artist, so he gets a lot of his inspiration here too."

Muriel took a sip of champagne. "Saxton tells me you're also a fisherman? Do you do that for a hobby?"

I glanced at Doyle and caught a smile on his face. "I do now, but I was raised here and fishing was my family business."

Muriel only nodded.

Saxton raised his glass. "I want to propose a toast. To my daughter. Thank you for agreeing to see me, and I love you."

As we touched glasses I saw the moisture in Resa's eyes as she said, "I love you too."

Muriel I could certainly do without, but it was easy to see that the father/daughter reunion was going very well, and I was thrilled for Saxton.

Just then Muriel leaned into Saxton's arm as she looked up at him with a sultry expression. "And you'll just have to get out to Seattle now and start spending more time with *our* daughter. I would think you could write there as well as here."

What? Was she trying to entice him to move out to the West Coast to be near her?

"Well, I don't know about that," he said. "I'll definitely get out there for a visit, but Cedar Key is my home now."

Right. You tell her, Saxton. And besides, the closest salon that could cater to somebody like Muriel was a one-hour drive away. Not that she'd consider moving to a place where she had to question what one *does* here.

Somehow we managed to get through dinner conversation with Doyle acting as a buffer.

When the crème brûlée and coffee were served, Saxton leaned over and whispered, "You look gorgeous in that outfit."

I sent a silent thank-you to Chloe just as I caught the sour look on Muriel's face.

She reached for his arm as if divorce hadn't canceled out ownership on her part and said, "So, Sax, what will we be doing tomorrow? Are there any other places for me to shop, or are those little gift shops all you have?"

Sax? What was with this *Sax?*

Doyle laughed. "Well, if you're looking for Neiman Marcus, you won't find it here on this island."

From the neutral expression on Muriel's face, it was clear she didn't find that humorous.

"I'm afraid we only have the art galleries and gift shops, Muriel," Saxton said, without an ounce of sorrow in his tone.

"Besides, I want to spend more time with Dad. He said we could take the Island Hopper out tomorrow and take a ride up the Suwannee River."

Muriel let out a sigh. "Well, then I guess I'll spend the day on the beach reading. I get seasick and have no tolerance for boats."

Why am I not surprised? I thought.

By the time we finished dessert I had formed the opinion that I liked Saxton's daughter a lot. Throughout the evening, she'd gone out of her way to ask me questions and tell me about her position with the computer firm in Seattle. She also mentioned her husband, Jake, a lot and it was obvious that they had a close relationship.

When we got up to leave, she hugged me again and said, "I've already told Dad that I'll be back again next year and I'll be bringing Jake with me. So I look forward to seeing you again."

I wasn't sure which I was impressed with more—the fact that she shared this with me or the fact that she somehow assumed her father and I would still be together in a year.

Saxton leaned over to touch my lips before pulling me into an embrace. "If it's okay with you, I'll drop Resa and Muriel off first at the B and B and then take you home."

"That would be great. Thanks," I said, and followed him to the parking lot.

I turned to say good-bye to Doyle. "And I'll see you on Thanksgiving, if not before. My aunt will also be there, and she's bringing some photos of my mom. Maybe that will help jog some memories."

"Maybe so," was his reply.

When I turned around to get into Saxton's car, I did a slow boil. That nasty Muriel had managed to grab the passenger seat for herself, leaving me no option but to join Resa in the backseat.

Conversation was brief on the short distance, and before leaving the car, Resa leaned over for another hug. "Now, you take care," she said. "I'll be in touch through my dad, and I look forward to seeing you next year."

I got out to join Saxton in the front seat and realized that Muriel hadn't even uttered a good-bye to me.

Saxton turned the car around and headed down Second Street.

"I love your daughter," I told him with honesty. "She reminds me a lot of you."

He nodded. "Thanks. Yeah, I'm pretty proud of her, even though I had very little to do with her upbringing."

He then let out a chuckle. "Her mother leaves a lot to be desired though. Whew! She was pretty difficult when I was married to her, but now . . . as you can see, she sure didn't mellow with age."

Relief swept over me. Silly, I know, but all evening I had a nagging thought that he might regain interest in her. His words allowed me to know that my fears were unfounded.

I leaned over to kiss his cheek. "I love you, Saxton Tate the third. I love you very much."

29

Any nervousness I had about getting together with my aunt quickly vanished the moment she opened the door of her cottage at the Faraway Inn.

Stella Baldwin didn't look much different than she had two years before at my grandmother's funeral.

Tall and slim, her silver hair was styled in a chic cut that fell to her cheeks. With her good looks and upbeat demeanor, she didn't strike me as a woman pushing seventy.

She pulled me into a tight embrace while saying, "Come in. It's so good to see you again, Berkley."

I walked into the combined bedroom, kitchen, and sitting area and saw a little Yorkie hop off the bed to greet me. Stella reached down to pick up the dog.

"This is Addi. She's my BFF."

"She's adorable," I said, putting out my hand for her to sniff. "I love her scarf." I laughed at the small pink bandana that had *Girly Girl* monogrammed on the front in a deep rose color.

"I was just going to make some tea," Stella said, walking to the kettle on the stove without putting the dog down. "Will you join me?"

"Sounds good." I went to sit on the sofa and spied a gorgeous piece of needlepoint. A half-finished European street scene was secured in a wooden frame. "Oh, this is beautiful. I didn't realize you also did needlepoint," I said at the same time the thought hit me that I actually didn't know very much about my aunt at all.

"Oh, yes. It relaxes me and I've been doing it for years. I know you knit, but do you do any needlepoint?"

I nodded. "Yes, my Gram taught me when I was little, and I just recently returned to it. Knitting will always be my first love, but I enjoy the needlepoint for something different. Did you have a good drive to Cedar Key?" I asked as my aunt placed tea bags in two mugs.

"I did. And when I hit that first bridge coming onto the island, well, I can see why you love living here."

I laughed. "Yeah, the view from the Number Four bridge has that effect on a lot of people."

Stella filled the mugs with boiling water. "But how on earth did you find this place? I'd never heard of it before you called and told me you lived here. I haven't seen much of the island yet, but it seems so . . . out of the way. Quaint."

"Thanks," I said, taking the mug she passed me. "Well, the way I found this place is one of the reasons why I wanted to get together with you."

Stella settled herself in the rocker across from me as her perfectly shaped eyebrows formed a V.

"I'm not sure how much of this story you know about, if anything. But forty years ago my mother came here for an entire summer."

"Really? I don't recall her leaving Salem with you."

"That's just it. She didn't. She came alone and left me with my grandmother. They still lived in Maine then, and by the time my mother returned, we had relocated to Salem. Do you know why she would have come here?"

Genuine surprise covered Stella's face. "Gosh, no. But then, you have to remember that I wasn't in touch with my mother or sister very much, except for letters. Your uncle Rudy was in the military and we traveled a lot. What year would this have been?"

"It was 1972. I was five years old."

Stella thought for a moment. "Rudy and I were living in England during those years. But it seems odd that my mother didn't tell me Jeanette had left town. I wonder why she would come here?"

"That's what I'm trying to find out. Neither my mother or grandmother would talk about it. I was hoping that you might be able to fill in some pieces of the puzzle." I went on to tell her about the postcards.

"My goodness, we have a genuine mystery in the family that I wasn't aware of." She let out a deep sigh. "I can't imagine why they wouldn't tell you the reason she came here, but then, Jeanette was always an odd duck."

"In which way? Tell me about her, because I'm beginning to think I didn't know my mother at all. Did you know my father?"

Stella shook her head. "That was another strange incident. First of all, I was shocked that Jeanette actually chose to leave Maine and go to college on the West Coast. She was always more of an introvert. And then, to drop out of college during her last semester and not graduate . . ."

"What? I never knew that. I just assumed she did graduate."

Stella shook her head. "No, silly, isn't it? To go to college for four years and then not graduate. She dropped out and went back to Maine, but then of course she was pregnant with you at that time, so I figured that was the reason. And, no, I didn't know your father at all. Your grandmother told me he was from Houston, apparently from a wealthy family. I imagine he did graduate from Berkeley and then was either drafted or enlisted, but he ended up in Vietnam and your grandmother said he was killed there before you were even born."

"Hmm, that's the story they told me too."

"You sound like you have doubts."

"Well, it just seems odd that my mother wouldn't really talk about him either. I know they weren't married, but you'd think she'd have at least one photo to show me of him."

"Oh! That reminds me," Stella said, jumping up to run into the bedroom. "I did find a few pictures, and I happen to have one of your mother and father, taken at Berkeley the year before you were born."

I felt a chill go through me. Forty-five years. Forty-five years and I was finally going to see what my father looked like?

She came back and sat beside me on the sofa. "Here it is," she said, passing me a blurry black-and-white photo.

Both of the people looked like strangers to me. Here was my mother, a young woman of twenty-one, with long, straight brunette hair falling to her shoulders. She wore bell-bottom jeans and a sweatshirt with *Berkeley* written across the front. Pulling her into a possessive embrace was a young, good-looking fellow. Blond hair reached to his shirt collar in the style of the sixties, and he had a self-assured smile on his face. I brought the photo closer to try and pull some recognition from the stranger smiling at the camera. But there was nothing about him that resembled me.

I blew out a deep breath of air. "They made a nice couple, so I wonder why my mother would never talk about him."

"I honestly don't know. Your grandmother only mentioned him when she told me Jeanette was pregnant and then when he was killed in Vietnam. Other than that, I don't know anything else about him."

"What was my mother like growing up? Did she have boy-friends then? What did she want to do with her life?"

Stella leaned back against the sofa cushion and sighed. "Well, she was always quiet. We were only eleven months apart in age, so we were in the same classes at school. I was the loud, outgoing one, but Jeanette was shy. That's probably why she always had her head in a book or she was writing."

"Writing? My mother liked to write?"

"Oh, gosh, yes. She wrote poetry and short stories. She majored in English at college. I think she wanted to be a journalist."

Another surprise about the Jeanette Whitmore that I didn't know.

"But she was what I always called a troubled soul. She had a fear of everything—of herself with doubts, of people, probably just a fear of life. It was like she wanted to succeed but she had a fear of failure and just found it easier to withdraw, I guess." Stella shook her head. "It's kind of sad when you think about it. Such a wasted life. Have you questioned people here on the island? Surely somebody must remember her from that summer."

"I've asked a lot of the locals and nobody can remember a twenty-seven-year-old woman who came here that year. But now that I have this photo, it might help."

"Oh, I have one more for you," Stella said, passing me another black-and-white snapshot. "Taken when you were about a year old, I'd say."

I saw my mother sitting on the front steps of the house we'd lived at in Maine. Both arms were wrapped protectively around me as I sat on her knees, and a huge smile covered her face.

"She looks happy," I said.

"Oh, I think she was. The few times I saw her after you were born, one thing I can say for certain—she adored you and she loved being a mother."

Then why would she leave me for a whole summer?

"I'm really beginning to feel like I didn't know her at all. I just don't get it."

Stella took a sip of her tea. "Yeah, Jenna could be a puzzle. That's for sure."

My head snapped up as I stared at my aunt. *"Jenna?"*

"Oh, yeah, she used to go by that nickname when we were young. My name ended in an *a,* and she thought Stella and Jenna sounded more like twins than just sisters. Anybody that knew her growing up called her Jenna."

"Oh, wow! Could that be why nobody knew a Jeanette Whitmore? Maybe that's the name she used here on the island, and if she changed her first name, it makes sense that she might use a different last name as well."

"You could be right. How did she sign those postcards she sent to my mother?"

"Only J. No names at all."

Stella reached over to pat my hand. "You could be onto something here."

30

When Jill arrived the following day, I still hadn't questioned anybody about a woman named Jenna. Part of me was scared that it would be another dead end, so I decided to let go of it until after Thanksgiving and just enjoy the holiday.

I had offered Jill my bedroom, but she insisted that the pull-out sofa was fine for her. We sat cross-legged on the queen sofa bed, a bowl of chips between us and glasses of wine on the table.

"Except for the wine, this reminds me of the sleepovers we'd have when you'd come to visit me after you moved to Salem."

I nodded. "Yeah, but my mother was so strict and would let me come there only once a year for a weekend during the summer."

"I know. But at least we could keep in touch the rest of the year with our letters back and forth. Okay—catch-up time. Tell me all about the ex-wife, what you learned from your aunt yesterday, everything!"

I laughed, took a sip of wine, and shared all the details.

Jill shook her head. "Wow, there's certainly a lot going on in your life. I'm sure you're not sorry Muriel is gone. She sounds like a piece of work. Good riddance to her, I say. And there's no doubt that Saxton feels the same way."

I nodded. "Yeah, I have to admit . . . I think I was a bit jealous of her at first. But by the end of the evening I knew she wasn't right for him."

Jill patted my hand. "Now, look, girl. I hope any doubts you have had are gone. Don't second-guess yourself like you always do. From what you've told me, it sounds like this is the real thing for you."

I smiled. "Yeah, I think you're right."

"Show me the photos of your mom."

I jumped up to get them from my bedroom and passed them to her.

"Gosh, your mom didn't look anything like this when I knew her. Look at her, with those bell-bottoms and long straight hair—she looks like a typical product of the sixties. And this is your dad? Good-looking guy, but you definitely resemble your mom more."

"Yeah, I thought so too."

"And still no more pieces to the puzzle?"

"Nope, and I'm going to let it go until after Thanksgiving. I'll go to the knitting group next week and take the photos. So we'll see what happens."

I woke the next morning with an extra fullness to my heart. My best girlfriend was sleeping in the next room and my aunt was just a few streets away. There's a lot to be said for having a history or shared blood with people. I hadn't known my aunt very well at all, but after spending time with her two days before, I felt a connection. In very subtle ways, I saw a likeness to my mother that made me feel good. Made me feel that although she was gone, a part of her still remained.

Knocking on the door caused me to jump up and tiptoe out into the living room where Jill was still sleeping.

"Hey," I said, opening the door to find Chloe standing with a tray filled with juice and muffins.

"Oh, no, I woke you, didn't I? I'm so sorry, but I thought you gals might like some breakfast."

"That's so nice of you," I whispered. "Jill's still sleeping, but . . ."

"No, I'm not," I heard her say.

I laughed. "Oh, good. Come on in, Chloe. I've been anxious for you to meet each other."

Jill sat up, rubbing her eyes, and yawned. "Not the best condition to meet, but I've heard so much about you, so just ignore my sleepy appearance."

Chloe laughed and headed to the kitchen to set down the tray. "I've heard a lot about you too. So nice to finally meet you, Jill."

"Just let me pop into the bathroom and I'll join you shortly."

I went to start the coffee as Chloe arranged the juice and muffins on the table.

By the time Jill had joined us, I had the mugs filled with the dark brew.

"It was nice of you to bring this over," Jill told Chloe before taking a sip of coffee. "Oh, you haven't lost your touch, girlfriend. Wonderful coffee."

"Help yourself to juice and muffins," Chloe told her. "So I bet you guys had fun visiting last night."

"We did," I said, and glanced at the clock over the fridge. "My God! It's nine already! I had no idea we slept so late."

"Well, we were up till after two." Jill reached for a muffin and nodded. "These look delicious. Thanks, Chloe."

"What time are you due at Saxton's?"

"Not till three, so we don't have to rush. What time is Maude doing dinner?"

"At two. I'm looking forward to spending the day and evening with Grace and Lucas. I haven't seen much of her since they got back."

I explained to Jill that they'd been in France since late April.

"I haven't even seen her at all," I said.

"Well, she'll definitely be at the knitting group a week from tonight. Said that she has lots of things to tell us."

"I want you to meet my aunt while she's here too. Maybe we can do lunch over the weekend."

"That would be fun. Count me in. It was great to meet you, Jill, but I have to run. Time to get my pies out of the oven. Have a wonderful dinner and I'll see you soon."

"Thanks again," I hollered as she left.

* * *

As Jill, my aunt, and I climbed the stairs to Saxton's deck I held my breath that his house would be in order and I wouldn't be embarrassed by his normal clutter.

He greeted us on the deck with a huge smile and hugs for all of us. I could see the two large tables had been pushed together and were covered with the tablecloths and napkins I'd brought over the day before. Doyle and Saxton had also managed to do a good job of getting the table set, complete with candles and flowers.

"Doyle's already here, but the others should be along shortly. Come on in," he said as we followed him through the open French doors.

Introductions were made as I quickly glanced around and smiled. No stacks of magazines and newspapers, no socks strewn around, no sense of disarray. Yes, there was hope for this man after all.

I noticed that Doyle's gaze seemed to linger on my aunt. Well, she was a very good-looking woman, and today she looked exceptionally sharp with a gorgeous, long burnt orange silk skirt and black silk blouse.

He drew his eyes away from her to announce, "Saxton put me in charge of the bar and I'm serving mimosas. Do I have any takers?"

"Definitely," Jill and I said at the same time, and laughed.

Lola came running from the back of the house to greet everyone, and my aunt bent over to pat her. "What a sweet dog," she said. "I bet my Addi would like her."

Saxton smiled. "Yes, Berkley told me you came with your little Yorkie. You should have brought her."

"Oh, thank you," she said, accepting a champagne flute from Doyle. "But I think she's worn out from all this ocean air. She was napping away when I left."

Leigh and her daughters, followed by Mr. Carl and Raylene, arrived a few minutes later and our group was complete. I had prepared everything the day before, and I could smell the wonderful aroma of turkey filling the air. Leigh had brought a sweet potato casserole along with a pumpkin pie, and Raylene had brought a green bean casserole and pecan pie, so our table was also complete.

After our mimosas, combined with conversation, Saxton and I

shooed everyone out to the table while we went to work in the kitchen mashing potatoes, slicing the turkey, making the gravy, and getting biscuits out of the oven.

A little while later, I carried a tray of bowls out to the deck. "Just about ready," I said.

"Are you sure we can't help?" my aunt asked for the third time.

I laughed. "Nope, we're all set, but we'll use you later for cleanup duty."

Saxton placed the large platter of turkey on the table as I went back for more items. Within a few minutes both tables were overflowing and we sat down next to each other. I looked around and swallowed the lump in my throat. Here I was having the large Thanksgiving dinner that I'd always yearned for. Here I was sitting beside a man who loved me the way I had always wanted to be loved, with my best friend, my aunt, and some wonderful Cedar Key people—all because of my mother.

"Okay," I said, reaching for Saxton's hand on one side of me and my aunt's on the other. "Time to give thanks for all that we've been given." Hands clasped around the table as heads bowed. "Dear Lord, thank you for this beautiful day, this wonderful food, but most of all, thank you for allowing me to find my way to Cedar Key. Amen."

"Amen," everybody chorused.

"This looks like a mighty fine dinner," Mr. Carl said. "Miss Raylene and I are very pleased to be here with you."

As bowls and platters were passed around, everybody began eating and chatting.

Doyle looked across the table at my aunt. "How long are you here for, Stella?"

"Until Wednesday, so I hope to see the entire island."

"Well, if you gals don't have any plans on Sunday I'd like to take you out on my boat. The island's pretty small so you'll get to see all of it, but you might want to see it from the water and also some of the other islands."

"Oh, that sounds like fun, but Berkley is my tour director," she said, glancing at me.

"I think that would be great. Thanks, Doyle."

Conversation shifted to Leigh and her plans for a day care center. "So with the back support payment that's owed to me and my share of the sale of the house, after the first of the year I just might be able to rent something here on the island."

"That would be great," I said. "We'll keep our eyes open for rental property."

"Well, ya know . . . I do have that property on Third Street, near the Curl Up and Dye." Raylene fingered her napkin as all of us looked at her. Was this the same nasty woman I'd first encountered trying to ban Corabeth's books now offering assistance?

She looked at Mr. Carl, and I saw him nod as if to encourage her.

"It's not much and needs a lot of remodeling. Two cottages side by side. One could be used for your day care center, and you could live in the other one."

The expression on Leigh's face showed her surprise. "Are you serious? You'd be willing to rent me that property? I know exactly where you mean. I've walked past there many times thinking it would be the ideal spot."

"Well, if you're interested, we can discuss it. But as I said, it will need sprucing up. Hasn't been lived in or used in a long time."

"I'm pretty handy with remodeling," Doyle said. "I'd be more than happy to help you out."

"Same here," Saxton told her. "I'm not sure how handy I am with that kind of work, but I'd be happy to help you too."

I caught the excitement and said, "Oh, me too. I can swing a paintbrush pretty well, and I'm good with wallpaper and just general cleanup."

Leigh wiped her eyes with her napkin. "My goodness, I never expected this. Okay. That would be great. Miss Raylene, why don't I take you to lunch next week and we'll discuss this. Thank you."

I smiled. That's how things happened on this island. Somebody needed help and the community chipped in. I remembered the story that Chloe had told me about Mr. Al and how his house and property had been such an eyesore that a few disgruntled residents felt he should be put into a nursing home and the property sold. But that had not happened. The entire community had banded together and cleaned up the property, and Mr. Al still lived there with his precious dog, Pal.

By the time dessert and coffee were served, everybody was filled with good food and good feelings.

"Okay," Mr. Carl said, tapping his spoon against his coffee cup. "I have a little announcement that I'd like to make."

All of us looked up expectantly.

"I've ... ah ... asked for the hand of Miss Raylene here in marriage ... and she has accepted my proposal."

Laughter and cheering filled the deck as I jumped up to squeeze both of them in a hug.

"Oh, my goodness," I said. "I had no idea you two were planning to be married."

"Well," Raylene said. "We weren't. That is, I wasn't ... until Carl convinced me I'd be foolish not to accept his offer."

This brought forth more laughter as Saxton produced a bottle of champagne. "I think this calls for a toast."

With glasses lifted we wished Mr. Carl and Raylene a long and happy life together.

"So when is this special event to take place?" my aunt asked.

"We thought New Year's Eve day would be good," Carl said. "And my bride here ... well, she'd like to be married on the beach. Not a big to-do. Just a few friends, so we'd like all of you to be there."

"That would be great," I said, and looked at Jill and my aunt.

"I'm not sure I'll be able to get away from the farm, but I'll be here in spirit." Jill raised her glass to the smiling couple.

"Oh, I'll definitely come back if my niece will have me."

I leaned over to squeeze my aunt's shoulders. "Of course I will."

Conversation flowed around the table as I felt that lump in my throat again. It had been a wonderful Thanksgiving, and I had a feeling that each of us had something very special to be grateful for.

❧ 31 ❧

By the time Thursday evening arrived I had begun to feel nervous about approaching the knitting group with the photos of my mother. Part of me was scared that I'd hit another dead end—but part of me was scared that I wouldn't. And all of a sudden I wondered if maybe it wasn't better to just let sleeping dogs lie, as Raylene had said months before.

I let out a deep breath, stuffed the photos into my knitting bag, and then headed down Second Street to Yarning Together.

"Ah, Berkley," Dora greeted me. "Did your company get off okay? It was such a pleasure to meet your aunt and Jill last week."

I nodded as I found a spot on the sofa next to Suellen. "Yes, Jill flew back Tuesday and my aunt left yesterday. But she'll be back for Raylene's wedding."

"Speaking of which," Chloe said. "Before she gets here, do you think we should have a little shower or something for her?"

Maybelle put her knitting in her lap and looked up. "And what, pray tell, does one give to a bride pushing eighty?"

Chloe and I laughed as Suellen said, "Longevity?" which produced more chuckles.

Dora shook her head. "You gals are terrible," she said, but I saw the grin on her face. "Yes, I think we should do something, Chloe. You and I will discuss it. We don't have much time between now and the wedding, so maybe a gathering here the week between Christmas and New Year's. And no more making fun of poor Raylene. Maybe Mr. Carl is the love of her life, and finding that person is a very serious matter."

I exchanged a glance with Suellen, feeling properly admonished by Miss Dora.

An hour later the room was filled with women knitting away on socks, afghans, sweaters, scarves, and hats. A feeling of peace and camaraderie enveloped me. I let out a deep sigh and decided now was the time to produce the photos.

I placed the lace socks in my lap and reached into my knitting bag. Clearing my throat, I said in a loud voice, "I wonder if any of you could help me." I held up the photos. "My aunt brought me two photos of my mother. One was taken when she was still a student at Berkeley and she would have been around twenty-one or two, and the other one was a few years later. Does anybody recognize her?" I passed the photos to Chloe on my right.

Various comments filled the room as the photos were passed from hand to hand.

"Oh, look at those bell-bottom jeans."

"Everyone seemed to wear their hair that way back then."

"What a nice couple they made. Such a handsome fellow."

"Aww, what a sweet little thing you were," Flora said. "Wait." She pulled the photo closer and adjusted her glasses. "By golly, I think this is . . . Oh, Lord, what was her name?" She looked over at Dora as I held my breath.

Dora got up to look at the photo that Flora held out.

Flora waved her hand in the air. "You know . . . that girl . . . the one that rented my apartment." She looked directly at me. "*Your* apartment."

I let out my breath at the same time that Dora said, "Yes. You're right. Her name was Jenna."

Flora snapped her fingers. "That's it! Jenna Walsh. That was her name."

My hands felt clammy and I gripped the side of the chair. "So you *do* know her? You remember her? And what do you mean *my* apartment?"

A hush fell over the room as all eyes were on Flora.

"This girl came to the island one summer. And yeah, it probably was about forty years ago now, but I distinctly remember her. She rented the apartment that you're now living in."

I could feel my heart racing.

"But you told us her name was something else," Flora said. "That's why we couldn't remember her."

I gripped the chair arm tighter and nodded. "Right. I just recently found out from my aunt that as a child she went by the nickname of Jenna, so she must have used that name when she came here. But Walsh? I don't know why she would have changed her last name."

"Sounds like she didn't want anybody to know who she really was," Dora said.

"What do you remember? Why did she come here? What did she tell you?" I could feel forty years' worth of questions tumbling out of me.

Chloe reached over and patted my arm.

"Well," Flora said, and I could almost see her mind going back in time. "I got a phone call one day from a young woman asking if she might rent the apartment she saw on the sign at the Market. The window of the Market is where everyone advertised things for rent or sale. Still is. Anyway, I said sure, and I remember meeting her at the corner of the building outside on Second Street."

"My God," I said. "So you mean to tell me that I'm now living in the very apartment that my mother once did?"

Flora nodded. "I know. Talk about coincidence, huh? So I took her upstairs and she said, 'It'll do.' Those were her exact words. I remember because she didn't say it's nice or I like it or anything like that. Only 'It'll do.' Almost like the place itself was only going to provide a means for shelter, not a proper home."

"What did she tell you? Did she say where she was from? Why she was here?" Again, the questions began tumbling out.

Flora shook her head. "Nope. I can't say that I remember anything like that. She rented the apartment immediately. It was furnished back then, and she only had a small suitcase with her. I do remember that, because I wondered why she only had clothes and no personal belongings. She did have a car. Didn't use it much because she never really left the island. Just walked everywhere."

"She must have worked somewhere," I said. "How did she pay her rent?"

Flora nodded slowly as if trying to recall more information stored in her memory. "Right. She did work and she paid her rent on time every single week that she was here. And then toward the middle of August, I remember she called me and gave me a two-week notice. Said she'd be leaving by the end of the month. But I don't remember where she worked, do you, Dora?"

Dora looked at the photos again. "Gosh, I didn't know her that well. But didn't she work as a waitress over at one of the restaurants on Dock Street? I'm almost certain that she did."

"I think you're right," Flora said. "But I honestly can't say where."

"You might question Doyle," Dora told me.

"Doyle Summers?" I said with surprise.

"Yes, his parents owned a restaurant there. It's a start. He might recall who she is from the photo and be able to help a little more."

I nodded. Well, at least I had definitely established that my mother had been here. The postcards had initially proved this, but hearing these two women actually recall her existence on this island made it all the more real for me.

"Thank you," I said, taking the photos from Dora's hand and replacing them in my knitting bag. "Thank you so much," I told them, but all of a sudden I felt a sense of deflation sweep over me. Yes, it had taken eight months to finally establish the fact that my mother had been here, and a few women even remembered her. And adding to the puzzle was the realization that I was actually living in the very same apartment that she had. But I quickly realized that despite these women recalling my mother's stay in Cedar Key, I really wasn't any closer to finding out *why* she came here in the first place. Why she left me for an entire summer to do so. I knew that the next piece to my puzzle might be Doyle Summers.

Two nights later I sat with Saxton on the deck of the Black Dog waiting for Doyle to arrive. I nervously took a sip of wine and felt Saxton pat my leg.

"He should be here shortly. It'll be okay."

A few minutes later Doyle joined us. After he had a glass of wine in front of him, he said, "So what's up? What's the reason for getting together?"

I let out a deep breath and passed the photos of my mother across the table. "My aunt gave me these. I have now found out from Flora that my mother rented her apartment during the summer she was here—the very apartment that I'm living in. She and Dora said they thought my mother worked as a waitress at one of the restaurants on Dock Street. Do you remember her?"

Doyle remained silent as he stared at the pictures, his eyes going from one to the other. He placed them on the table in front of him, never taking his glance away, then took a sip of wine and said, "She's very pretty."

I was stunned by the fact that this was the first time I'd heard somebody refer to my mother as *pretty*. "But do you remember her?"

"Yes . . . I do. Jenna Walsh. She worked at my parents' restaurant."

"What? She did?" I leaned farther across the table. "What can you tell me? Do you know why she came here? What did she tell you?"

Instead of answering my questions, he said, "I can tell you that there's a lot more to this story. I also think that over time you'll probably find your answers, and I feel it has to be you that discovers them."

I had been trying to secure those answers for forty years. Wasn't *that* enough time?

"What do you mean by that?" I questioned.

"What I mean is, everybody reacts to family secrets in a different way. Some people feel the truth will set them free. Others aren't able to accept what actually happened."

"You mean like, be careful what you wish for?"

"Exactly. Listen, you're off work Monday. I'd like you and Saxton to come over to my place. About seven, for a few drinks." He stood up, gulped the last of his wine, and said, "See you then."

32

The next few days crawled by, and despite constant badgering of Saxton, he assured me he didn't have a clue what was going on.

"I had no idea that Doyle even knew your mother," he told me over coffee at the coffee café on Monday morning. "I definitely would have said something."

"Why couldn't he just tell me what he knew the other night? Why do we have to go to his place?"

Saxton shrugged. "I can't answer that question either."

Suellen came to our table to refill our coffee. "So tonight's the night, huh? Hopefully, you'll finally get some answers."

I had brought Suellen, Chloe, and my aunt up to date over the weekend. They were just as intrigued with the story as I was.

"I certainly hope so," I told her.

Later that afternoon my aunt called.

"I must say, Berkley, this is really turning into quite the family mystery. Do you think your mother and Doyle were involved? You know, in a romantic way?"

"Well, he said there's more to the story than I realize. So, that would indicate they had to have been close, I think."

"You know, I recalled something this morning. An incident that would have been right around that time. Actually, I think it was May of that year. Rudy was being transferred somewhere and I'd gone home for a few days to spend some time with my mother and Jeanette. I was awakened one morning by their loud voices in the kitchen. I was surprised, because they normally got on exception- ally well and it was obvious they were having a disagreement."

I clenched the phone tighter. "Really? What was it about?"

"I can now only remember my mother saying something about how wrong it was and that my sister needed to face facts. Then Jeanette started crying and that was the end of it. And of course, none of this was mentioned to me."

"Hmm, I wonder what that was all about?"

"I honestly have no idea, but I thought it might help with putting another piece to the puzzle."

I was beginning to feel I was getting so close—yet, so far.

Saxton and I arrived at Doyle's house on Andrews Circle at pre- cisely seven o'clock. I had never been to his home before, but had always admired the house tucked back behind the black wrought- iron fence, surrounded by so many trees and bushes that it always reminded me of the Secret Garden.

Doyle seemed to have a somber expression as he opened the door, and we entered his living room. A large room, enclosed by floor-to-ceiling windows on three sides, which gave an unob- structed view of the dock and water beyond.

My gaze scanned the room, which had an old-fashioned feel to it with chintz-covered chairs and sofa, bookcases, and an easel set up near the window with a half-finished watercolor of pelicans swooping over the Big Dock. It was then that my eyes went to the extremely large painting over his fireplace.

A boat in the middle of the water, with the skyline of Cedar Key in the background. Standing on the boat was a young woman. Her long brunette hair was windswept, giving her an exotic look. She wore shorts and a cotton blouse; her head was thrown back, reveal- ing a huge smile that radiated pure joy. I could almost hear the laughter through the painting.

I got goose bumps as a feeling of familiarity came over me. Continuing to stare, I slowly walked toward the painting, and gasped. It was my mother. I was sure of it.

I spun around to find Doyle with a pained expression. "Yes . . . It's her," he whispered. "It's my Jenna."

His Jenna? He was right. There was a lot more to this story.

"Have a seat. Let me pour us each a glass of wine and then . . . we'll begin."

My mind was racing, but I refrained from blurting out the million questions that I had. Saxton sat beside me on the sofa, patted my knee, and looked as surprised as I felt.

Doyle passed us a wineglass and then took the chair that directly faced the painting. Holding his glass up, he said, "Here's to Jenna. Somebody that I'll never forget."

I glanced up at the painting and felt a multitude of emotions. But the strongest one was that I could not ever recall seeing my mother look like that. Happy. Her face exhibiting pure bliss. She had a certain sense of confidence that the artist caught perfectly, in the toss of her head, the uplifting of her chin, hair caught by the breeze, arms straight up in the air as if to say, "Life is good."

"I met Jenna the day after she arrived here. I happened to be in the restaurant when she came in to fill out an application for a waitress job. A lot of people don't believe in love at first sight. I can emphatically say . . . it is possible. Because it happened to me. I was at the counter, turned around, and there she was. I knew in a heartbeat that something shifted inside of me. That I'd never again be the person I was before I turned around and saw her. And I could almost feel that she felt the same way. We made mundane talk about the job, the hours, that sort of thing. But the entire time I felt like I was enveloped in a . . . cocoon. Like the entire rest of the world had simply drifted away. Conversation from guests at the tables was muffled, making me feel like we were the only two people left in the world."

Doyle stopped to take a sip of his wine while I tried to comprehend what he was telling me.

"Jenna got the job, and we began seeing each other immediately.

She had a sadness about her. I saw it in her eyes, and sometimes a quietness would come over her. She told me she was from Maine, that she had come here because she had been ill and needed to recover."

I leaned forward on the sofa, gripping my wineglass. "Ill? My mother hadn't been sick. What did she mean by that?"

"There are all kinds of different ways of being sick, Berkley." He let out a deep sigh. "I know you're not going to be happy about this, but I'm not at liberty to tell you the rest of the story."

Anger began surging through me. "What! That's it? That's *all* you're going to tell me? Obviously, you know why she came here and you *won't* tell me?" I felt on the verge of tears built by years of frustration.

Doyle stood up, patted my hand, and walked to a small wooden chest on the desk. "It isn't that I won't tell you, Berkley. I *can't*. It's a promise I made many years ago."

My anger now mixed with confusion as I saw Doyle remove a yellowed envelope from the chest before sitting back down.

"You're determined to find your answers. And you will. But you have to be patient. I hope that you'll trust me and trust your mother. She gave me this letter to give to you a few months before she died and..."

"Before she died?" It was getting more and more difficult to wrap my brain around everything he was telling me. "You were in Salem? You came to see her?"

He shook his head. "No, not Salem. I met her at the Cape. We had arranged that trip months before. It was the first time we had seen each other again after forty years. But during that time we had never lost touch." He leaned over to pass me the envelope. "This is for you. Your mother wrote it. It was no mistake that you found those postcards, you know. She could have thrown them all out... and you wouldn't be here right now. But she felt you did deserve answers—she just wasn't able to give them to you."

I fingered the envelope in my hand and looked down to see my mother's familiar scrawl with my name on the front. "Can I open it now?" I asked in a voice that didn't sound like mine.

Doyle nodded, and I carefully slit open the envelope. I removed two pages of stationery and held them so Saxton could read along with me.

> *My dear Berkley,*
>
> *If you're reading this, then I'm no longer here with you. And if you have these pages in your hand, then you did what I thought you would. You followed the trail and it has led you to Cedar Key—where I managed to keep all of my secrets hidden.*
>
> *I know you were angry with me for leaving you behind the summer that you were five years old. I know you desperately wanted the answers as to why. I simply wasn't brave enough to give them to you. I knew when you found the postcards that you would pursue it and finally find the answers.*
>
> *You need to know that Doyle was the love of my life. He was my soul mate. That one person on earth that was meant for me. Unfortunately, due to circumstances, we were not able to be together. But that doesn't mean we ever stopped loving each other. Therefore, I have entrusted him with my secret. When we saw each other again on Cape Cod, we had lengthy discussions about all of this. We are both at peace with what is. I hope eventually that you will be too.*
>
> *Doyle knows my story. He knows why I came to Cedar Key. He knows why I returned to Salem. But he has promised that until you finish the rest of the journey, he will not tell you what happened.*
>
> *So, my daughter, I want you to be the one to actually find out what happened. Not with somebody telling you, but with you seeing it for yourself. You will need to return to Maine, because that's where the answers are. Go to the Curtis Memorial Library in Brunswick. Ask to see the microfilm of the newspapers from May and June of 1972. And you will find your answers. Please don't ask Doyle for the information. He has*

promised to abide by my wishes. And when you return to Cedar Key, as I know you will, then sit with Doyle and get the rest of the story that he and I shared.

When you find the answers, I can only hope that you will forgive me. That you'll forgive my fear, my cowardice and my choices. Because above all, you need to know that I love you so very much, from the bottom of my heart. Doyle may have been the love of my life, but you, Berkley, were what sustained my life.

All my love always, Mom

I realized that by the time I finished reading the letter, tears were streaming down my face. Doyle jumped up and put a box of tissues in my lap. I swiped at the tears, trying to absorb what I had just read.

I let out a deep breath. "So you have the answers and won't . . . can't . . . tell me? I have to make a trip to Brunswick to find out?"

Doyle nodded but said nothing. I looked at Saxton.

"When do you want to leave?" he asked, and I felt my heart turn over. I wasn't going to have to complete this journey alone. Saxton was going to be there for me. Every step of the way.

Later that evening after Saxton had left, I sat curled up on the sofa sipping herbal tea. I looked over at the urn that held the remains of my mother. I knew for certain that I had not known this woman at all. I knew Jeanette Whitmore, mother, daughter, sister, chocolate shop owner. But Jenna Walsh, the woman? I didn't have a clue who she was. But I was going to find out.

Saxton and I had discussed it and decided that with Christmas only a few weeks away and then Mr. Carl's wedding, we would fly to Maine on New Year's Day. He would make the arrangements for our flight and book a place in Brunswick for a few nights. The answers were all beginning to come—and I was very grateful that I had Saxton in my life, by my side, to share them with me.

❧ 33 ❧

I thought I would go crazy with the impatience of waiting to get on that flight from Tampa to Maine. But all of the holiday activities managed to keep me busy. Christmas in Cedar Key brought an extra amount of tourists to the island, and all of them seemed to find their way to my chocolate shop. Handmade chocolates make a special Christmas gift. I had to put in increased orders with Angell and Phelps to make sure I had plenty on hand. And I was busy in my own kitchen making up double batches of my signature chocolate clams.

Saxton and I attended the Christmas party that the Historical Society sponsored, along with other parties that various merchants held. But the big party I was looking forward to was the one that Dora was having at her home a few evenings before Christmas.

I normally had lunch with Saxton most days, but today was his day to be at the school for the reading program with Lola. So I decided rather than go upstairs to my apartment, I'd hop across the street to the coffee café and just get a baked good for lunch.

I was happy to walk in and see Grace sitting with Chloe. She jumped up to give me a huge hug.

"I was beginning to think you really hadn't come back from Paris at all," I told her. "Are you feeling better now?"

Grace laughed. "I know. I'm so sorry I couldn't make the knitting group, but I'll be there tonight. I promise."

"And you're finally going to share some news? Tell us all about your trip and everything?"

"Absolutely."

"And of course you can't give me a hint now, right?"

Chloe laughed. "Hey, you've waited years for information about your mother. You can wait till tonight to hear from Grace."

"That's right," Grace said. "Chloe filled me in about Doyle and your mother. And now you have to go to Brunswick?"

"Thanks, Suellen," I said as she placed my usual coffee in front of me. "And can I get a blueberry muffin too? Yup, we have a flight to Boston on New Year's Day. Then we'll rent a car and drive to Jill's place in North Yarmouth for a night before heading up the coast to Brunswick."

Grace shook her head. "Amazing story so far. You never knew anything about Doyle?"

"Nothing. But then, I knew very little about any of that summer."

"Tell her about the painting," Chloe said.

"Doyle did a gorgeous painting of my mother. On his boat. Actually, he'd taken a snapshot, and then when she left the island he had the picture to refer to. I was blown away by it. Not only the talent, but how he captured a mother I never knew. She looked so carefree and happy in the painting. Something I didn't see much of when I was growing up."

"Such a shame," Grace said. "It's so sad that they never got together again permanently. I wonder why not. They were obviously very much in love."

"Well, I'm hoping to find that answer too after I go to Maine. My mother said in her letter to get with Doyle after I return and he'll give me the details."

"At least they did see each other once more before she died. Call me sentimental, but that makes me feel good."

I nodded. "Actually, it makes me feel good too."

* * *

I arrived early at the yarn shop and walked in to find only Dora there.

"Hey," she said, coming to give me a hug. "Glad you could make it."

"Are you kidding? Tonight's the night Grace has some news for us."

"That's right. She's been under the weather since she got back. I think she caught that bug going around the island. I just hope she's not going to tell us that she and Lucas are moving to France permanently."

I poured myself a cup of coffee from the newly brewed pot. "Oh, no. I didn't even think of that. Gosh, I hope not. I like Grace a lot. I'd hate to see her leave."

"And I've heard all about your news on your mother, Berkley. I'm so happy for you. That you're beginning to find some answers."

"Yeah, it's taken a long time, but things are finally getting pieced together. I just hope whatever I find in Maine won't be too devastating. My mother said she hoped I'd be able to forgive her, so it might be something I'd rather not know after all."

"Oh, I don't know about that." I saw a faraway look in Dora's eyes. "I've always felt it's better to know. No matter how difficult, I think we're better off knowing. It's the worst thing in the world to always wonder. To never have answers as to why something happened."

I didn't miss the wistful tone to her voice, but before I could question her, four of the knitting ladies walked in. Grace arrived a little while later. All knitting projects got put in our laps as we all leaned forward and said, "Well?"

Flora piped up with, "Yeah, I heard you have some news for us, and inquiring minds want to know."

Grace laughed and set aside the cabled beige afghan she was working on to stand up. Clapping her hands together, she said, "Well, actually it's Lucas and I both that have this news to share with you."

"Oh, no!" I blurted out. "You're not moving to France, are you?"

She waved her hand in the air. "No. Definitely not, because . . . Lucas and I are having a baby."

Stunned silence filled the room for a few seconds, and then everybody began talking at once.

"Oh, my God. You're pregnant?"

"And you thought at thirty-seven your chances were gone."

"Well, that's a sexy Frenchman for ya."

"When are you due? How do you feel?"

Grace held both hands in the air as she joined our laughter.

"I know. Isn't it amazing? I really did think that at thirty-seven my chances were pretty slim. I'm due in April and . . ."

"April?" Dora said. "You don't even look pregnant!"

"Oh, but I do," she said, lifting the loose-fitting sweater she was wearing to reveal a medium size bump in her tummy. "I've just been trying to hide it till I could tell all of you. The only ones who have known were Chloe and Aunt Maude."

"And lemme tell ya, it's been damn hard not slipping and saying something," Chloe said.

Maude laughed. "I have to agree."

"Congratulations," I told her. "And you're feeling okay?"

"I had some morning sickness while we were still in France, and I was feeling better till I caught something right after Thanksgiving. But much better now and . . . it's a girl! We're having a daughter."

This news brought whoops and more laughter.

"Well, I'll be," Flora said. "That just proves, never say never. I'm so happy for both of you."

"So the island will have two new residents come spring," Ava said. "My baby boy is due in March and you're April."

"And they can both come to my day care center when they're a bit older," Leigh said.

Monica jumped up to give Grace a hug. "I'm just thrilled for you, but don't go trying to up me by having quadruplets."

Grace laughed. "No chance of that. I'm only carrying one baby girl."

"Any names picked out yet?" I asked as I resumed knitting on my lace socks.

"We've chosen Solange...Solange Genevieve, after Lucas's daughter."

"What a beautiful name," Dora said. "Solange Trudeau. Very nice, and I like that you chose Genevieve in memory of her sister. Lucas must be over the moon about all of this."

"Oh, he is. He's waiting on me hand and foot. I'm sure he's thrilled I'm finally telling you tonight, because he's been chomping at the bit to tell his own friends he's going to be a father."

"Enjoy the pampering," Monica said. "Once the baby gets here, that'll slow down a bit. Although I do have to say, Adam is really incredible with the triplets. He knows they're a lot of work and is always trying to pitch in."

I looked around the room and felt the joy and happiness all of us were sharing. Which made me wonder why my mother had never returned to Doyle. Had she done so, I could have finished my growing up years right here on Cedar Key. But she had chosen otherwise. And I was getting more and more anxious to find out the reason.

After more baby talk, the conversation switched to Dora's upcoming party and who would bring which covered dish, dessert, or snacks. After that was figured out, Maude said, "Raylene, how are the wedding plans coming?"

We had held a mini-shower for her a few nights before, and she had been like a blushing bride when she opened some of the frilly and sexy nightwear, but it was all in good fun and we knew that Raylene had appreciated it.

"Very well," she said. "And...I asked Corabeth to stand up for me, and she agreed."

All heads swiveled toward Corabeth. The woman who wrote erotica? The author whose books Raylene at one time wanted banned?

"Yup," Corabeth said, obvious pride in her voice. "I'm to be a bridesmaid. Can you imagine? And Mr. Carl insists it's all due to Berkley's chocolates."

Everyone laughed, but for once, I wondered... was there any truth that my chocolates did in fact bring about good changes in people? I'd probably never know for sure, but it gave me a good feeling that I might possibly have given something back to this island I was growing to love more and more.

❧ 34 ❧

During the holidays, with all the events going on, it gave one a chance to dress a little more formally than usual. I had decided to wear my long black velvet dress with black strappy heels. Just as I had sprayed Chanel No 5 on my neck, I heard Saxton at the door.

"Oh, my," he said, pulling me into an embrace. "Berkley, you look stunning."

I took in his tan sport jacket, white shirt, and chocolate slacks and said, "You look pretty good yourself." And he did. I loved to see a man with a shirt and sport jacket, and Saxton carried it off exceptionally well. I realized that this was the first time either of us had been out together so formally dressed.

"If you'll take the cake plate, I'll get the spinach pie," I told him. Pistachio cake with green frosting and my grandmother's spinach pie recipe was my contribution for Dora's party.

We arrived at Dora's house to find Christmas lights blazing outside and in. My first Christmas in Cedar Key, and I loved how the light displays in Florida rivaled any in the northeast. Dora's bushes, pine trees, and walkway sparkled with multicolored lights.

We entered her spacious living room to find a crowd had already gathered. In the corner was a tree touching the ceiling, complete with white lights, red bows, and assorted ornaments.

"Welcome, welcome," Dora greeted us. "Come on in."

"Your outside lights and tree look beautiful," I told her.

"Thank you. All due to my grandsons' efforts. I don't know what I'd do without them this time of year. They always come to help me decorate. You can put that in the kitchen, straight through the house to the back, and then I'll introduce you to my daughter and grandsons."

Saxton followed behind me as we wove our way through groups of people chatting and laughing, nodding and smiling as we went.

"Ah, more food," Sydney said. "We'll find a spot here on the counter."

I saw casseroles, sliced ham and turkey, various salads, and a separate table for desserts filling the kitchen.

"Thanks," Sydney told me. "The bar is outside on the patio, so go help yourselves to a drink."

I followed Saxton out the French doors to a large flagstone patio where more couples and groups milled around. We made our way to the bar, and Saxton poured us each a glass of red wine.

"Here's to our first Christmas together," he said, touching my glass.

"Cheers," I replied, and looked around. I spied Chloe, Grace, Lucas, and Maude in one group and headed toward them.

"I think congratulations are in order for the father-to-be," I told Lucas, holding up my glass.

"Yes, I must say, I think fatherhood will agree with you," Saxton said, and I saw the embarrassed look on his face as he quickly realized this would not be Lucas's first time becoming a father.

But Lucas brushed it off, accepting Saxton's handshake. "Yes, I think we have an exciting time ahead," he said, placing a kiss on Grace's cheek.

Strains of Christmas carols drifted out from the house where a group had gathered around Dora's piano, and I saw her heading toward us followed by a woman and two young men who appeared to be early to midtwenties.

"Berkley, I want you to meet my daughter, Marin, and her sons, Jason and John. And all of you know Saxton."

Marin extended her hand to greet me with a smile. "Oh, yes.

We're all quite familiar with Cedar Key's popular author. And I've heard all about your chocolate shop, Berkley. I'm anxious to get down there tomorrow."

Dora's grandsons extended their greetings and then excused themselves.

"I'd love to have you stop by," I told her. Marin looked to be in her late fifties, and I saw a striking resemblance between her and her cousin, Sydney. I recalled the story that Grace had told me about Sydney finding her biological mother a few years before. Sybile Bowden was Dora's sister, and Sydney and Monica had welcomed the newfound family that had come into their lives. I briefly wondered if this was the sort of thing I might discover in Brunswick. Did I have extended family that I wasn't aware of?

"Is your husband here?" I asked.

Marin shook her head. "No, I'm afraid Andrew has been under the weather. He really hated to miss this gathering."

"Be right back," Saxton said. "There's Rob, and I want to speak with him about the reading program with the dogs."

I saw Suellen talking to a group and wandered over to join them.

"Hey," she said. "I don't think you've met Mitchell. This is my friend, Mitchell Thomas."

I shook hands with a tall, distinguished-looking man about Suellen's age. We chatted for a few minutes before being joined by Chloe, holding the hand of a man who looked vaguely familiar.

"This is Cameron. He owns the jewelry shop downtown, but I'm not sure you've ever met."

"No," I said. "But I've heard about you from Chloe. Nice to meet you."

Conversation flowed, and I saw that Saxton was now chatting with another group near the French doors. That was when I spotted Doyle. Standing by himself at the end of the patio, looking out toward the water.

I walked over to join him. "Can I intrude?" I asked.

"Berkley," he said, a smile lighting up his face. "You look great."

Doyle wasn't as formal as Saxton and a few of the other men, but gone were his normal cutoffs and tee shirt. He was wearing a black turtleneck and dress slacks, and with his silver ponytail he looked more bohemian than hippie.

"Thanks. Nice party."

He nodded. "I take it you're not upset with me?"

"For being with my mother one entire summer or for not telling me before now?"

He chuckled before saying, "Both."

"No, how could I be upset with you? I'm glad that my mother had somebody like you in her life, even if it was only briefly. And as far as not telling me—well, you promised that you wouldn't. But I still have a few more questions that you *can* answer. That night that you first met me at the Black Dog—did you know I was Jeanette's daughter?"

"I had a pretty good idea when I first saw you, yes. You may not see it, but there's a definite resemblance to Jenna. And when you told me you were from Salem and owned a chocolate shop, then I knew for sure."

"And yet you waited months before telling me there was a connection? Why?"

Doyle let out a deep sigh and then took a sip of wine. "It was one of the things that Jenna and I had discussed last year before she passed away. She felt pretty certain that somehow you would make your way here. But she wanted to be sure that you were ready to begin getting your answers. So she told me to wait awhile, get to know you, see if maybe you'd give up trying to piece together why she came here. Although I've never been a father, she said she trusted that when I felt the time was right, she wanted me to tell you about us and to give you the letter."

"What made you think the time was right now?"

"When you reconnected with your aunt. Having her come here. You were still searching for those answers. You hadn't given up at all, and I knew you weren't going to. So I did what Jenna asked. When you showed me those photos, I knew the time had come for you to learn the entire story."

"And yet, you can't tell it to me now?"

"I can't," he said softly. "Saxton told me you have a flight booked to New England on New Year's Day. You'll have your answers soon enough, Berkley."

"And after I do, will you answer any further questions that I might have?"

"I will."

We were both silent for a few minutes, gazing out at the water as the night air filled with the scent of lantana.

"My mother liked it here, didn't she?"

"Very much. I think when she came here, it was the one time in her life she felt complete."

I glanced up at him. "And you loved her very much, didn't you?"

Doyle nodded.

"Then why did you let her go?"

"Sometimes loving somebody means that you have to let go. When you fall in love with that one special person, there are no guarantees, Berkley. Sometimes the circumstances just won't allow it. It doesn't mean you ever stop loving them. It just means you're not able to be together."

I felt his sadness. Sadness for what never was.

Saxton came up behind me, slipping his arm around my waist. "Hey, sweetheart, I wondered where you disappeared to. How're you doing, Doyle?"

Doyle nodded. "Fine. I'm okay," he said, and I watched him walk back toward the house alone.

In that moment, I felt a surge of love for Saxton. For the person that he was to me. For the person I was when I was with him. But most of all, because not only had we found each other, we were able to be together and share that love. Unlike my mother and Doyle.

35

I awoke Christmas morning, turned over, saw Saxton's face, and smiled. We had decided to spend Christmas Eve and Christmas Day at his house because he had more room for a small tree and our wrapped presents.

Almost as if he felt my gaze on him, he opened his eyes. A smile covered his face as he said, "Good morning, beautiful. Merry Christmas."

"Merry Christmas to you," I said, snuggling into the crook of his arm.

"So have you been a good girl? Think Santa was good to you?"

I laughed. "Oh, I'm not sure about that. I have a tendency toward being naughty."

I felt Saxton's hand slip down my body. "I like it when you're naughty."

"That was delicious," Saxton said as he took another sip of coffee.

"I'm glad you enjoyed it. I thought omelets and grits would hold us till dinner later at the Island Hotel. I'm glad you booked there for us, rather than cook here."

"I thought it might be a good idea since you want to drive around visiting and dropping off your chocolate."

I had put together my signature clams in gold boxes tied with red ribbon and bows. Just a little gesture for my friends.

"Now, let me help you clear this table and we'll go inside to see what Santa's left for us under the tree."

It was a fun time and brought back memories of my childhood Christmases. The excitement and surprise with each gift un-wrapped.

Saxton was pleased with the books and hand-knit sweater, scarf, and hat that I'd made for him. He had also gotten me newly re-leased novels that he thought I'd enjoy, along with a new bottle of Chanel No 5 and some wonderfully fragranced shower gel and lo-tion.

I jumped to give him a kiss. "Thank you so much. You've made Christmas very special."

"Well, it's not over yet," he said, producing a small box wrapped in silver paper with a red bow on top.

My surprise must have shown on my face as I reached for it.

"Go ahead," he told me. "Open it."

My heart skipped a beat because I knew it was a ring box. I loved Saxton. I did. But engaged? An engagement led to marriage. Marriage was great for some people, but Saxton knew my feelings on this topic.

I removed the paper and flipped open the blue velvet box to see an incredible ring staring back at me. An oval-shaped garnet stone, surrounded by diamonds in an antique setting.

"My birthstone," I whispered with surprise. "It's gorgeous."

"You like it?"

"I love it, Saxton. Thank you so much."

He removed the ring from the box and reached for my left hand. "I'd like to think this is a promise ring. Wearing it will mean that we've made a promise to each other to always be together. The ring makes it official."

He slipped it onto my third finger, and I held my hand out in front of me to admire the beauty.

"I accept," I said, as I felt moisture stinging my eyes. "I absolutely accept. I love you, Saxton, and I'll always love you." But even more important than the ring was the fact that he *did* know me. Really know me.

He pulled me into an embrace as his lips found mine. "And I will love you all the days of my life."

After we had showered and dressed I was placing my candy boxes into a shopping bag when Saxton came up behind me. He placed a kiss on my neck.

"Are we about ready to begin our Santa run?"

"Yup, I'm all set. We'll hit Monica's house first. I have another bag with gifts for the kids, and then we'll head to Maude's house. Next stop will be Dora's, and then on to the Lighthouse to drop off chocolates for Sydney and Noah. Oh, and we need to make a stop at Doyle's house too. I have chocolates for him."

"Oh, we're definitely stopping at Doyle's, but we'll make his place our last stop."

I saw a twinkle in his eye and laughed. "What's this about? I have a feeling it's more than me just dropping off chocolate."

"Be patient," he told me, a grin covering his face. "You'll see."

Monica's home was the epitome of Christmas afternoon with children. Cardboard boxes were strewn about, with wrapping paper, ribbons, multiple toys, and in the midst of it were Monica and Adam looking happier than I'd ever seen them.

Adam laughed and said, "If you can make your way through, come on in. As you can see, mayhem descended here this morning."

The triplets were tottering around grabbing toys from each other, laughing and displaying the excitement and delight of Christmas.

Monica looked up from the sofa where she was sitting beside Clarissa Jo. "Ah, welcome to the madhouse. Merry Christmas."

I laughed and shook my head. "My goodness, it looks like Santa was very good to this house."

Clarissa ran over to me, opening a tote bag for me to peek inside. "He was. Look at the new circular needles and yarn he brought me."

I fingered the various fibers and colors. "Oh, I think you'll be quite busy over the next year with such a great stash."

Adam brought a tray of coffee, and we managed to find a seat not occupied by toys or gift wrap.

"Oh, what's that?" Monica said, jumping up to come over and grab my hand. "It's gorgeous, Berkley."

"Thank you. It's a promise ring from Saxton. It seals a promise that we'll always be together."

"How romantic. Congratulations," she said.

After we finished our coffee, we were on our way to Maude's house. Everybody was gathered in her kitchen when we walked in. I distributed my candy and then Saxton and I joined them for a glass of wine.

Chloe was the first to spy my ring, and I received more congratulations.

"I'm so happy for both of you," Grace said. "And thank you so much for the chocolate. It seems since I got pregnant, I crave it even more."

"You're booked for dinner at the Hotel, right?" Maude asked.

"Yes, four o'clock, so we'd better get going. We have a few more stops to make."

We arrived at Dora's to find Maybelle, Marin, and Dora's grandsons. I was surprised that Marin's husband wasn't there.

"I hope your husband is feeling better," I told her.

A worried expression crossed her face. "No, he really isn't. He's scheduled for some tests next week."

After coffee and one of Dora's delicious blueberry scones we were on our way to Sydney's.

"No more food for me," I told Saxton as we drove down Rye Key Drive. "I won't be able to eat dinner later."

The Lighthouse came into view and I marveled, as I always did, at the unique structure. Built from the plans of the Hooper Strait Lighthouse in Chesapeake Bay, it stood majestically against a background of sky and water. The house sat atop stilts with a full set of stairs leading to the deck that surrounded it, enclosed with a railing.

Saxton pulled the golf cart into the gravel drive, and as we climbed the stairs, I stopped halfway to admire the view over the water, with sandbars peeking out and pelicans swooping to grab their daily rations.

"Merry Christmas," Sydney greeted us.

"Hey, good to see you guys," Noah said, joining Sydney.

"It's such a gorgeous day," she said. "Why don't we sit out here on the deck. Can I get you something to eat or drink?"

I put my hand in the air and laughed. "Thanks, but no thank you. I think we've just eaten and drunk our way around the island, and we're due at the Hotel for dinner at four. I just wanted to drop off some chocolate for you."

"Oh, that was so nice. You know I'm addicted to it," Sydney said. "Yeah, we're due at Dora's for dinner at three."

"And don't you leave a week from today for Maine?" Noah asked.

"Yes." I nodded. "I'm just not sure what I'll find when I get there."

"My story of finding Sybile was astonishing, but yours is proving to be quite a mystery. Any ideas why your mother came here?"

"Nope. And Doyle is sworn to secrecy for the rest of the story until I go up to Maine and check those newspaper microfilms. I can't even imagine what I'll find out."

"Nervous?" Sydney asked.

"I am." I let out a deep sigh. "I mean, of course I want to know . . . but . . ."

I felt Saxton's hand on my knee.

"Right," Sydney said. "Fear of the unknown."

After chatting awhile longer, we made our way to Doyle's house. He opened the door with a huge smile on his face. "Come on in."

We followed him into the living room, where I saw a crate in the corner containing the most adorable puppy I'd ever seen.

Rushing over to it, I knelt down and stuck my finger between the wire bars. "Oh! Doyle! You got a puppy for Christmas?"

Saxton laughed as he came over, opened the door of the crate, and said, "No. *You* got a puppy for Christmas." He picked up the little black fur ball and put it in my arms as he leaned over to place a kiss on my lips. "Merry Christmas, Berkley. I hope you'll like her."

I looked down into the most soulful dark eyes and then up at Saxton. "Really? For me?"

He nodded. "Yes, for you. I know how you like Lola, and you had hinted that you might like a dog. We know Sigmund gets along fine with my dog. So I wanted you to have your own."

My eyes filled with tears as I snuggled her close to me. "It's a girl?"

"Yes. I got her at the Levy County Humane Society. She's only about ten pounds but is full grown, and she's eight months old. She's part poodle, part Maltese and God knows what else. A sad story—her owner passed away and the niece brought her to the pound."

"Aww, you lost your owner?" I kissed her forehead and cuddled her tighter. "Well, I'll be your new mama. Oh, Saxton, thank you so much."

"We have to thank Doyle too. He's the one that helped me by hiding her for a couple days here at his house."

I walked over and placed a kiss on his cheek. "That's going above and beyond friendship," I said. "Thank you for keeping her here."

"If you didn't come soon, I was thinking about keeping her myself," he joked.

"Any names in mind for her?" Saxton came over to pat her.

"Yes," I said. "Yes. I'm going to call her Brit. For British. Your heritage."

He put his arm around me. "I like that. Very much."

I held her away from me so I could see her better. "She's such a pretty pup. And she seems like a good girl."

"Oh, she is," Doyle said. "Sleeps well. All housebroken. I think you'll enjoy her a lot."

"And Uncle Doyle here has even offered to keep her while we're in Maine."

"That's really nice of you," I told him. "Where're you going for dinner today?"

"Dora invited me. I think she's a little concerned about her son-in-law, so I'll see if I can cheer her and Marin up a bit."

"Yeah, Marin mentioned he's been sick. I hope it isn't anything serious."

Doyle nodded.

"Well, thank you for keeping the surprise," Saxton said. "But I think we need to get Brit here home and settled before we leave for the Hotel and dinner."

❧ 36 ❧

We got back to my apartment following dinner to find Brit sleeping away in her crate. As soon as she heard our voices, her eyes popped open and her little tail began wagging. I reached down to scoop her up.

"Aren't you just the best girl," I cooed to her. "I'm sure she has to go out. Feel like a walk?"

"Definitely," Saxton said. "I could stand to walk off that great dinner."

"I know." I attached the pink leash to Brit's pink collar. "Wasn't that heart of palm salad just delicious?"

"All of it was. All set?"

I followed him down the stairs, and just as we turned onto Second Street Saxton's cell phone rang. I could tell by the smile on his face and his voice that it was Resa.

"Merry Christmas to you too, darlin'," he said, and I looked up at him and smiled. "Yes, she was pretty surprised. We're walking the pup now. Berkley named her Brit."

My smile increased as I realized he had shared my surprise with his daughter. That made me feel good. They continued talking as we strolled over to City Park.

He hung up and said, "As you know, that was Resa and she said to be sure and wish you a Merry Christmas too."

"You have a great daughter, Saxton. I like her a lot."

"I'm glad because I know she likes you."

We walked around the park and then back to my place.

"Tomorrow I'll come over with Lola so she and Brit can get to know each other. I'm pretty sure they'll be fast friends."

As we walked into my apartment the phone was ringing, and I answered to hear Jill.

"Merry Christmas, girlfriend. I hope it was a good one."

"The best," I said, and went on to tell her about my ring and Brit.

"I'm so happy for you," Jill said. "And I really hate to burst your bubble, but . . . I take it you haven't caught the news or any weather updates today?"

"Hmm, no. Why? What's up?"

"Well, they're predicting a blizzard up here midweek. It's not looking so good that you'll be flying into Boston a week from today."

"Oh, no. Geez. How bad?"

"Pretty bad. They're saying over a foot of snow New Year's Eve into the next day."

"Well, we might not have a choice. We'll probably have to reschedule."

"Yeah, I'm really sorry. I know how anxious you are to get up here and figure out the rest of your story."

True. I was. But part of me was a tiny bit relieved too. I was beginning to feel more and more uneasy about what those newspapers might contain.

When I hung up, I filled Saxton in on the news.

"Gee, that's a shame," he said, going to flip on my TV to The Weather Channel.

We heard pretty much what Jill had just relayed to me.

"Well, let's give it another day or so, keep up with the forecast, and take it from there," Saxton said. "I can always cancel the hotel and we can rebook the flight for whenever you want."

"Sounds good," I said.

* * *

By the time my aunt arrived three days later, our trip had been canceled. The New England area was getting belted with a good old-fashioned nor'easter.

"That's such a shame," my aunt said as we sat sipping tea in her cottage at the Faraway.

"Yeah, looks like Mother Nature had other plans for me."

Saxton sat beside me with Brit in his lap. "I told Berkley that whenever she wants to go up there will be fine. We're going to reschedule."

"Oh, good," Stella said. "Now that you've come this far with your inquiring, you have to get the rest of the story. Imagine . . . Doyle and my sister." She shook her head. "I feel bad, though, that the relationship never had a chance to grow."

"I know. It really is sad."

"And I can't even begin to imagine what newspaper articles might tell you. What on earth could that have to do with you and your mother?"

I shook my head. "I'm as stumped as you are."

Addi came over to sniff Brit, and I smiled.

"I think they like each other."

"Oh, Addi is very dog friendly. I think she feels like the big sister," Stella said, as Saxton placed Brit on the floor.

"I think you're right," I told her as I watched both dogs chasing each other around the table.

"She's just adorable. I'm really glad you have a dog, Berkley. Addi is my best friend. I just don't know what I'd do without her."

Saxton nodded. "I feel the same way about my Lola. Dogs are remarkable with the joy and unconditional love they give us."

"Are you going to get her into that reading with the children at school like Saxton does?"

"I thought about it. Saxton said we can go to Gainesville for the obedience classes. Brit seems pretty bright, so I think she'll do well."

"That's such a great program," my aunt said. "I should really look into that in my area. I suppose I could squeeze out a few more days of my week for another activity."

I laughed. "I can't believe what a social butterfly you are."

"Hey, life is for the living," she told me. "May as well take advantage of it and live life to the fullest."

"Ditto on that," I said, thinking my mother was gone much too soon. Before she had a chance to really enjoy it—with Doyle.

My aunt got up to open the windows in the sitting area. "Such a beautiful day. It has to be in the seventies. Hard to believe a blizzard is going to hit New England. Are all the plans in place for the wedding?"

"As far as I know. It'll be held at four o'clock on the beach at City Park and then a reception following at the Community Center. There should be quite a crowd."

"I think it's just great that a couple pushing eighty is taking a leap with marriage. Not that it's unheard of today, mind you. I just recently read somewhere that a couple in their nineties decided to get married in the nursing home where they resided."

"And the thing is, more people are living longer today, so why not?" I said, even though such an official and legal exchange wasn't something I wanted or needed in my life.

Saxton reached over and squeezed my hand. "There's no age limit on love."

Precisely, I thought, *and that's what our relationship is all about. The love we share.*

The love that was displayed as Mr. Carl and Miss Raylene stood on the beach proved what Saxton had said. They positively glowed. It was almost embarrassing to see the way they looked into each other's eyes as they repeated their traditional vows.

Raylene had chosen an ankle-length dress of soft lavender. She was barefoot, with a purple hibiscus flower clipped to her white hair. Carl, wearing a tan dress shirt and dark brown slacks, was also barefoot. They had chosen the marriage lady of Cedar Key to perform the ceremony.

I stood beside Saxton and glanced around. Neither Carl nor Raylene had had children, but the large crowd that was gathered was very obviously *family* to them.

"I now pronounce you husband and wife" was followed by

hooting, cheering, and laughter. Somebody had brought a dozen white balloons, and these were now released up into the sky over Cedar Key while the crowd clapped.

It seemed like most of the island had turned out for the event, and all of us went the short distance to the Community Center to help Carl and Raylene celebrate.

When everyone arrived and a glass of champagne had been placed in each hand, Carl tapped his glass with a fork for attention.

Holding his glass up, he said, "I want to thank all of you for coming today to see us become man and wife." Looking in my direction, he said, "And I want to especially thank Miss Berkley for those magical chocolates that she makes."

I knew my face was turning crimson as laughter and clapping filled the room, but if Mr. Carl thought it was the chocolates, it was fine with me.

A wonderful wedding buffet was set up, and after filling our plates we found a table where my aunt and Doyle joined us.

"This was such a nice wedding," my aunt said. "I'm very happy to be here."

"I'm glad you could come too," Doyle said.

Call me a hopeless romantic, but something in the way he said that caused me to look at Saxton with raised eyebrows. He shrugged, but gave me a smile. Was something going on here that I wasn't aware of?

After the meal, the band began playing music. From some of the dance steps on the floor, it was difficult to think so many of the couples were over seventy.

"Care to dance?" I heard Doyle say to my aunt.

"I never refuse an offer from a handsome gentleman," she said.

My God! My aunt was flirting with Doyle Summers.

I sat and watched him lead her onto the dance floor, where they proceeded to glide around, perfectly in sync, to a waltz.

"Well," I said. "That's interesting."

Saxton laughed. "You're not being a prude, are you?"

"Of course not. I just didn't realize . . . I didn't know there was an interest there."

"I didn't want to say anything to you after your aunt's Thanksgiving visit here, but Doyle had questioned me about her. If she was single or seeing anybody."

"No! And you didn't tell me. What else did he say?"

"He said he thought she was an extremely attractive woman. And I didn't tell you because there wasn't *anything* to tell."

I nudged him on the arm. "Men! Of course there was something to tell me. That's very significant, you know. That he finds her attractive."

Saxton threw his head back laughing. "You are such a romantic."

We both shut up as my aunt and Doyle returned to the table. The next song was a cha-cha, and before I could blink, Doyle had her back up on the dance floor.

"He's quite the Fred Astaire, isn't he?" I said.

"I believe he's found his Ginger Rogers. I heard that Doyle has always been quite the dancer."

"Well, I'll be darn."

"I'm no Fred Astaire, but care to join me on the floor?"

I lifted my hand in the air and, with an exaggerated tone, said, "But, of course, my handsome man."

❧ 37 ❧

The forecasters had all been correct. New England got almost two feet of snow, and the farthest north states of Maine, New Hampshire, and Vermont got the most. Great for skiers, bad for travelers.

My aunt ended up staying on the island a few days longer than she had intended. I couldn't help but wonder if this was due to Doyle. She didn't say anything. I didn't ask.

By the time she left, though, it was obvious that some sort of attraction was going on with her and Doyle. He had taken her out to dinner a couple times, and one day they even drove into Gainesville together for a movie.

Walking down Second Street to Yarning Together for our Thursday night knitting group, I smiled. It was nice when people hooked up. People who enjoyed each other's company, enjoyed doing the same activities together. This made me feel sad for my mother. She had a chance to have this—but for some reason, she made a different choice.

I walked into the yarn shop to find most of the women already gathered and knitting away. I was always impressed with the level of expertise they displayed. Flora was working on a very intricate lace sweater for her daughter in the most yummy shade of pistachio green. Dora was working on an entrelac hat in vibrant colors of peach, pink, and lavender. And I saw Grace knitting away on a pink baby sweater that had small white lambs across the top.

"Hey, good to see you, Berkley," Chloe said, looking up from a pink basketweave blanket I knew was for her sister's baby.

I settled down beside Dora and removed the beige cable mittens from my bag.

"For Jill?" Dora questioned.

"Yup. With all that snow up there, I'm sure she can always use more mittens."

"But what happened with your trip?" Flora asked.

"We've postponed it till March. Looks like it's going to be a bad winter up there, and we don't want to have to cancel again."

Flora nodded. "Right. Why give up this gorgeous weather here for snow and ice," she said, and everyone laughed with agreement.

"It's getting to be that time of year again," Dora said. "We need to start thinking about our vendor's table for April and the Arts Festival. Any ideas what we should make?"

"I think the Cedar Key scarves were a big hit," Corabeth said. "Maybe we should make those again."

"I agree." Raylene took a sip of her tea. "We ran out in practically no time."

"That's fine with me," Dora said. "It's such a nice pattern. Okay. If everyone is in agreement, then we'll do the Cedar Key scarves again this year."

"Oh, did you hear?" Raylene asked. "I'll be leasing my property to Leigh for her day care center."

"That's wonderful," I said. "Where is she tonight?"

"Said she had a lot of things to get in order. She's really going to have her hands full getting the property in shape, I'm afraid."

Dora nodded. "But a lot of people have volunteered to help. We should set a date on a weekend and we can all pitch in."

"I know she'd like some murals done on the walls," Raylene said. "Maybe we can see if somebody at the Arts Center would be willing to help."

"Right." Chloe reached for another skein of yarn to attach. "We should plan on next month. I think Leigh said she hopes to have her inspection by the state around May and possibly open in June."

After an hour of knitting, Dora announced it was time for snacks. "Raylene brought brownies tonight."

"I wanted to make something more fancy, but . . . well, Carl and I have been so busy."

"Right," Flora said with a snicker. "Newlyweds are usually pretty busy."

The room erupted in laughter as Raylene got up to assist Dora. Her face had turned beet red as she stammered, "Oh, no. Well . . . that isn't what I meant. . . ."

"Come on, Raylene," Dora said, pulling her toward the back room. "They're just teasing you."

When we got situated with tea, coffee, and brownies, Maybelle announced that she had some news.

"You know my goddaughter, Victoria, who I've mentioned?"

"Oh, right," Corabeth said. "The one you haven't heard from in so long."

Maybelle nodded. "Yes. Thirty years it's been." She took a sip of her tea and sat up straighter in her chair. "Well . . . I have heard from her."

"That's wonderful," I said. "Any chance you'll be getting together?"

I saw the look of happiness that crossed Maybelle's face. "There is. Victoria is single with a four-year-old son, Sam. They live in upper state New York, where Victoria owns a needlepoint shop. She said with the economy so bad things have gotten pretty slow, but she's holding on. Victoria told me she always remembered me, but because of the bad feelings on her mother's part, she never pursued getting in touch. When Dorothy passed away last summer, Victoria said she felt the time had come for us to reunite."

"Such a shame that feud caused Victoria to drift away," Dora said. "When do you think you'll see her?"

"She's hoping to visit this summer with Sam. It would be so great. She was only ten the last time I saw her."

"That's wonderful news," Flora said. "I love to hear about people reconnecting. And you and Dorothy couldn't patch up your differences, huh?"

Maybelle shook her head. "I'm afraid not. I was certainly willing, but she could be pretty stubborn. We disagreed on something and . . . well, that was the end of our friendship."

"What a shame," Grace said, looking at her sister. "I'm sure glad that Chloe and I were able to get through our differences."

"You and me both," Chloe replied. "Friendships and family are so important. Holding grudges and being stubborn certainly accomplishes nothing."

"And you said she owns a needlepoint shop? That's interesting. I've been tossing around a few ideas with Chloe." Dora winked in her direction.

"Hey, no holding back," Flora said. "Come on. Tell us what you two have up your sleeve."

Dora laughed. "Well, nothing is definite and it's all in the planning stages right now, but . . . I'm thinking of purchasing the empty shop next door. Breaking through the wall and adding a needlepoint shop to Yarning Together."

"Really?" I said. "I just recently returned to doing some needlepoint. That's a great idea. Many yarn shops carry both."

"Oh, I agree," Corabeth said. "I haven't done needlepoint for years, but it would be nice to have a different project when I want something other than knitting."

Chloe smiled. "See, Dora, I thought it would be well accepted. And you said that Marin is quite accomplished with needlepoint. She might be willing to help out. I think we should do it."

"You could be right. Well, when I get a chance I'll look into it. The property is listed with Pelican, so we'll start there and then . . . who knows. This could turn into a very exciting new venture for me."

The look on Dora's face made me hope that she'd be able to make the addition happen.

Before I left the shop I purchased enough of a yummy shade of ocean blue cotton to knit my required Cedar Key scarves for the Arts Festival, and then headed home.

As soon as my key hit the lock I heard Brit yipping. I certainly loved Sigmund, but the wagging of a tail and excited barks surpassed a nonchalant feline greeting.

"Hey, sweetie," I said, opening the door to release my little bundle of black fur. No doubt about it, I was a proud dog owner and Brit was the best gift that Saxton could have given me.

"Let me get your leash and we'll take a walk," I told her before scooping her up and heading back downstairs.

As we strolled along Second Street, thoughts of my mother floated into my mind. She had walked this very street, lived where I did, and had even met some of the people that I now knew. Once again, doubts nagged at me. Would I be sorry for delving into the past? Her past. Or would my mind finally be at ease with something that had haunted me for so long? No matter what, within eight weeks I'd have my answers.

❦ 38 ❦

On a Saturday morning in mid-February residents of the community came together to work on Leigh Sallenger's new day care center.

I arrived on the golf cart with Saxton to find quite a crowd had already assembled, and I saw Doyle and another man hanging the brightly colored wooden sign SUGAR AND SPICE DAY CARE from the porch eave.

"Looks like the work is well under way," I said, getting out of the golf cart and balancing a box of muffins while Saxton grabbed the second box.

"Mornin'," Doyle said. "How's the sign look?"

I nodded. "Terrific. I think you earned yourself a muffin and some coffee. We stopped at Island Girl Cakes to pick these up for the crowd."

Leigh greeted us at the door with a huge smile. "Lord, did I hear you say Island Girl Cakes? You mean to tell me I get all this help plus those yummy muffins?"

"You do," I said, walking in and placing them on a table. "Coffee ready?"

She pointed to the large coffee urn and nodded.

I looked around and saw people painting walls, hanging border print, and doing other assorted tasks.

"Hey, Berkley," Chloe said, coming from a back room and spying the box of muffins. "Oh, tell me those are from Island Girl Cakes!"

I laughed. "Yup, they are. Come and help yourself."

"Everybody," Leigh hollered. "Time for a coffee break before we continue working."

I marveled at how many people had showed up to help both inside and out. I saw Dora through the window with Maude. They were busy planting some flowers and bushes between the two cottages. I rapped on the window and motioned for them to come inside.

"Grace and Lucas will be along shortly," Maude said, reaching for a muffin. "Berkley, you have to come and see the beautiful mural that Josie's working on in one of the back rooms."

I grabbed a muffin, filled a cup with coffee, and followed her.

"Oh, wow," I said as my eyes took in the pastel colors of what was going to be a meadow filled with lambs. "Josie, this is gorgeous. I had no idea you were such an artist."

She laughed as she brushed a strand of hair from her face. "Yeah, my mother might be the author but I got my creativity with drawing and painting. I think this wall will look great when I finish. Leigh said this is the room where the cribs will be for the babies, so she wanted the softer colors in here."

"It's going to look super. Go grab a muffin and some coffee though. Everybody's taking a break."

I wandered into another room and saw somebody at work using primary colors to paint numbers and letters on the wall. And on the other wall Suellen was painting the animals from Winnie the Pooh.

"I'm amazed at the talent here," I said. "Suellen, you're a born artist."

She stood up from kneeling to work on Pooh's honey pot and stretched. "Oh, not really. I've been drawing all my life, but I wouldn't consider it prize material."

I shook my head. "I don't agree with you. Geez, I'm not sure what I can contribute. I can't even draw a straight line."

"You said you can swing a paintbrush. Your job is to paint the other two walls in here. Leigh wants one in a bright red and the other one yellow. Paint cans and brushes are in the corner."

I took the last bite of my muffin and nodded. "That I can do," I told her, and set to work.

I was halfway through the second wall when I felt Saxton come up behind me and place a kiss on my neck.

"How're you doing here? The walls look great. But it's going on two o'clock. Ready for lunch?"

"Two o'clock? I've been working for five hours? No wonder I'm hungry."

He laughed. "I've been helping the guys put the fence up in the backyard. We have it just about finished. Let's go grab something at the Pelican and then come back for a couple more hours."

"Sounds good, but I'll probably need a massage after all this bending and stretching."

He grabbed my hand as we walked outside to the golf cart. "I think that can be arranged for later this evening," he said with a twinkle in his eye.

After a quick lunch we returned back to Third Street, where Leigh greeted us with the news that Ava had delivered her baby that morning.

"Did you hear?" she asked. "Ava had her baby boy this morning."

"Are they okay? Isn't she too early?"

"Just two weeks early, and both mother and little Jonah are just fine. He might have to stay a day or so longer, but he's in good health."

"I'm so happy to hear that. And I love the name Jonah. Ava must be so thrilled."

"She is," Grace said, coming from a back room. "I just got off the phone with her. She assures me childbirth is a piece of cake."

I looked up to see Dora, Chloe, Maude, and Leigh exchange a glance.

"Right," Grace said. "I know enough to know that all new mothers say that. I think once that baby is put into your arms all thoughts of the labor and delivery seem to vanish."

Lucas put his arm around her. "You'll do just fine, *ma chérie*. I'll be there with you for all of it."

Seeing the love that they shared made me realize that maybe there was something to this parenthood stuff after all.

"Congrats to Ava and Tom," I said, heading back to my wall. "But I have to get that painting finished up."

By the time all of us returned to the day care center on Sunday morning, we had made quite a dent in the remodeling. The rooms looked cozy and inviting for babies and toddlers alike. Somebody had built a window seat in one of the rooms with bookshelves to each side. Floors had been sanded and polished, and in the toddler room Doyle and Saxton were helping to lay the tile. I had managed to help with the border print that now hung around the top of the various walls. All with a baby or storybook theme.

"This looks incredible," I told Leigh.

"It does, and I never could have accomplished any of this without all the help."

"When does the furniture and stuff arrive?"

"I still have a lot to get done here on my own, so there's no rush yet. I'll have my inspection in May and then hopefully open in June as I planned. But I'm thrilled that I was approved for my small business loan. I've managed to get some cribs and things from people in the community. That's been a big help financially. I have to go to Toys R Us and get toys and games and that sort of thing."

"How many children are you planning to have?"

"I'll be approved for ten, but that won't be for a while, until I can hire more help. Paula will be able to help me only part time while she's working on her degree. So when I open I'll start with just four or five. A couple of the girls who are graduating in June approached me about working as an assistant. I could use the help, but first I'll have to see if I'll be able to afford their salaries."

"So it'll all take time," I told her. "But I'd say you're on your way. A year from now . . ."

I was interrupted by the sound of Dora crying in the next room. "Oh, dear Lord," she screamed.

Leigh and I ran in to see Dora clutching her cell phone, surrounded by Monica, Sydney, and Grace.

By the look on their faces, I knew it wasn't good news.

"What's wrong?" I asked.

"That was Marin on the phone," Sydney explained. "She's at Shands Hospital in Gainesville. Andrew was rushed there about an hour ago . . . and . . . they lost him. A heart attack."

My hand flew to my mouth as Sydney escorted Dora to a chair.

"Oh, my God! What can we do?"

The room began filling with other volunteers who heard the commotion.

Dora took a deep breath as tears streamed down her face. "Marin. I have to get to Shands and be with Marin."

"None of you are in any condition to drive," Doyle said. "Come on, I'll drive you."

"I'll call Noah. Monica, can you go with Aunt Dora? Noah and I will be right behind you."

"Yes. I'll call Adam on the way to let him know what's going on."

We watched helplessly as they rushed out to Doyle's car. Within minutes Noah pulled up to get Sydney.

"Here," she said, passing me a set of keys. "Could you do me a huge favor and go to Aunt Dora's and feed Oliver?"

"Of course I can," I assured her, giving her a hug. "Just go. We'll take care of Oliver."

Just like that—a life was snuffed out, leaving behind sorrow and grief.

An hour later Saxton and I pulled into Dora's driveway. When I unlocked the door, we were greeted by Oliver.

He sniffed and looked behind us, and I knew he was looking for his beloved Dora.

"Come on, fellow," I told him, leading the way to the kitchen. "Time for your din din."

Monica had quickly instructed me on his food before she left, and I got his bowl, dry mix, and a can of Pedigree.

While I got it ready Saxton patted Oliver and tried to make him feel better. "Dora will be back later, buddy. Not to worry. We won't abandon you."

Oliver's curiosity about Dora's absence didn't diminish his hunger. He chowed down every morsel and then sat in the middle of the kitchen floor looking at us.

"Let's get his leash and take him for a walk," Saxton said.

We walked slowly around Andrews Circle with Oliver sniffing here and there.

"Poor Marin," I said. "This had to have been such a shock for her."

Saxton nodded. "Yeah. She knew he wasn't feeling well, but I'm sure she didn't expect this. He didn't even get a chance to get in there for those tests that were scheduled for the end of the month."

I shook my head. "I know. It's so sad. Life can change in a heartbeat."

When we got back to Dora's the phone was ringing. I grabbed it to hear Monica's voice.

"I thought I might catch you there. Thank you so much, Berkley, for going to take care of Oliver."

"I'm glad I could help. How's Marin holding up?"

"Not good, I'm afraid. It all happened so fast. We'll be leaving here shortly. Marin is coming back to Aunt Dora's to stay. So I wanted to let you know we're on our way and you don't have to stay there."

"Okay. We fed Oliver and took him for a walk, so I think he's all set."

"We really appreciate your help. We'll be in touch soon."

I hung up the phone and realized that *this* was what being part of a community was all about. Something as simple as helping out with a dog during a time of crisis.

❧ 39 ❧

There was a large group of people from Cedar Key who made the drive to Gainesville for the funeral of Andrew Kane. It was an unseasonably warm day, and the sunshine somehow made a difficult time a little easier.

Dora had planned an open house back at her home to thank everyone for coming.

When we arrived we saw Marin talking to a group of people and waited our turn to give our condolences.

She was composed, although her face showed the fatigue and sorrow of the past few days.

I gave her a tight hug and tried to find the words that are always so awkward in the loss of a loved one.

"Thank you so much," Marin said, and I could tell she was struggling to be brave. "Andrew was such a good husband and father. My one comfort is that he didn't linger or suffer. And now . . . my life has been turned upside down with him gone."

I nodded. "It has to be so difficult, but I'm sure in time you'll figure out what you're doing."

"I know, and for right now I've decided to stay here at my mother's house. I just can't bear to go back home . . . without Andrew there."

That made sense to me. I gave her another hug, and Saxton and I moved away to allow others to offer their sympathy.

We mingled in the crowd, offering our condolences to Monica, and then I spied Sydney talking with a woman about her age. Tall and slim, with a salt and pepper braid hanging down her back, she looked vaguely familiar.

Sydney turned around, saw me, and motioned for me to join them.

"Berkley, I'm not sure if you've met my best friend, Alison Marks. Ali owns the B and B here on the island, but she and Paul have been off traveling for almost a year."

I extended my hand in greeting. "It's so nice to finally meet you. I've heard about you from Monica and Sydney."

"Yes," Sydney said with a smile covering her face. "Believe me, Ali was my salvation when I first came to Cedar Key. Took me in and allowed me to heal."

Alison laughed. "Well, I may have taken you in, but the healing . . . you had to do that on your own."

"Are you planning to stay around here now?" I asked.

"I'm not entirely sure. Paul and I have a place in the historic district, but I think I've finally made the decision to put the bed and breakfast up for sale. I know it's not a great time in the home market, but I'm not in any rush. And I'm very fortunate to have such a great staff to run it while I've been away."

"I wish you all the best," I told her, and then offered my sympathy to Sydney.

"Thank you. I'm really hoping my cousin will decide to live here permanently. I think it would be good for her with her family and friends here."

I agreed, but I also knew that sometimes it's very difficult trying to make a life changing decision after the death of a loved one. Had it not been for finding the postcards, I'd probably still be living in Salem, running the chocolate shop there. But I was convinced that fate had other plans for me.

I turned around to catch the wink and smile that Saxton threw my way and I had no doubt that no matter what I discovered in Maine, I was meant to be here on Cedar Key with him.

I walked into Yarning Together a couple of weeks later to find Dora alone, stocking shelves with some delicious-looking new yarn.

"Just what I'm looking for," I told her. "A new project to take on my flight tomorrow."

She turned around and smiled. "I just got this order in, and I don't think you'll be disappointed. What do you have in mind?"

I wandered over and began fingering the soft fibers as my eyes took in the various colors.

"Well, I have six Cedar Key scarves done, so I'm a little tired of working on scarves."

Dora laughed. "You'll probably want something that will be small enough to knit on the plane. How about an ascot?"

"Oh, good idea. I have a great pattern for one and it's very simple with mostly knits and purls. Okay, I think I'll take some of this dusty rose lace merino and maybe the turquoise cotton pima."

"Good choices," Dora said, taking them to ring up at the counter.

"How's Marin doing?" I asked.

Dora let out a sigh. "Well, as to be expected, she has her good days and bad days. When I lost my Henry, it was different. He'd been sick for well over a year, so I had some time to prepare myself. But poor Marin. It all happened so fast. It's going to take a while for her to come to grips with all of it."

I nodded. "It's wonderful that she has you. I'm sure staying with you is a comfort to her."

"I like to think so, but no matter how much family or friends try to help, I'm afraid this is a journey each of us has to walk alone. People mean well, but losing a loved one is something we just have to experience on our own."

"I'm sure in time Marin will make some decisions and go forward."

Dora passed me the bag of yarn. "That's one good thing. She's already trying to make some plans. It seems she might put her house in Gainesville up for sale and live here permanently."

I recalled what Sydney had said. "That would make some people very happy."

"Well, the thing is, she had retired from teaching at the university last year. With Andrew due to retire this year, they had lots of plans for travel and being together. So she's a little concerned about finding something to keep her busy. She's fortunate that financially she'll be fine, but it's the empty hours she's worried about."

"Yeah, I can understand that," I said, knowing full well that I welcomed the work in my chocolate shop and the additional time spent with filling orders for my spun yarn.

"So you're off for Beantown tomorrow."

"I am, and I'm happy to hear the temps are in the sixties and no snow in sight."

Dora laughed. "Nervous?"

"A little, but also excited to finally be able to fit all the missing pieces into my puzzle."

"So you're not sorry you came here last year and decided to find your answers?"

Without hesitating, I said, "Oh, no. Not at all. No matter what, I have no doubt that I was meant to come to Cedar Key. Living here has surpassed my expectations and Saxton...I know now that I'd been searching for him all my life and I didn't even realize it."

Dora patted my hand and smiled. "Nothing can be better than not only finding that one special person, but also being able to be together. Enjoy the moments, Berkley, because I'm afraid the older we get, the less those kinds of moments come to us."

Once again, I detected a wistful tone to her voice.

The 737 circled and made its final descent into Boston's Logan Airport. I felt Saxton squeeze my hand as I looked out the window and saw the Prudential Center, State Street Bank, Boston Harbor, and Georges Island. Moisture filled my eyes as it always did when looking down on my roots from the air. I felt the soft bump as the wheels hit the tarmac a few seconds before hearing the flight attendant announce, "Welcome to Boston. Please remain seated with your seat belt fastened until we reach the gate, and thank you for flying with us today."

I let out a deep breath and smiled up at Saxton. "Well, here we are."

Once the seat belt sign was off, I gathered up my knitting and the one small carry-on in the overhead, and Saxton and I made our way into the terminal and downstairs to the rental cars.

The check-in process went smoothly, and before I knew it we were leaving the airport and heading for I-95 north. My excitement was building at the thought of seeing Jill and my beloved alpacas, Bosco and Belle. It had been exactly one year since I'd seen them.

A little over two hours later I spotted Rumination Farm farther up on the right.

"There it is," I said, pointing a finger, and heard the excitement in my voice.

The large white farmhouse was situated quite a distance back from the road with a long gravel driveway leading to the front door. A two-story clapboard with a sprawling porch, the house with its surrounding eleven acres looked like the quintessential New England postcard.

Before Saxton even had a chance to shut off the ignition I saw Jill come bounding out of the house and down the stairs.

I ran to greet her, and we threw our arms around each other. I'm sure anybody watching would have thought we were two teenage girls giddy with excitement.

"I'm so happy you're *finally* here. Hell, it's only taken a year to get you back," Jill said, giving me another hug.

She ran over to Saxton, gave him a bear hug, and said, "Okay, let's get your luggage inside. I'm so glad you agreed to stay here for your first night."

Saxton and I had decided to stay with Jill to allow us more time to visit and then drive the short way to Brunswick the following day.

We each grabbed a piece of luggage and headed for the front door.

"Nice place," Saxton said, looking around the foyer with the hardwood floors, braided rug, and antique tables.

"I know," I told him. "I just love this house. It belonged to Jill's grandparents, and when they died she inherited it and turned it into the alpaca farm."

"Why don't you show Saxton around while I put the finishing touches on lunch. Then we'll go out so you can see Bosco and Belle."

"Living room's in there," I said, pointing to the large room on my left.

He peeked in the doorway to see the fieldstone fireplace dominating one entire wall, cushy chocolate brown leather furniture, and antique lamps and tables.

"Dining room over there," I told him, nodding to the right. "Kitchen is behind the dining room, and Jill's bedroom suite is in back of the living room. Guest rooms upstairs," I said, reaching for a piece of luggage and climbing the gorgeous staircase in front of us.

"I gave you guys the guest room on the right," Jill hollered from the kitchen. "Nice and private in case you get frisky."

"Very funny," I hollered back with a laugh.

Saxton followed me down the hall to the large bedroom. It was just as I had remembered it. I had been allowed to come here a couple of times to spend the night with Jill when my mother and I still lived in Topsham. And I recalled my yearly visits as an adult visiting from Salem.

A huge mahogany four-poster with a beautiful white lace duvet and handmade quilt folded at the bottom of the bed took up one wall. An oak rolltop desk sat in front of the double windows, and a small sitting area with two cushy chairs and a mahogany table between them was situated next to the bathroom suite.

"Beautiful room," Saxton said, looking around.

"It is. I'm so glad Jill decided to keep the house and live here herself."

Saxton pulled me into an embrace. "There's a lot to be said for these older houses. Maybe it's because I'm from England, but I've always been partial to them."

I kissed his cheek. "Me too, and I always thought it was because I'm from New England, but I find them much more appealing than the modern houses. Okay, all set? Let's go down for lunch and then we'll show you around the property outside."

◈ 40 ◈

"Oh, Jill," I said, blotting my lips with a napkin. "You outdid yourself on that clam chowder. I don't know, but I think you could give Tony's Restaurant a run for his money in the chowder competition."

Jill laughed, then took the last sip of her wine. "No, thanks. I only make it for myself and those I love. But I am a bit prejudiced toward clams right out of the Atlantic. Gabe brought these to me last night so I could get the chowder going."

Gabe? This was the first time I'd heard her mention this name. "Who's Gabe?" I asked with interest.

"Oh . . . well . . . I was kinda waiting till you got here to tell you. I've started seeing somebody. A really nice fellow. Nothing serious . . . but . . . I like him."

She reminded me of a flustered teenager, and I chuckled. "Okay. Time for details."

"Well, we met right after I got back from Thanksgiving in Florida and . . ."

I cut her off. "What? Four months ago and you're just getting around to telling me *now?*"

"Technically, three months ago. In December. He owns a seafood restaurant a few miles up the coast and I just happened to stop in there for lunch one day. He's also the chef and came over to the table to see if my scallops were okay. So we started chatting and well . . . next thing I know, he's asking me out. I figured what the heck. We had a really nice time and, um . . . well . . . the rest is history."

"You've been holding out on me, Jill. Shame on you," I said, laughing. "But I'm really happy for you. Do I get to meet this beau while I'm here?"

"Actually, I did invite him for dinner this evening. So, yes, you'll be able to give your approval."

"Great. Okay, let me help you clean up. I'm dying to show Saxton around."

"No, no. I can handle it. Go show him around and I'll join you out there shortly."

I took Saxton's hand and led him out the back door. I took a deep breath of the brisk March air and pointed across the field.

"That old barn is what Jill converted to her yarn shop. She does all the spinning and dyeing of the yarn in there. And there's the alpacas," I said, nodding toward two pens enclosed with fence across from the barn. "Let's go find Bosco and Belle."

As we got closer, I spied them immediately. One tan and one beige. Alpacas can be skittish, and I knew it had been a year since I had seen them, so I approached the fence cautiously.

"Hey, babies," I said softly, holding out my hand. It took a bit of coaxing, but after a few minutes Bosco came closer, followed by Belle.

"They're really gorgeous," Saxton said, following my lead and speaking softly. "What a beautiful coat they have."

I nodded. "Yeah, nice and wooly, and it makes perfect yarn. Jill will shear them in the spring. Come on, sweetie, come closer."

After a few more minutes Bosco was at the fence, Belle at his side, and I was able to pat them and nuzzle the top of their fuzzy heads. Alpacas weren't like dogs, but I had no doubt that they remembered me. We spent some time giving them attention and then I said, "Come on. I'll show you the yarn shop."

We walked across the path to the restored barn, and I opened the door on the huge room. One side was set up as a working area with spinning wheels, bundles of fleece, and roving. The other side was the shop where the yarn and accessories were sold. Large enamel tubs held skeins of various colors and fibers. Baskets were overflowing with alpaca and cotton. Racks displayed finished sweaters, scarves, blankets, and afghans. Up three steps from the main room was an area that held a long granite table with wooden chairs.

"That's where Jill holds all of her knitting classes and gatherings," I said.

Saxton shook his head. "I'm impressed. She has quite a business here. And she runs it all herself?"

"She takes care of the alpacas herself, but she just recently hired an assistant a few days a week to help out in the shop and with some classes. This has always been Jill's dream, ever since I can remember."

"There's a lot to be said for making dreams come true."

"You think? Some days I'm not so sure about that."

I turned around to see Jill had joined us, and laughed. "Oh, come on. You know you love it."

She nodded. "I do, but I'm really glad I've now hired Becky. It gives me a few free hours now and then. Did you see Bosco and Belle?"

"Yeah, they look great, and I do think they remembered me."

"Of course they do. Alpacas are smarter than people think. I just put a pot of coffee on. Thought we could have some with the cranberry bread I made this morning."

"Sounds great," I said as we followed her back to the house.

We spent a relaxing afternoon chatting and catching up on news. The aroma of a New England boiled dinner began to fill the house.

"Let me just go check how dinner's coming," Jill said. "More coffee?"

"If you don't mind, I'd like to go back outside and see those alpacas again. They're fascinating animals." Saxton stood up and followed us to the kitchen.

"They are," I said. "Go ahead and I'll join Jill for another cup of coffee."

I settled myself at the counter while she lifted the lid on the huge pot holding the smoked shoulder, potatoes, carrots, turnip, and cabbage, creating an even stronger aroma.

"God, that smells good," I told her. "I can't remember the last time I made that."

"I know. It's pretty simple to put together and it's always good. If you don't mind, I'm just going to roll out the dough for the biscuits. Gabe said he'll be here about five, so I planned dinner for five-thirty."

"Sounds great," I said, as I watched her flour a wooden board and begin rolling out dough.

"You seem happy, Berkley."

Her statement took me by surprise. I refilled my coffee mug and looked at her.

"I am happy."

"What I mean is, I think Saxton has a lot to do with your happiness. You seem . . . well . . . *changed* since you've met him."

"Really? In which way?"

She hesitated for a moment. "More relaxed. Less stressed. Not as . . . obsessive."

I noticed she didn't look at me when she said this but continued to concentrate on cutting out circles of dough for the biscuits.

I let out a deep sigh. "Well, despite what you've always said, I've never considered myself obsessive. Or compulsive. But yeah, you could be right. Saxton makes me *feel* different."

"More secure?"

"Oh, now I'm also insecure?"

Her head shot up. "I didn't mean that in a bad way, Berkley. Honest. It's just that since we were kids, you've always tried so hard to be independent. To the point where once we got older, I used to wonder if it was a mask. A cover-up for how you really felt."

I hadn't ever given this much thought, but Jill could be right.

"I suppose so," I mumbled, as I realized that since meeting Saxton I had let go of a lot of my quirky behavior. I no longer needed the light on at night when I slept—even if Saxton wasn't spending the night at my place. I had been able to let go of having everything placed precisely where I'd put it. My list and notes—I'd probably always be a list maker, but I had made changes in many ways.

"I just want you to know," Jill said, wiping her hands on a towel, "no matter what you find out in Brunswick—it won't define who you really are. Whatever it was, it was your mother's life. Not yours. You had nothing to do with anything that happened. I mean, I think it's pretty obvious that whatever you're going to find out—it won't be good news. Otherwise, your mother and grandmother wouldn't have gone to such lengths to keep it away from you. But, Berkley, just keep it in perspective."

"I will," I said, and hoped that I was right.

"That was really delicious, Jill," Saxton said. "There's nothing like true home cooking."

"I agree," Gabe told her as he reached over to pat her hand.

"Thank you so much for making this." I shot her a smile both for the dinner and for my approval of Gabe.

I liked him a lot from the moment he entered Jill's kitchen, a bottle of wine in one hand and a bouquet of spring flowers in the other. Tall, average looking, and very personable. He had one of those personalities people were naturally drawn to. Genuine and sincere, much like Saxton, and I thought he was the perfect match for my best friend.

"Thank you. All accolades gladly accepted. And now . . . How about a piece of homemade apple pie to finish it off? I have coffee to go with it."

"Great, I'll help you," I said, leaving the dining room to follow her into the kitchen.

"I like him, Jill. Gabe seems like a really nice guy, and I think you two are well suited."

"I've been thinking the same thing. You know, it's really strange. When you least expect it, when you're truly not searching for anybody in your life . . . boom . . . it just happens. In walks Mr. Right."

I laughed. "I know the feeling exactly," I said, thinking back to the day I found Saxton sitting on the pavement in front of my chocolate shop waiting for me to open.

Following dessert and coffee, we went into the living room,

where a huge fire was blazing in the fireplace. I curled up next to Saxton on one sofa, and Gabe and Jill took the other one. We passed a pleasant few hours conversing, and then Gabe said he needed to get going.

"I have a big day at the restaurant tomorrow. Lots of bookings, so I'll need to get an early start. If you get a chance, before you head back to Florida, come by for dinner. On the house."

We assured him we'd try to make it one evening before leaving.

By ten o'clock Saxton and I were ready to call it a night.

"Sleep as late as you want," Jill told us before heading to her room downstairs. "I don't have any classes or anything tomorrow, but I'm usually up pretty early to tend to the alpacas."

I joined Saxton in the comfy bed and curled up in his arms. Snuggled beside him, with the duvet and fluffy pillows, I felt like I was in a cocoon. A protective cocoon. And I wondered what tomorrow would bring. What would I find in those newspapers at the Brunswick library? Now that I was hours away from the information that I had craved for forty years, I could only hope that Jill had been right—that I'd be able to accept whatever it was I was about to find out.

❧ 41 ❧

I awoke to find Saxton staring at me, a smile on his face. "Good morning, beautiful. Sleep well?"

I returned his smile and touched his cheek. "I don't think I woke once. How about you?"

"The same. I love you."

I slid over closer. "I love you too. Be right back," I said, scooting out of bed and heading for the bathroom.

I returned a few minutes later and saw the bedside clock read six thirty-five.

"I bet Jill's already outside feeding the alpacas," I said, snuggling back in next to him. "How long have you been awake?"

"Since about six."

"You've been staring at me for a half hour?"

"I love staring at you," he said in a husky voice as I felt his hand slide down my body.

Following a delicious breakfast of pancakes, Vermont maple syrup, and rich, dark coffee, we said our good-byes to Jill and headed to Topsham, where Saxton had rented a cute little cottage for our three-night stay.

After we got settled in he said, "How about we find a place for lunch and then hit the library?"

Spring can be a bit slow arriving in New England, but we had a sunny day with temps in the midsixties, and everywhere I looked I saw crocuses and other flowers peeping out of the ground. Leaves were beginning to fill all the trees in Topsham, bringing back a multitude of memories from my early childhood there.

"After lunch I'd love to drive past the house where I lived with my mother and grandmother."

Saxton locked the door and we headed to the car.

He gave my hand a squeeze. "This is your trip, Berkley. Just tell me where you'd like to go."

After we finished a delicious bowl of fish chowder we headed toward Elm Street, a short distance from our cottage on Main.

Saxton drove slowly, waiting for my instructions.

"A little farther up on the left," I said.

I saw the yellow clapboard one-story house and pointed. "There," I told him.

He pulled into a spot across the street as I leaned over and stared at my childhood home. Forty years had passed since I'd seen it, but except for the exterior color little else had changed. A nondescript two-bedroom, one-bath house. A house I'd been whisked away from at age five to begin a new life in Salem, Massachusetts.

I let out a deep breath. "It was white when we owned it, but . . . it doesn't look any different." I noticed the bushes along the walkway that had seemed so small when I lived there had now grown about waist high. Two Adirondack chairs were positioned on the small porch, and the front door had been painted a lemony shade of yellow. I also expected to see my grandmother opening the door in welcome.

When I remained silent, Saxton reached for my hand. "Are you okay?"

I nodded. "Yeah, it just seems so odd seeing the house again." I felt moisture stinging my eyes as memories overwhelmed me. I cleared my throat. "Okay. On to Pleasant Street and the library."

We easily found a parking spot and walked the short distance to the brick structure built in 1904. Climbing the stairs to the original wooden door with glass panes, I had a flashback of coming here with my mother to borrow books from the children's section.

Saxton followed me upstairs where the reference area was located, and I spotted a woman about my age behind the desk, where a small nameplate told me her name was Barbara Murphy.

She looked up and smiled as we approached. "Can I help you?"

"I hope so," I said, and went on to explain I was looking for microfilm of a 1972 newspaper.

"Do you have a particular month in mind? That would help to narrow the search."

"Yes, May and June."

She went to retrieve two small canisters containing the microfilm, directed us to a machine, and said, "If you need any help at all, just give a holler."

With shaking hands, I put the microfilm on the spool, turned on the machine, and stared at the front page of the *Times Record*. Quickly scanning the headlines, I saw nothing of interest that jumped out.

Saxton peered over my shoulder. "Try the next day."

Three tries later I pulled up the front page for May fifteenth, and as soon as I saw the headline I got a sick feeling in the pit of my stomach. Instinct kicked in—and I knew this was the beginning of my family secret unraveling.

Houston Man Slain in Shoot-out with Police

My hand flew to my face as a wave of nausea came over me. "Oh. My. God. This was my father."

I felt Saxton's hands on my shoulders as I read the article out loud in a strained voice.

"On Wednesday morning police were alerted to a quarrel at the Brunswick Motel between Alden Sharpe and his girlfriend, Jeannette Whitmore. Whitmore was in the office with Ann Brown, proprietor of the motel, when they arrived.

"According to Brown, Sharpe had checked in a few days before and that morning she heard raised voices coming from the room. A few minutes later she stated that Miss Whitmore came rushing into the office, her face bruised, and screamed for Brown to call police because Mr. Sharpe had a gun in his possession.

"Police attempted to talk with Sharpe through the locked door when a shot was fired, hitting Officer Thomas Frost. Frost is in critical condition at Maine Medical Center. More shots were exchanged, one of which fatally wounded Alden Sharpe."

Dizziness overtook me as my brain tried to comprehend what I was reading. My father shot a police officer? He was shot and killed by the police? He hadn't died in Vietnam as I'd been told? I felt the tears streaming down my cheeks and heard sobbing, which came from deep inside of me.

Saxton attempted to get me away from the machine, and I looked up to see Barbara Murphy come rushing over.

"Is she ill?" she asked. "Let's take her into the small conference room over here."

I was dimly aware of being led a few steps with Saxton holding me up. As I felt myself being lowered into a chair, I heard him say, "She's just had some shocking news. Could you get her some water, please?"

He knelt in front of me, grasping my hands tightly in his. "It's going to be okay, Berkley. I'm here for you, and we'll get through this. Take some deep breaths."

A minute later Barbara returned with the water, and Saxton assisted me with taking a few sips.

Barbara put a box of tissues on the table beside me, and slowly I began to regain my equilibrium.

Dabbing at my eyes, I said, "I don't believe it. How can that article be correct? How could my entire life have been one huge lie?"

Saxton squeezed my hand. "That's not true, Berkley. It was your mother's lie. Not yours."

I shook my head, trying to make sense out of what I'd just learned. "So my father was killed in a shoot-out? And why was my mother's face bruised when she ran into that motel office? I don't understand any of this."

I heard Barbara gasp and looked up.

"Oh, my God. You're Berkley Whitmore, aren't you?"

I looked at her closely, but she didn't look familiar to me at all. "Do I know you?"

"Yes. Well, no. Not exactly. Your mother was Jeanette Whitmore, right?"

I nodded.

"My mother is Rose Langley. Well, she was Rose Castle when she knew your mother. They went to college together, at UC Berkeley. My mom is originally from Bath, and they met at college because they were roommates. Your mother never told you what happened with your father? I can't believe you're just finding out this story now. I'm so terribly sorry." She reached over and patted my shoulder. "If there's anything at all that I can do, please let me help."

"There is," I told her as I began to feel steadier. I went on to briefly explain my story, the family secret that had been kept from me and how I had recently started to search for the answers after my mother passed away. "And now—it seems I have even more questions than I did a year ago."

"You're right. There's a lot more to Jeanette's story. Would you like me to contact my mother? She lives in Topsham, and I know she'd love to see you and be able to explain some things to you."

Her kindness and concern brought a fresh flood of tears as I nodded. "God! That would mean everything to me. Thank you so much."

"You stay right here. I'm going to call my mom right now. I'll be right back. Are you in town for a while?"

"Yes," Saxton told her. "We're here two more nights. Longer, if necessary."

I shook my head as Saxton pulled up another chair to sit beside me. "Of all the things that I thought I might find out, I just never thought it could be something as violent as this. My God, do you think he had that gun with plans to shoot my mother? And what was she doing there with him at that motel to begin with? I guess it's pretty easy now to figure out why she told me he was killed in

Vietnam. What mother wants to have to tell her daughter something like this?"

A few minutes later Barbara returned. "My mother would be thrilled to see you, Berkley. I think she's also upset at the way you had to find this news. She wants to know if you'd like to come by her house tomorrow morning. She'd love to meet with you sooner but she already has plans for the rest of the day."

A feeling of gratitude washed over me. "Thank you so much. Yes, tomorrow morning will be fine. This is so nice of both of you."

"I'm off work tomorrow, so I'll be there too. My mom lives on Elm Street, farther up from where you did. Here's the address and her phone number if you need to call her. She said any time after ten would be great." She passed me a piece of paper with the information. "Would you both like some coffee? Can I get you anything?"

"No, thanks," I said. "But I would like to get a copy of that newspaper article. I didn't even get a chance to finish reading it."

"You stay here as long as you need to. I'll go make a copy of that for you. As I recall, there was only one other article about the shooting in the paper a few days later, but that was mostly about the police officer's recovery. He did live, although he passed away just last year from cancer. I'll be right back."

I let out a wry chuckle. "Well, at least I can rest easier knowing my father wasn't a cop killer."

Later that evening I was curled up on the sofa with a cup of herbal tea and Saxton beside me. He knew I was in no condition to go out for dinner, so he made a run to the grocery store and cooked steaks on the grill, baked potato, and salad for supper at the cottage. I felt his hand reach for mine.

"Doing okay?"

I nodded. "I guess so. It's just so much to take in, and I still don't even have the full story. I just can't believe my mother experienced something like that, and the more I think about it, I don't think there's any doubt that she was a victim of domestic abuse."

"I'm sure you're right, and tomorrow you'll get some more answers."

❧ 42 ❧

I didn't sleep well at all. When I did manage to drift off, I had crazy dreams about violence, somebody running, lots of turmoil. I'd wake to feel Saxton beside me, knowing he wasn't getting much sleep either.

I opened my eyes to see sunshine streaming through the blinds. The bedside clock told me it was eight-fifteen, so I must have managed a few hours of sleep. I felt Saxton stir and turned to look at him.

"Good morning, handsome. I love you."

"Oh, how I love you, beautiful. Good morning."

"Why don't you try and get a bit more sleep? I know I kept you up most of the night. I'll go start the coffee."

"Nah, I'm fine, but coffee sounds great."

Saxton had picked up some cinnamon buns and Danish at the local bakery the evening before, and I put those on a plate as the coffee brewed. I heard the shower being started in the bathroom at the same time the phone rang.

"Berkley, I really hate to bother you, but I didn't hear a thing from you yesterday and I was getting a little concerned. Are you okay?"

I smiled when I heard Jill's voice. "I'm sorry. I just wasn't up to talking to anybody after I left the library. Yeah, I think I'm okay. Still kind of numb, I guess." I went on to fill her in on the details of what I'd discovered the day before.

"Holy shit! I sure never thought you'd find out something like that about your father. We always thought he died in Vietnam."

"Yup, we did. I'm now wondering if your mother knew. She had to, Jill. These are small towns around here. It was in the papers and people talk. Unfortunately, she's gone now too."

"I know. Well, if she knew anything, she never told me a thing. But she was never a gossip, and she knew you were my best friend, so it makes sense she wouldn't say anything. But yeah, I agree, I'm sure she knew all about it. I was so upset when you moved away so fast, and now I do remember her telling me that sometimes people just had to do what was best for them. Of course, at five years old, it made no sense to me at the time."

I felt Saxton come up behind me, encircling me in his arms. He smelled of soap and toothpaste and aftershave. I turned around and placed a kiss on his lips.

"Well, we're meeting with my mother's old college roommate this morning, so hopefully I'll gather some more pieces to this puzzle."

"Listen, I know tomorrow is your last night at the cottage. But if you have all of your info by tomorrow, I'd love to have you guys come here instead. You can get to Logan for your flight the next day just as easily from North Yarmouth as you can from Topsham."

"That would be great. Let me talk to Saxton and I'll call you back later tonight."

At precisely ten o'clock we pulled up to the home of Rose Langley. Although a little larger, her house resembled my old one.

We were greeted at the door by Barbara. "Come on in. It's good to see you again. My mom's in the kitchen."

She led the way down the hallway to the back of the house, where a woman in her late sixties was pouring coffee into china cups. Shorter than Barbara and with a smart silver hairstyle; there was no doubt they were mother and daughter.

Rose scooped me into a tight embrace. "Oh, Berkley. It's so

good to finally meet you. You have no idea how many times I've thought of you and wondered what became of you and your mother."

Rose Langley was one of those people who, when you met her the first time, you felt like you'd known her forever.

"Thank you so much for letting us come over. This is my friend, Saxton Tate," I said.

Handshakes were exchanged, and she indicated for us to have a seat at the table. Barbara produced a platter of blueberry muffins.

"Oh, my goodness. Are those the Jordan Marsh muffins?"

Rose laughed. "They certainly are. I think everybody in New England got that recipe during the sixties."

"Jordan Marsh was the big department store in Boston," I explained to Saxton. "They had a bakery where they sold these incredible, humongous blueberry muffins. Somehow the recipe got out, and every housewife around New England got a copy of it."

Saxton laughed. "Secrets always have a way of getting out, don't they?"

I caught his meaning and smiled.

Rose and Barbara joined us at the table, placing coffee in front of us. "Help yourselves to the muffins," Rose said. "Now—where to begin?"

"Could you start at the beginning? How you met my mother at UC Berkeley?"

Rose took a sip of coffee and nodded. "I grew up in Bath, just a few towns away, but I never knew your mother when I lived here. Strange enough, we had to travel across the country to meet up. We weren't originally assigned as roommates, but when we got there, there was a mixup and, long story short, we ended up sharing a room. I think we connected right away because of our Maine roots."

"And you knew my father? You had met him?"

"Oh, yes. It wasn't long before everybody on campus knew who Alden Sharpe was. Came from money in Houston. I don't like speaking unkindly of the dead, but I never cared for him. I wasn't impressed with his wealth or his good looks. He was charming, okay, and I'm afraid he charmed the pants right off of your mother. Literally."

I smiled at her outspoken honesty.

"They met within the first month of classes. Alden was a bit older than us though. He was in a graduate program. But somehow he hooked up with Jeanette. To be honest, I was a little surprised. Your mother was quiet, a bit shy, and I wondered what the attraction was for him. Oh, don't get me wrong. Your mother was extremely pretty. Actually, quite a few fellows had their eye on her."

More and more, I felt like I hadn't known my mother at all.

"But it wasn't long before I came to understand what the attraction was for Alden. In addition to her good looks."

I waited as she broke off a piece of muffin and chewed it thoughtfully.

"Yup, he had control over Jeanette. She was easy to mold to his liking."

"What do you mean?"

"Well, Alden had to be first in everything. He was arrogant. Had an air about him. Was known for giving some of the professors a hard time if they didn't agree with him. I think poor Jeanette was so caught up with the attention he showered on her, she was willing to do his bidding. She seldom disagreed with him. By the time our freshman year ended, she was completely infatuated with Alden Sharpe."

"So what happened?"

"Well, they began dating. We called it *going steady* back then. She wore his college ring on a chain around her neck. To the casual observer, they looked like the perfect couple. But I knew better."

I took a sip of coffee, digesting all that Rose was telling me.

"During that summer, Alden invited Jeanette to his parents' home in Houston."

"What? She met his parents? My grandparents?"

"Briefly. She was supposed to stay there a week before going home to Maine for the summer, but her visit only lasted a few days and she left. From what she told me, from the moment she got there she didn't feel comfortable. His parents weren't friendly to her at all. The house was huge, more like a mansion, she said. Servants everywhere. It was completely different from what Jeanette was used to, and I don't think she enjoyed it at all."

I felt anger surging over me. All that money. All that wealth. And I knew for a fact that not one penny of it had ever found its way to my mother. All of her life, my mother struggled financially, raising me. On her own. Alden Sharpe had never contributed anything toward my support.

"So did they break up?" I asked.

Rose let out a disgruntled sigh. "Quite the opposite. When they both returned to campus in the fall, they were connected at the hip. He never let her out of his sight. Very possessive. He even got into a few fist fights with a couple fellows that had the nerve to speak to her. Word got around campus fast, and pretty soon, about the only friend that Jeanette had left was me. Nobody wanted to tangle with Alden."

"So in today's world, he'd be considered a bully," I said.

"Exactly. But during our sophomore year, I began to notice things. Jeanette would come back to our room crying after an evening out with him. When I'd question her, she'd just say they had an argument but everything was fine. Then one night she came back and her face was terribly bruised. I insisted she be seen at the infirmary on campus, but she said it was nothing. She'd tripped on the pavement outside. The first incident, I believed. But after that, I knew better."

"Oh, my God! So he was beating her up?"

"I'm afraid so, and it never stopped. Right up till the end. He was a control freak, Berkley, and he had your mother exactly where he wanted her."

I now felt a different kind of anger welling up inside me. "But why the hell didn't she leave him? Just break it off?"

"If you've never been in a situation like this, you probably don't understand. That's easier said than done. An abuser manages to strip away every single ounce of a woman's self-esteem. She doubts herself constantly and even allows herself to believe that maybe she's the cause of the abuse."

I'd read articles about this. Seen movies about it. But I'd never given it much thought.

"A man like that can run a woman into the ground. And that's exactly what Alden did with Jeanette. She didn't trust him, but even worse, she no longer trusted herself."

But why didn't she just get away from him was the thought that kept going through my mind.

"I witnessed how he chipped away at her, a little at a time. Her confidence was gone and in its place was fear. She was terrified to leave him, Berkley. One night she came back to our room and I knew she was in terrible pain. She showed me her arm and said she'd fallen. Again. I didn't believe her for a minute and pretty much dragged her to the infirmary. She had a broken arm. That was when she finally began to open up to me."

"And that wasn't enough? She still wouldn't leave him?" I couldn't even comprehend staying with a man that had done this to me.

"It wasn't that she wouldn't. She *couldn't*. She was too filled with fear. She shared that he had threatened to kill her if she ever left him."

"Surely he didn't really mean that, did he? Why didn't she report this to the police?"

Rose let out a chuckle. "Oh, Berkley, I hate to tell you, but you are terribly misinformed when it comes to domestic abuse. Get on the Internet. Do some research. The laws we have now protecting women? We didn't have those back in the sixties and seventies. People can say what they want about the feminist movement, but believe me, it was that movement and organizations for women's rights that fought for what we have today to protect women. Battering women has gone on since the beginning of time. During the sixties and early seventies we didn't even have the term *domestic violence*. There was no such phrase. It was called battering or wife beating, and if, by chance, a man was to get arrested, it was for assault and battery."

I considered myself a pretty well-informed female, but I was feeling mighty uneducated on the entire scope of this issue and couldn't help but wonder if it was because by the time I hit my teen years, these laws were being put in place and more was being done to protect women. It certainly wasn't something I had grown up with, like Rose and my mother.

"Are you aware that the very first shelter for abused women wasn't even opened in Maine until 1973? Spruce Run was the first place that a woman in fear, like your mother, could find help. And that was a year after her tragic incident in Brunswick. But the good news is that it's still in existence today helping women."

I shook my head. "No," I said quietly. "I had no idea."

"It wasn't a good time for women, and I can attest to that fact. One night Jeanette returned to the dorm and again, Alden had beaten her up. She had quite a laceration on her head where he'd hit her with something. I was tired of the entire situation and was beginning to think I was as wrong as she was for not trying to do something. I didn't give her a choice. I called the police, said we had to to get to the emergency room. I sat with Jeanette in the back of the cruiser on the drive over and with my own ears I heard the cop in the passenger seat say, 'Well, you probably deserved it.' Probably *deserved* it? This is what a cop says to a woman who admits her boyfriend has beaten her up?"

The anger toward my mother that I'd felt earlier had now morphed into sympathy and understanding. Sympathy for her lack of resources. And understanding for what she must have gone through.

I shook my head as I felt Saxton reach for my hand. "And yet . . . and yet she got pregnant with me?"

Rose took the last sip of her coffee. "That was a blessing in disguise, believe me. I think after the emergency room incident, Alden tried to restrain himself, because she did give his name, but no arrest was made. She continued to date him, and in April of our junior year she got pregnant. She told me right away but didn't tell Alden until she had already figured out what she was doing. She knew his parents would never consent to him marrying her, and he sure as hell didn't want to be on their bad side. So she made the decision to leave school and go home to Maine with your grandmother, have the baby, and be on her own. Away from him."

"So she dropped out and never finished her senior year—because of me."

Rose nodded. "But it was her out, Berkley. It got her away from him. For a while anyway."

"Did he continue to bother her?"

"Not at first. After I graduated I had my degree as a social worker and came back to Maine, and she called me one day. You were about a year old. She seemed to be doing pretty well, working in the chocolate shop with your grandmother, raising you. We reconnected our friendship and used to see each other a lot. Two years later I married, and a year later I had Barbara, which gave us even more in common. When you were about four, she told me that she'd received a letter from Alden. He was still single and it sounded like things had gone sour working for the family business. He hinted that he'd like to come to Maine, see her again and see you. Mind you, in four years he hadn't shown one ounce of interest in you. I told her to be careful, and she assured me she didn't want a thing to do with him. Even though I saw that old fear returning to her eyes, I knew she meant it. She didn't want to see him or have anything to do with him."

"Then how did he end up here that May of 1972, a year later?"

"I'm afraid at this point my information is a bit sketchy. A week before he got here was the last time I saw her. She told me he'd written another letter and he was on his way to Maine. She prayed he was lying and just trying to scare her. I don't have any idea why she went to that motel room to meet him. I wish I did. The next thing I knew, it was on the news about the shooting, and within a few weeks I heard around town that all three of you were gone."

"My God, to think she went through all of this and felt she could never tell me about it. Now I need to find out *why* she wouldn't share any of this with me."

And I knew for certain that the rest of my answers were with Doyle Summers.

❧ 43 ❧

The small aircraft touched down at Gainesville Airport and I blew out a breath of air.

"Glad to be almost home?" Saxton asked.

"Yes. Very much so, but also very glad that I had you with me in Maine."

I was quiet on the drive to Cedar Key, but that was one of the things I cherished about my relationship with Saxton. He allowed me to have my quiet time and it felt comfortable.

Since my meeting with Rose, my mind had been swirling with the information I had learned. I had called both Jill and my aunt Stella to fill them in before I left Maine, and they had been as shocked as I was.

An hour later we approached the Number Four bridge just as the sun was beginning to set in the western sky. Now, more than ever, I could understand why my mother had chosen to come to this particular place. The beauty and solace surrounded me, and I felt my mother's presence closer than I had in a long time.

After dropping our luggage at my apartment, Saxton made a quick call to Doyle telling him we'd be over to get Brit and Lola.

After hanging up, he came to pull me into an embrace. "We

don't have to concern ourselves with supper tonight. Doyle said he's throwing some burgers on the grill and he made a potato salad."

"Great," I said. "Let's go. I can't wait to see Brit and Lola."

Walking into Doyle's house was pure pandemonium while the dogs greeted us. Brit jumped into my arms, wetting my face with kisses. When I put her down she ran over to Saxton, and Lola had run to me. Barking and tail wagging continued.

I put my hands up in the air, laughing. "Okay, okay, girls. Not that you missed us or anything."

Doyle joined my laughter. "I think it's pretty safe to assume that they did. But they were both very good, and Uncle Doyle here enjoyed the doggie sitting."

Once the dogs calmed down, he popped open a bottle of cabernet and filled three glasses.

"Here's to secrets being revealed," he said.

I lifted my glass. "I'll drink to that."

"Okay, let's go out on the patio while I fire up the grill and you can tell me everything."

After I brought Doyle up to date, he remained silent. From the look on his face, I was certain everything that I'd told him he was hearing for the second time.

"My mother told you all of it, didn't she?"

He nodded. "Yeah, but it's not any easier hearing it the second time."

"Can you start at the beginning, Doyle? She came here to escape my father, didn't she? But I don't really understand that part. He had already been killed."

Doyle took a deep gulp of his wine and sat down to join us. "Right. When Jenna arrived here, she was pretty fragile. Actually, she was going through a nervous breakdown. After I heard her story, I couldn't blame her. It was your grandmother's idea for her to get away. She knew that some of the Maine fishermen used to come to this island and she thought it might be the perfect place for Jenna to recover and heal."

"Okay, I get that. But . . . why didn't she take me with her?"

"She couldn't. That first week she arrived here, she could barely take care of herself, never mind a five-year-old daughter. Quite frankly, she couldn't function. I remember my mother was a bit hesitant about hiring her but decided to give her a chance. She was actually a good waitress. She was able to stay focused, and it was probably good for her to have something else to think about. She was dealing with a lot of baggage."

"The way my father was killed?"

"Right. At first, she blamed herself. Felt it was her fault. Over time, I was able to convince her that every single thing that had happened had been due to Alden Sharpe. Not her. She also felt guilty that you had lost your father—even though he had never once tried to see you or pay support for you."

"Rose Langley explained to me the way it was back then for women when it came to abuse. She said women didn't have the options that they do today."

Doyle nodded. "That's the absolute truth. Hell, I remember here on the island—we had a few men who would get drunk, go home, beat up their wives, and nothing was ever done to the husbands. Where was a woman going to go? She had her kids, no education, no training to support herself and those kids. It was pretty much a dead end and very wrong. At least today, there's shelters and laws to protect abused women. Unfortunately, Jenna made a bad choice and fell in love with the wrong guy."

"Do you think she really loved him?" This thought had been going through my mind the past couple of days.

Doyle took another sip of wine. "I think she thought she loved him in the beginning. I do remember something she said to me, though; that the love a woman finds when she's younger is not the same type of love she wants when she's older."

I looked over at Saxton and knew this to be true. When I thought back to some of the losers that I'd dated in my younger years and compared them to Saxton, there was no comparison.

"She could have reported him though. I'm not sure she even pressed charges for the incident when she was at college and had to go to the ER."

"Berkley, she was ashamed. Plain and simple. I think many

women were. It just wasn't something that was openly talked about back then. A friend of mine is a doctor. Do you know he told me that in the mid-1970s when he went to medical school the term 'domestic violence' was nowhere to be found in medical textbooks, published literature, or curriculum. It was a secret pandemic that wasn't addressed in the classroom or at the bedside, and as a consequence it remained largely unrecognized and invisible to the medical community."

I recalled that Rose had told me pretty much the same thing.

"Doctors and nurses today are trained to recognize the signs, to screen patients and focus on prevention and help. It certainly wasn't like that when your mother was going through it. It had been swept under the carpet for centuries."

"Do you know why she went to his motel that morning?"

Doyle nodded. "Alden called her when he got into town. She refused to see him. At your grandmother's insistence, she was in the process of getting a restraining order, but I have to say, I don't think they're worth the paper they're printed on. That morning, your grandmother had taken you and gone into Bath to do some shopping. Alden called again, but this time he threatened you and your grandmother."

I leaned closer in my chair as I heard myself gasp. "What do you mean?"

"He told her he had a gun and if she refused to come to the motel and meet with him, he'd use the gun on her daughter and her mother."

"Oh, my God! He would have killed us?"

"Who knows. He was pretty deranged. I have no doubt that in addition to being a drinker he did a fair amount of drugs as well. Jenna said she didn't have a choice. She had to go and at least try to talk him down."

"And all of these years . . . all of these years I never thought of my mother as being strong," I said, and felt shame creeping over me.

"Jenna Walsh was one of the strongest and most resilient women I've ever met. She went to the motel and another fight ensued. He began hitting her, pushing her into furniture, and she knew he'd probably kill her and then go after you and your grandmother. I remember when I was with her at the Cape last year, she said even though she knew she was dying, she had never felt closer to death than in those moments with Alden in that motel room."

I could feel the tears sliding down my cheeks.

"I don't know how she managed it, but she did manage to get the door open and run to the office. She said that every step of the way she was waiting for that shot to hit her back. The owner took one look at Jenna, locked the door, and called the cops—and you know the rest of the story."

I nodded as Saxton passed me a tissue. Letting out a deep breath, I took a sip of wine and dabbed at my eyes.

"I was right. I never did know my mother—not the woman that she really was. I always thought she was weak, filled with fear, unable to take any risks or chances. When in fact she took the biggest risk of all—putting her own life on the line . . . to save mine."

"But thank God it didn't come to that," Doyle said. "I have no way of knowing, but I'd say that's what a mother's love truly is. Protecting her child. No matter what. And that's what Jenna did."

I shook my head slowly. "I had no idea. And you think the reason that she never shared any of this with me was because she was ashamed? But she shouldn't have been."

Doyle shrugged. "People feel what they feel, Berkley. And yes, she told me she just couldn't ever tell you what really happened. I don't know this for sure, but I got the feeling that she thought you'd stop loving her when you heard the story."

Tears started sliding down my face again. "My God!" I said as I felt my heart swelling with love. "If anything, I love her even more after hearing all of this. She did it for *me*. All of it. Leaving college, raising me on her own, basically giving up her entire life—all for me."

Doyle reached over and patted my hand. "Don't feel bad. This is how she wanted it. Believe me. She came here to heal, to get over what had happened and start fresh when she went back. That was also why you moved so quickly with your grandmother to Salem as soon as Jenna came here. Neither of them wanted you growing up with that stigma surrounding you. It would have been difficult in school, hearing stories around town. They both wanted to protect you from that."

I nodded, finally fully able to comprehend not only why she wasn't able to take me with her that summer but also why we had to leave Maine.

"But," I said. "Fate intervened—and she met you when she came here. And you fell in love with each other. Why did she give you up? Why didn't she just bring me here and she could have been with you?"

Doyle took the final sip of his wine. "Believe me, I asked myself that a million times after she left. She wasn't even in touch with me again for about six months. And then she sent me a letter, trying to explain. Until that letter, I had hopes that maybe she would come back with you. But she told me she couldn't uproot you. Take you away from your grandmother. Subject you to another new environment. She said that she hoped I'd understand, and she wanted me to know that despite everything I would always be that one great love of her life. But she was gone to me. This was what she told me, and while I knew it was all the truth, I also knew there was another reason why she wouldn't return here with you."

I looked up and now saw tears glistening in Doyle's eyes as I waited for him to go on.

"I had no doubt whatsoever that she loved me as deeply as I loved her, but she was unable to trust me. Fully trust me. She had been too severely damaged, both physically and emotionally. The fear held her back. Fear of getting hurt again, fear of losing both your love and my love. You were everything to her, Berkley, and she couldn't risk trusting me enough to bring you here. What if it didn't work out?"

"So again—she did that for me. She gave up that love . . . because of me."

He let out a deep sigh. "She did it because . . . for her . . . it was the *right* thing to do. And I accept that."

I shook my head at the sadness of it all. The sadness for what she endured with my father. Sadness for secrets that women had to keep. But most of all, sadness for a love my mother was never able to fully experience.

Now it was my turn to pat Doyle's hand. "I'm sorry," I told him. "I'm so sorry for your loss."

❧ 44 ❧

I flipped the calendar page to April and realized that it had been almost thirteen months since I'd moved to Cedar Key. Looking around the chocolate shop, I smiled. It had taken me a full year to discover all the answers I'd been looking for. Some days I felt sorrow for what my mother had gone through, but during the past few weeks I'd come to realize that everything that had happened had been her choice. I may not have agreed with all of those choices, but they had not been mine to make. Above all else, I had also come to understand that my mother had lived her life on her terms. Looking back, I knew she was happy working in the chocolate shop, living with my grandmother, and watching me grow up. In many ways, I wasn't like her at all. But more and more, I was coming to see that I truly was my mother's daughter.

My smile broadened as I glanced over to two of the crystals on the table and saw somebody had touched them and they weren't in the precise location I'd placed them, and I chuckled. Because I had no desire to go over and set them right—they were fine just where they were.

I looked up as Mr. Carl entered the shop.

"Top of the mornin' to ya," he said, a huge grin covering his face.

"Hey, Mr. Carl. How's married life treating you?"

"Fine. Better than fine. I think Miss Raylene and I are still on our honeymoon," he said with a chuckle.

"May it last forever. What can I get for you?"

"My usual. Some chocolate clams and truffles from Angell and Phelps."

"You got it," I said as I began preparing the boxes.

"So how're *you* feeling, Miss Berkley? Starting to come to grips with why your mother came here?"

"I am, and I'm doing great. Thanks for asking."

"Yeah, sometimes the past can be difficult. But I still think it's better to know the truth."

I rang up the sale and smiled. "I agree with you on that one."

At twelve noon I turned my sign to *Be Back After Lunch* and headed across the street to the coffee café for lunch.

"Hey," Suellen greeted me. "Not that I don't love your business, but a muffin and coffee isn't a very nutritional lunch."

"You're very right. Give me a piece of that cheesecake instead."

She laughed as she went behind the counter.

"How's the mother-to-be doing these days?" I asked.

"Well, not much longer now, and Grace said it won't be soon enough for her. I swear she's carrying around a ten-pound baby. Poor thing, she's so uncomfortable."

We both looked up as Grace came in the door accompanied by Chloe. Suellen was right. Since I'd last seen her, Grace's tummy had increased in size. She waddled over to the table, leaned back, gripped the edge of the table, and sat down.

"Whew," she said. "That was an effort."

I shook my head. "Are you as uncomfortable as you look?"

"I positively am. I gave up trying to tie my shoes weeks ago. If I drop something on the floor at home, it stays there till Lucas gets home. Sleeping? Forget it. Out of the question."

"How much longer?"

"My due date is April fifth, but I got the great news yesterday from my doctor that I might be late. Isn't that jolly?"

I suppressed a giggle. "Just the news a pregnant mother does not want to hear. Sorry."

Chloe laughed. "Hey, I keep telling her it'll be worth it."

"Hmm," was all Grace said.

Suellen placed my cheesecake and coffee in front of me.

"I'll have a double of that," Grace said, pointing to my cheese-cake.

"Really?"

"No, not really. Give me a low-fat, low-calorie, low-taste muffin and some decaf. Boy, am I ever gonna splurge when I deliver this baby."

All of us laughed.

"And we'll all help you," Chloe told her. "So, Berkley, how's it going? You've sure been hit with some surprising news."

Grace attempted to adjust her position. "Oh, gosh, I know. Everybody has been filling me in. What a story, and your mother certainly went through a lot."

"She did, and I'm doing fine. Actually, probably better than I have been in years. I wanted to find out why she came here, and I wanted all the answers. I'm not sorry that I went searching. I think it's allowed me to get to know a side of my mother that I never knew."

"I can understand that," Grace said. "I'm not sure any of us daughters ever really know our mothers. I mean, we know them as *mothers*. But as women? I'm not so sure about that. Maybe we don't want to dig that deep, but you did and I applaud you for that, Berkley."

"Me too," Chloe said. "Gosh, if not for Aunt Maude I'm not sure we'd ever have understood about our mother. I resented her for so many years, but you know, I finally came to see that she did the best that she could. I don't think any child can expect more than that."

Grace nodded. "I can only hope that someday Solange will feel that way about me. I know I'm going to make mistakes, cause her to be angry with me, but I hope she'll see when she's older, I did the best I could for her."

"Exactly as my mother did for me," I said.

Suellen pulled up a chair and joined us. "Hey, I really hate to

bring this up . . . but . . . now that you have your answers and figured everything out, will you still be staying here in Cedar Key?"

Without hesitating, I said, "Oh, gosh, yes. Definitely. I can't
help but feel that Cedar Key is the legacy that my mother left to me.
If she hadn't come here, I'm sure I wouldn't be here."

"Oh, good," Chloe said. "We've been talking about it and were
concerned that you might go back to Salem."

"Yeah, and take your chocolate shop with you," Grace replied,
which brought forth laughter.

I shook my head. "No, the chocolate shop is safe, I assure you."

"Not to mention Saxton," Suellen said. "I mean, I can't see him
leaving the island, but if you were to go . . . well . . . no doubt he'd
follow."

"We both plan on staying right here, so not to worry. Any further word on Dora purchasing the shop next door?"

"Actually, yes. She's meeting with Pelican next week to discuss
the details. I think you know that Marin's house is up for sale, and
for right now she'll be staying with Dora permanently. She's pretty
excited about a needlepoint shop where she can help to run it."

"That's great," I said. "I know it must be difficult for her losing
Andrew, but it seems she's trying to go forward."

"Aren't we all," Chloe said.

I looked over at her and saw the unhappy expression on her
face. "What's up? I feel like I've been out of the loop here during
the past month."

"Cameron and I have had a . . . what would you call it? Parting
of the ways. Our relationship was going nowhere. I knew that. But
now he's decided to sell the jewelry shop and move to California to
be near his daughter and granddaughter."

"Oh, no," I said. "I'm really sorry to hear that."

"Hey, it might be for the best. You never know what's around
that next corner," she joked.

"I like your attitude. Well, I better get going. I have to take Brit
for a short walk before I reopen the shop." I placed some bills on
the table and got up to leave. "Be sure to take it easy, Grace, and
keep us posted on that baby."

"Will do," she hollered as I left.

* * *

I returned from Brit's walk, unclipped her leash, and made myself a cup of tea to bring downstairs with me.

Standing in the middle of my living room, I looked around. I still found it eerie that my mother had lived in these very rooms during that summer. She must have felt so lost, so alone, but being here had allowed her to regain her strength, deal with her choices, and come home to me.

My eyes fell on the urn that contained her ashes. I went over and touched the cool marble. It was time. The time had come to release her back into the universe, and I had an idea.

Picking up the phone, I called Saxton. "Any chance you could come over for dinner this evening?"

"Absolutely. What's up?"

"Do me a favor and call Doyle too. I'd like you both to be here. I'll see you at six," I said, hanging up with a smile on my face.

❦ 45 ❦

I hummed along to an old sixties song that was playing on the radio as I prepared a salad to go with the Swedish meatballs that were simmering and scalloped potatoes that were in the oven.

Saxton arrived a little before six with a bottle of red wine in one hand and a gorgeous bouquet of spring flowers in the other.

I leaned over to kiss his cheek. "You're too good to me," I told him.

"Ah, then my mission in life is being accomplished," he said, returning my kiss. "Smells good in here. What can I do to help?"

"Open the wine and light the candles on the table. Thanks."

Doyle arrived a few minutes later carrying a rum cake that I knew came from Island Girl Cakes.

"Oh, Doyle, you shouldn't have. But thanks for the great dessert. I didn't have a chance to make anything."

"My pleasure," he said, setting the heavy box on the counter.

Saxton filled three glasses and I lifted mine first. "Here's to great friendship," I said. "And especially to our friendship, Doyle."

"Thanks," he said, touching the rim of his glass to mine and Saxton's. "So what's this dinner all about?"

"Hey, can't a girl cook for two special men in her life?" I joked.

"No complaints from me," Doyle said. "It was just sort of last minute, so I thought something was going on." He looked at Saxton, who shrugged his shoulders.

"I have no idea what she's up to."

"Well, what I'm up to is . . . I think the time has come for me to let go of my mother and spread her ashes."

"Okay," Doyle said, waiting.

"I'd like to do something a little special. You know, have it be meaningful. I didn't have a formal wake or funeral, and I think my mother deserved that. When I came to Cedar Key with her ashes, I felt when the time was right that I'd do something."

"Sounds like a good idea," Saxton said. "What have you got in mind?"

I let out a deep breath. "Well, I was wondering if we could go out on your boat, Doyle? You said she loved it out near North Key. Maybe we could go there and spread her ashes in that area over the water. I'd like to have my aunt come down and be here for that. I'm not sure if Jill could get away, because it's almost shearing season, but at least my aunt could join us. And then maybe a dinner or something after."

"I think that's a wonderful idea," Doyle said. "It would be an honor to assist you. Just let me know when and if I can do anything in particular."

"Great. Well, I want flowers on the boat. I want the flowers to follow her ashes in the water. And maybe some music would be nice. I wonder if I should invite Suellen and Chloe? Suellen has a great voice and plays the guitar. Maybe they'll come too."

Saxton nodded. "I'm sure they will. I think they'd like to be invited. When were you planning to do this?"

"I was thinking early May. By then, The Arts Festival will be over and hopefully poor Grace will have had the baby."

"Sounds good to me," Doyle said, and I looked up to see a strange expression on his face.

"Something wrong?" I asked.

He shook his head and pointed toward the radio. The Righteous Brothers were singing "Unchained Melody" and the words filled the room.

"What is it?" I whispered, although I had a pretty good idea.

"That was our song," Doyle said softly. "It played on the oldies station on the radio that entire summer. Wherever we were. In the restaurant, in the car, at my place. And since Jenna died, I hear it and can feel her close to me. Silly, I know."

The haunting lyrics continued to fill the room.

I went to hug him. "It's not silly at all, Doyle. Many people don't believe that after somebody we love passes on their spirit can communicate with us in many different ways. But I do. It could be the wind or maybe a butterfly, and sometimes it's via the airways." I felt goose bumps on my arms and had no doubt whatsoever that my mother's spirit was with us. "She's here, Doyle. I believe she's trying to let us know that she loves us, and she'll always be close, if we're open to it and pay attention. I've felt her spirit in this way only a few times since she passed, but maybe that's because I've been too busy trying to discover her secrets."

He returned my hug and nodded. "Thank you for understanding," he said as the song ended. "I think she approves of your farewell for her, and I'm glad that I can be a part of it."

"Me too," I told him.

I hadn't been to knitting night since I'd returned from Maine, so I was looking forward to the gathering the following week.

I walked in a little after seven to see everybody seated except Grace.

"No," Chloe said before I could ask. "She has not had that baby yet. Four days late and counting. She's home with Lucas praying for labor to start."

I laughed as I sat down. "I'm sure it won't be much longer. Today's the ninth."

Flora placed a pink cardigan sweater in her lap and looked up. "We've only gotten bits and pieces of your story, Berkley. You have to fill us in on your trip to Maine with all the details."

"Yes," Dora said. "I was so sorry to hear your mother was a victim of domestic violence."

I nodded. "Yeah, it was quite a surprising story," I said, and went on to share the information that I'd learned.

The women shook their heads as comments flowed.

"I remember those times well," Flora said. "We had our share of wife beating here too, but like you said, most of the time it just wasn't talked about."

"Right," Dora said. "At least now it's out in the open and women have resources and help. Forty years really isn't that long ago, but it was so much different back then regarding women."

"Oh, I can vouch for that," Maybelle said. "Being a Copa Girl and looking back, I sometimes feel we were really owned by the club. Don't get me wrong, we weren't treated badly and the owner made sure the patrons behaved themselves. But still . . . it wasn't an easy time for women."

"True," I said. "I feel we still have a way to go, but so much has been accomplished since then with women's rights."

"My goodness, how scary that must have been for your mother. The morning she met your father at the motel and realized he really did have a gun with him. I can certainly understand why she wouldn't want to tell her daughter about that," Dora said.

I nodded. "Right. Instead she let me believe that he'd been killed in Vietnam. I'm not sure that I'd have been able to cover for him like that. He wasn't a good person, and yet she protected him."

"Oh, I don't know about that, Berkley." Dora looked up from her knitting. "As a mother, I have to say, I think she was protecting *you*."

I heard the murmurs of agreement. She was right. What child wants to grow up knowing her father had threatened lives and did end up shooting a police officer? Had I found this out when I was younger, to be honest, I'm not sure how I would have dealt with it.

"You're right, Dora. And Flora, I wanted to thank you."

Her head popped up. "Me? Whatever for?"

"For being so nice to my mother when she came here. You rented her the apartment and I know you were kind to her. She certainly needed some kindness shown to her at that stage of her life."

Flora nodded. "She was a sweet young woman. Quiet but personable. I'm glad she found what she needed on this island, especially Doyle."

"Oh, I wanted to tell you. I've decided to spread my mother's ashes on the water. Over near North Key, where she and Doyle used to go a lot."

"What a great idea," Dora said.

"When do you plan to do this?" Corabeth questioned.

"The beginning of May. We're going to go out in Doyle's boat." I looked at Chloe and Suellen. "I'd love you both to join us, if you could. And I'm going to have my aunt come down and maybe Jill. We'll probably do a dinner after."

"I'd love to come," Chloe said.

"Oh, me too. Thank you for including me." Suellen shot a smile my way.

"But wait," Dora said. "Your mother was a part of our community, even if it was only for a summer, and now you're a part of this community. I think we'd all like to help you with your farewell. I have an idea . . . Grace should certainly have delivered that baby by the end of the month. Why don't we all gather at my house after you go out on the boat? We'll have a celebration of life. For your mother and also for Grace's baby."

"Oh, Dora," I said as my vision blurred with tears. "I couldn't let you do that. That's so much work."

"Work?" Raylene piped up. "How can it be work if all of us pitch in to help?"

"Right," Flora said. "It'll be a labor of love and we'll enjoy every minute of it."

"Then it's settled," Dora said with a smile. "A celebration of life at my house early May. That is, if you approve, Berkley."

I got up to hug Dora. "I approve. I wholeheartedly approve, and thank you."

I was awakened the next morning by the ring of my cell phone and answered to hear Chloe's voice.

"I'm an aunt," she said, and I heard the excitement in her voice. "Five days late, but I have a niece. Solange Genevieve Trudeau made her entrance into the world at two-thirty this morning. And Suellen wasn't far off on the weight. Nine pounds and five ounces."

I sat up in bed laughing and crying at the same time. "Oh, my God! I'm so happy for all of you. Are they okay?"

"Perfect. Lucas said they'll both be home tomorrow, and Cedar Key has another new resident."

Yes, life was good. Very good indeed.

✃ 46 ✃

As I sat in Grace's living room holding Solange in my arms, I thought about motherhood. Not in relation to myself—instead my thoughts flowed to my mother. I pictured a girl in her early twenties, holding her newborn daughter. I tried to imagine the fear and concern she probably had about raising that daughter alone. I stared at Solange peacefully sleeping away, and yet she was so vulnerable—dependent on Grace for every single need—and for the first time, I fully understood how brave and strong my mother had been.

"She's gorgeous," I whispered. "So perfect." I held her awhile longer before giving her back to Grace.

"Thank you," Grace said, and gazed down at her daughter. "She's our precious gift."

Even though the circumstances were much different, I knew without a doubt that I had been a gift to my own mother. A gift that she protected and loved. I glanced up and saw Saxton send me a smile.

"You need to get your rest," I said. "So we're going to scoot along. If you need anything at all, just give me a call."

Grace laughed. "Thanks, but between Chloe, Lucas, and Aunt

Maude, I think they have everything covered. And thank you so much for the gorgeous knitted crib blanket."

I nodded. "Take care, and I'll see you soon."

When we left Grace's, Saxton and I headed back to my apartment. I made a fresh pot of coffee and we settled on the sofa with Brit beside me.

"You're quiet," he said. "Everything okay?"

"Yeah. Holding Grace's baby made me reconsider motherhood."

"For yourself? Are you thinking you might want a child now?"

I laughed and patted Saxton's hand. "No, not for me. Even though you might be willing to become a father again, at forty-six, I think I'll pass on that." I ruffled the top of Brit's head. "I'm content to be a doggie mom. I was thinking about my mother and how difficult all of it must have been for her. Dropping out of college, involved in an abusive relationship, returning home pregnant, and then raising me without any assistance from my father. She really was fortunate to have my grandmother, but I'm sure it was still hard."

He nodded. "I agree, and I think what Doyle said is true. She was a lot stronger than you ever realized."

"Strange how we can sometimes come to know somebody better in death than we did in life."

Doyle's boat slowly moved out of the channel and we headed north as I sat clutching the urn containing my mother's ashes.

I glanced at Aunt Stella and smiled. Reconnecting with her was another thing that I could thank my mother for. Our relationship had grown and become solid over these past months. Finding out about her sister's past had been as much of a surprise for Stella as it had been for me. I recalled what she'd said the night before: *I could have tried harder to be a better sister, but the past is the past. What I can do now is go forward and continue to build my relationship with you.*

She was right. We can't undo the past. Mistakes are made. Words are left unsaid. Risks are not taken and what we're left with is the present. It isn't the past that counts, but rather what we choose to do with our remaining time. I glanced at Saxton, and once again I was grateful that he had crossed my path—allowing me to spend that time with him.

I was also fortunate to have Jill, Chloe, and Suellen in my life. Jill had insisted on flying to Florida for a few days to attend my mother's memorial. She said the shearing of the alpacas would still be there when she returned.

Chloe and Suellen had helped me through a difficult time from the moment I'd arrived on the island. They encouraged me and supported me as I began to put pieces of my puzzle together, proving to me once again how precious and valuable female friendship is.

I looked up at Doyle as he stood at the wheel steering the boat toward North Key. He was another gift that I'd been given from my mother. I never knew my father, but if I could choose a substitute, it would be Doyle. He had loved my mother without reservation, even when she wasn't able to fully return that love.

I heard Suellen begin playing the chords of "Against the Wind" on her guitar. I had chosen the Bob Seger and the Silver Bullet Band lyrics because they seemed appropriate and the 1980 hit had been one that my mother had played over and over on her record player. The words were now very meaningful to me. My mother had found her shelter, had found her healing and recovery right here in Cedar Key.

I watched as we approached North Key and knew it was time to finally release her back to the universe. The evening before, I had asked Doyle if he would assist me. I now saw him walk toward me and reach for my hand.

"Ready?" he asked, and I nodded, following him to the bow.

As we held the urn and loosened the top, my aunt, Chloe, and Saxton dropped stems of red roses into the water as Suellen's music filled the air.

In that moment, despite the sunshine and warmth, a strong wind began to blow. Doyle and I looked at each other, smiled, and released the ashes.

"Rest well, Jenna," he said. "Be at peace with my love."

I felt the tears sliding down my face. "And with mine," I said, before leaning over to place a kiss on his cheek.

* * *

We arrived at Dora's house to find it filled with people and received a warm welcome from everybody. Dora managed to usher all of us out to the patio, where her grandsons were circulating with a tray of champagne flutes.

Conversation ceased as Dora clapped her hands together and reached for her glass. "I want to thank all of you for coming today," she said as I looked around and saw all the people that had become so special to me. Mr. Carl was standing beside Miss Raylene, Leigh was there with her daughters, Sydney and Noah were next to Monica and Adam, the women from the knitting group stood clustered together in addition to so many other Cedar Key residents. "Because today is a celebration of life. Life is a special gift," she said. "And we're welcoming the new life of Solange Genevieve Trudeau."

Everyone looked to where Grace was seated with Solange in her lap and Lucas kneeling beside them as applause broke out.

"And we're also celebrating the past life of Jeanette Jenna Whitmore, Berkley's mother. During a very difficult time in her own life she found her way to Cedar Key, seeking solace and comfort. I have no doubt she found that here, and she has now passed on this special place to her own daughter." Dora lifted her flute in the air. "Here's to Solange and Jenna—a beginning and an end to life."

Cheers and applause filled the patio area as once again I felt moisture stinging my eyes.

"Enjoy all the food on the buffet table," Dora said. "But most of all, always enjoy the moments."

Saxton touched his glass with mine. "To your mother," he said. "And to her very special daughter who never gave up."

I smiled and took a sip of champagne before touching the rim of his glass again. "And to you, Saxton Tate the third, for coming into my life and helping me to see just how great life can be."

I saw Doyle standing with a group laughing and talking and was reminded of the Wheel of the Year that hung on my wall. I began to fully understand why that piece was so important to my mother. Why it was the one thing, besides me, that she had taken home with her from Berkley. The wheel depicted the annual cycle of the earth's seasons. It had been a little over a year since I'd come to Cedar Key—filled with doubt and uncertainty, searching for answers that had eluded me for over forty years. And during the past year, not only had I found my answers but I'd found so much more. I wasn't the same woman who had arrived on Cedar Key. I had changed. Grown. And had learned so much about both people and life.

I recalled the words from Ecclesiastes in the Old Testament, *To everything there is a season, a time for every purpose under heaven. A time to be born, and a time to die.*

Leaning over, I placed a kiss on Saxton's lips. "I love you," I told him. "Everything in life happens in its own time. Everything happens for a reason. I'm glad I finally understand the meaning of this."

"So am I," he said as he pulled me close.

Author's Note

Like Berkley, I lost my mother in 2005 to the complications of hemochromatosis. Therefore, this little known disorder has affected me personally and I wanted to make my readers aware of the diagnosis and treatment options. More information can be found at the American Hemochromatosis Society: www.americanhs.org.

Although Berkley's mother experienced domestic abuse in the 1960s, unfortunately it is still an issue that affects many women. However, we do now have resources available for women who need assistance, and the Internet has a vast amount of information and help.

Most of the places of business mentioned in my novels are real, but Berkley's chocolate shop is a figment of my imagination. Call it wishful thinking on my part due to my love for quality dark chocolate.

Island Girl Cakes is very real, though, and owned by Cedar Key native Jan Allen. It is located on SR 24, and I can vouch for the incredibly delicious cakes for sale at Jan's shop.

My good friend, personal assistant, and expert knitter Alice Jordan was kind enough to design a Cedar Key scarf that the knitting group at Yarning Together made for their fund-raiser. We wanted to share the pattern for that scarf here with you, my wonderful knitting readers.

Cedar Key Scarf

DESIGNED BY ALICE JORDAN

Supplies:

2 skeins 50G 100% cotton
Size 6 needles

Cast on 30 stitches.

Row 1: K30
Row 2: K3, P24, K3

Then, follow instructions for the pattern rows below.

Pattern Rows:

Row 1: K4, P3, K3, P3, K3, P4, K3, P3, K4
Row 2: K4, P3, K1, P1, K1, P4, K1, P1, K1, P3, K1, P1, K1, P3, K4
Row 3: K8, P1, K5, P1, K6, P1, K8
Row 4: K3, P5, K1, P1, K1, P4, K1, P1, K1, P4, K1, P1, K1, P2, K3
Row 5: K4, P1, K1, P1, K4, P1, K1, P1, K4, P1, K1, P1, K9
Row 6: K3, P7, K2, P5, K2, P5, K2, P1, K3
Row 7: K 30
Row 8: K3, P24, K3
Row 9: K3, P24, K3
Row 10: K3, P24, K3

Repeat pattern rows 1–10 to desired length, ending with Row 8.

Bind off.

POSTCARDS FROM CEDAR KEY

Terri DuLong

ABOUT THIS GUIDE

The following questions are intended to
enhance your group's reading of
Postcards from Cedar Key.

Discussion Questions

1. Did you think Berkley's relocation to Cedar Key in order to uncover a family secret was justified?

2. Discuss the character of Saxton Tate III in relation to Berkley. Did you feel they shared chemistry when they first met? Why or why not?

3. How did you feel about Berkley's compulsive behavior? Do you have certain rituals that you adhere to? What do you think is the difference between compulsive behaviors and habits?

4. What was your initial feeling toward Raylene Samuels? Discuss her demand to ban Lacey Weston's books. Do you think it's ever justified for a book to be banned?

5. This story had quite a few dogs. Discuss how dogs weaken or enhance a story in a novel. Do you enjoy reading about the dogs owned by various characters in a book?

6. Discuss Berkley's signature chocolate clams. Do you think they contained magical qualities produced by Berkley's grandmother's plant?

7. What was your impression of Doyle Summers? Did your impression of him change as the story unfolded?

8. Toward the end of the story there seems to be a connection between Doyle and Berkley's aunt, Stella Baldwin. Do you think there's a chance for that relationship to progress?

9. How did you feel about Muriel, Saxton's ex-wife, and his daughter, Resa? Do you think he was right to contact his daughter after so many years?

10. Being judgmental is one of the issues covered in the story. Raylene judged Lacey Weston and her books. Berkley was judgmental in her lifelong assessment of her mother. What

do you think accounts for people forming their opinions of others without more information? Do you agree or disagree with the saying "Never judge another until you've walked a mile in their shoes"?

11. Miss Maybelle is introduced in this story. Discuss her character and the potential for her to have a stronger part in future stories.

12. When Berkley finally discovers the answers she's been searching for, the truth is much different than she anticipated. Do you feel she regretted trying to put all the pieces together? Why or why not?

13. Discuss your thoughts on seeking out answers to family secrets. Do you think they should always be pursued? Or, as Raylene said, is it sometimes better to let sleeping dogs lie?

14. Domestic abuse is still a major issue for women around the world. Discuss the events that Berkley's mother experienced in the 1960s and compare them to what might have happened today in relation to the court system, resources available, and so on.

15. Do you think women today are more aware of domestic abuse? And if so, what do you think accounts for this?

16. Based on the four books in the Cedar Key series, discuss which character you'd most like to see featured in the fifth book.